SOFTLY

Also available from Headline Liaison

Voluptuous Voyage by Lacey Carlyle
Dark Deception by Lacey Carlyle
Magnolia Moon by Lacey Carlyle
Sensual Storm by Lacey Carlyle
The Journal by James Allen
Love Letters by James Allen
Aphrodisia by Rebecca Ambrose
Out of Control by Rebecca Ambrose
A Private Affair by Carol Anderson
Autumn Dancing by Adam Chandler
Portrait in Blue by Lucinda Chester
Vermillion Gates by Lucinda Chester
The Paradise Garden by Aurelia Clifford
The Golden Cage by Aurelia Clifford
Green Silk by Cathryn Cooper
Sleepless Nights by Tom Crewe and Amber Wells
Hearts on Fire by Tome Crewe and Amber Wells
Seven Days by J J Duke
Dangerous Desires by J J Duke
A Scent of Danger by Sarah Hope-Walker
Private Lessons by Cheryl Mildenhall
Intimate Strangers by Cheryl Mildenhall
Dance of Desire by Cheryl Mildenhall

Killing Me Softly

Laura Aspen

HEADLINE
Liaison

First published in 1996 by
HEADLINE BOOK PUBLISHING

A HEADLINE LIAISON paperback

10 9 8 7 6 5 4 3 2 1

All characters in this publication are fictitious and any resemblance to real persons, living or dead, is purely coincidental.

ISBN 0 7472 5426 5

Typeset by Avon Dataset Ltd, Bidford-on-Avon, Warks

Printed and bound in Great Britain by
Cox & Wyman Ltd, Reading, Berks

HEADLINE BOOK PUBLISHING
A division of Hodder Headline PLC
338 Euston Road
London NW1 3BH

Killing Me Softly

Prologue

'Not a word,' he said. 'And when I enter you, you're not even to moan.'

Nikki felt an involuntary shiver go through her as she looked up to meet the gaze of the man who stood opposite her. Eyes the colour of polished mahogany bored unblinkingly into her own and, blushing, she looked down at the carpet.

'Should I run?' she wondered, knowing that the door behind her was locked. But she knew she didn't want to run, as surely as she'd known, from the moment she first saw him in the hotel lobby, that she couldn't leave. She couldn't simply pay her bill and catch her plane, couldn't go anywhere on earth except to his room. To his bed.

He'd stood next to her as she was checking out. Handing her credit card to the desk clerk, she had turned to look at him, noticing his thick black hair, high cheekbones and sensual, mocking mouth. It was then that she had first looked into his eyes – dark, dangerous and framed with a sweep of black lashes so rich as to be almost feminine.

When he moved towards the lift she had followed. And now he stood facing her. There was only the ticking of the clock and the slight scent of gardenias in a vase on the bureau nearby to distract her as he came closer.

Nikki felt his breath on her neck as he lifted his fingers to trace the hollow beneath her earlobe. She felt a deep rush of pleasure as his fingers stroked the soft curves of her throat.

He began to unbutton her jacket, sliding it from her

shoulders in one expert movement. She noticed his long and elegant fingers as his hand moved towards her breast. At his touch, her nipples hardened and a thrill of pleasure ran through her. She felt the moistness between her legs and a gentle throbbing which was sweeping away all restraint.

As he lowered his mouth to cover her own, she smelt the scent of his skin and was aware of nothing but her own hunger. She willed him to plunge his tongue deeper into her. Her body was on fire as she felt his hard erection against her skirt. She longed for the waiting to be over, ached to feel him moving urgently inside her.

Lifting her up, he carried her across to the bed. He slipped off her skirt, slid her panties down over her smooth brown legs and spread her wide apart. She stared up at him, at the bulge of his erection straining against his trousers as he stood over her – powerful, menacing and silent.

He took off his tie and tied it tightly around her mouth.

Not daring to move, she watched as he stripped, gasping silently at the size and firmness of his penis which rose from between his slim hips.

Kneeling between her legs, he gazed steadily into her eyes and licked his index finger. She felt the moistness inside her grow as he brushed her glistening clitoris with the most gentle of movements. 'I can't stand this,' she thought, 'I shall come too soon.' But no sooner had he touched her than his hand moved away.

He pinched her hard on each nipple, sending waves of pleasure and pain coursing through her. Raising her buttocks with his hands, he plunged himself into her with one powerful thrust, filling her more completely than any man had done before.

She felt his balls slapping against her as he thrust deeper and deeper.

Then his body tensed and his climax was on him. As he came, so did she, carried on a tide of pleasure so thrilling that she knew nothing would ever be the same again. Her forbidden moans were hidden beneath the deep groan which shook his whole body as she closed her eyes and tried to fight her way to the surface. 'I must wake up,' she thought as she felt him shudder. 'I must wake up.'

Chapter 1

Nikki was glad she'd left home early. The journey so far had been horrendous, though as she came up the steps at Green Park underground station and emerged into a perfect spring morning, she looked forward to the walk which would take her through the park, across Marble Arch and along Brompton Road to arrive by nine a.m. on the doorstep of Maison Naturelle, the Knightsbridge beauty salon in which she was senior beauty therapist and Madame Etoile's second-in-command.

Though the sun was shining there was still a chill in the air and, glancing at her watch, she shivered and turned her collar up against the wind which whipped across the grass, flattening it like a hand across cat's fur.

There'd been another tube strike. Not an all-out, close-the-network kind of strike, but one of those infuriating stoppages where some trains ran and others didn't. From the Earl's Court flat she shared with Chris, it had taken her an hour to get this far. And now she had to walk the rest of the way. No matter. She'd allowed plenty of time.

The frost had melted from the grass and little droplets of water glittered in the sunlight. Thrusting her hands deeply into her pockets, Nikki walked on past the banks of daffodils and beds of crocuses, past joggers and businessmen, pigeons and skylarking lovers catching a fleeting kiss as they parted on their way to work.

Nikki smiled wistfully to herself and thought about Chris.

She'd woken that morning full of desire, reaching out in that delicious half-dreaming state between sleeping and waking, expecting to find Chris lying next to her so that she could run her fingertips down his chest, stroking him into wakefulness, feeling his cock rise beneath her touch.

Chris would have made love to her then. Or at least what passed for making love these days. In recent months the routine had been the same: licking and squeezing her breasts for about thirty seconds, slipping inside her and thrusting for about three minutes, coming, kissing her, rolling off, stroking her hair, falling asleep. She could set the alarm clock by it.

Things hadn't always been this way. When they'd first met, she'd found it impossible to be in the same room with Chris without feeling flustered. The touch of his fingers alone would send shock waves coursing through her body. Whenever he was near, the delicious throbbing in her clitoris would make her self-conscious, making her feel that other people would sense her confusion and guess her secret. At one time she even thought that the swelling between her thighs would be visible to others. 'Like a bandy cowboy,' she'd thought, blushing.

Their love affair had started with an old-fashioned courtship. Chris hadn't made a move until they'd really got to know each other. Trips to theatres, intimate dinners and autumn afternoon walks had run their slow and sensual course towards that Sunday afternoon when, sitting on the floor in his flat drinking wine and listening to Billie Holiday on the stereo, he had reached across for her hand, pulled her gently to her feet and led her into his bedroom.

On that cold grey afternoon Chris had driven her to a pitch of desire she'd only dreamed of, taking complete control, building her slowly to a pleasure more intense than anything she'd ever experienced.

This gentle and thoughtful man had stood before her, undressing her expertly and in seconds, loosening his shirt with one hand while the other sought the zip on her skirt, his mouth all the while exploring her soft skin as the clothes fell from her and more of her eager body was exposed to his touch.

All Nikki's shyness had evaporated as she felt Chris's lips touch her throat, his fingers reaching inside her bra, groping for her nipples, turning their soft pink tips to hard little buttons with the slightest touch. Her body strained against his as they stood together, his penis brushing her leg as his hands moved to trace the contours of her backside. His fingers slid into her panties, pulling them down over her thighs. Then he unhooked her bra so she stood before him naked, her body on fire though he'd hardly really touched her.

He'd carried her to the bed and laid her down, telling her how beautiful she was. He'd kissed her eyelids, her mouth, her throat and, all the time, his huge erection was just out of reach, driving her mad with desire.

She'd never been so wet! The tops of her thighs were slippery, the lips of her vulva swollen and parted wide. She was longing to take this man inside her, this man whose pale blond head was, at last, moving down to kiss the soft mound of golden hair between her legs. His tongue slid gently inside the parted lips, teasing the very tip of her clitoris with rapid flicking movements of his tongue which caused her to cry out with longing. Her deep wet cavern throbbed and her legs parted wider still as she pulled his head closer. His tongue slipped easily into her entrance, lapping the soft walls of her vagina till she felt she would come, her body tensing as the waves of pleasure washed over her.

Lifting his head, he had smiled up at her and moved his body further up the bed till he was poised over her. His huge prick hovered above her parted legs, his fingers stroking the inside of her wet thighs, just out of reach of her burning clitoris, teasing her.

She had stared up at him imploringly and, leaning across to kiss her slowly on the lips, he had taken his prick in his hand to circle the entrance to her vagina, dipping the fat, round tip into the juices of her desire. Nikki had raised her hips off the bed to take him as he slid inside her in a deep, slow thrust which filled her aching passage and made her gasp. She clung to him as he plunged inside and tightened her body around him as his thrusts grew faster. She felt his prick grow harder and longer inside her, its head swelling as he pumped further into her. Nikki's muscles contracted in spasms of pleasure, holding him tight as he rammed her full of his musky manhood.

He'd fucked her hard that first time. Like two people dying of thirst they clung together, drinking in the pleasure of each other's bodies. As he drove his swollen cock into the velvet shaft that enveloped him, Nikki dug her fingernails into his small, firm buttocks, giving herself up to the mounting tide of orgasmic sensation that spread through every pore of her skin, down to the very tips of her fingers.

She had longed to suck him dry with her body that first afternoon. To close herself around him and never let him go. To possess him completely and forever.

Later, curled in the crook of his arm, Nikki had lain awake listening to his breathing. Safe, warm and satisfied, she'd kept quite still, basking in the knowledge that soon he would wake and make love to her again. Tentatively, she'd reached across to touch the hair on his chest. 'The chest of an athlete,' she'd thought – muscular, compact, golden.

Lifting the sheet gently from his sleeping body, she'd looked at his penis lying at rest against his left leg, surrounded by its thick forest of curly hair. Just a little while ago that had been inside her. Three times its present size, hard and eager, he had slid it into her, causing the pleasure she now felt between her damp thighs.

Looking at his body, Nikki had longed for him to wake, her hunger growing as she massaged her breasts and slid one hand down to touch the tender folds of her labia and stroke her clitoris with the gentlest of movements. She felt her passion and desire sweep over her in a hot wave of longing.

Sliding down the bed, she'd stopped when her head had reached the top of his thigh. Close to his penis, the sweet, arousing smell of him filled her senses and, unable to stop herself, she leant across and carefully took the tip of him between her lips. The soft touch caused his prick to stir and grow.

Glancing up anxiously, Nikki hoped she wouldn't wake him. Amazingly, he did not stir. Emboldened by curiosity, Nikki continued her gentle explorations, stroking his cock with her tongue, pushing back the hood of flesh at its tip to discover the hard, silky roundness that lay beneath.

Still he did not wake! Chris's cock stood firm and straight, rising from his body like a golden dagger.

Nikki propped herself up on her elbow and, with one hand still pinching her breasts, closed her eyes and took the full length of him between her lips. He filled her mouth and the muscles of her jaws began to ache as she sucked and licked, breathing steadily as his cock pushed in and out. His body seemed to be moving in time with her own and she was sure he was thrusting gently as she sucked him, yet still he slept on.

Nikki manoeuvred herself so that, with Chris still in her mouth, she could reach between her legs with one hand while still caressing her breasts with the other.

Her senses on fire, Nikki masturbated. She surrendered to the feelings which swept over her, the silky hardness against her lips, the softness between her legs and the electric current which united these sensations as she rubbed her taut, pink nipples.

Still Chris slept. Nikki felt her body shiver and her breathing quicken as her orgasm began, her vagina throbbing against her fingers. She felt him stir, grunting in his sleep, but he did not wake.

Suddenly his arms reached down to her, lifting her off his cock and pulling her across his body. His erection was as hard as a length of wood beneath her.

Sitting astride him, she took his fat cock inside her, opening her inner lips with her fingertips and spreading her thighs to take him as deeply as her body would allow.

Nikki began to move her pelvis, pressing him deep inside her vagina, her clitoris rubbing against the top of his prick, her hands on her breasts, pinching and stroking. As the throbbing intensified and she felt her orgasm begin, his eyes opened sleepily and Chris began to moan.

They came together, the intensity of their coming blending as their bodies melted in unison.

Nikki kissed his face in a thousand little butterfly kisses. 'You were asleep so long,' she said.

Smiling up at her, Chris tweaked the end of her nose. 'No I wasn't,' he said, 'I was awake all the time.'

That was the beginning of their closeness. A voyage of discovery that had brought them to know all there was to know about each other's bodies. But that was then. A lifetime ago.

Nikki sighed deeply as she thought back over the last few months. Preoccupied with his work, Chris's efforts at lovemaking had become perfunctory. Sometimes they had gone for months with no more than a goodnight kiss. And when they *did* make love . . . Nikki felt the tears starting behind her eyelashes as she thought back to this morning.

Why didn't he seem to need her any more? She longed to feel like she did when they'd first met, first lived together. She needed to know that she was loved. But was she?

It was barely daylight when she'd got out of bed. Chris was at the kitchen table, sorting through his portfolio, blond hair flopping over a face that was unusually stern. She'd leant over him, brushing the top of his head with her lips, smelling the sweet, sleepy smell of his skin.

She'd longed to open the bathrobe he was wearing and spread herself astride him, straddling his thick, firm cock and taking her pleasure from the body she knew so well.

Instead, feeling it was best not to disturb him, she'd prepared the breakfast silently while he carried on with his work.

'That was some dream you were having,' said Chris, looking up. 'I felt like waking you up and asking to join in.'

'Well, why didn't you?' she thought as she busied herself with the coffee cups, fighting the wave of ennui that threatened to engulf her.

After a hurried breakfast and a quick shave, Chris had set out for the studio. She hoped it would all go well for him today. She really did.

As she'd heard the door shut behind him, suddenly and unexpectedly she'd felt bitter and resentful and instantly ashamed. She was being selfish. After all, she knew what his career meant to him.

Walking past Harvey Nichols, Nikki began to think of the day ahead. A fairly mundane group of clients were due in for treatments, with the notable exception of the Contessa. Though many of her clients were rich, in Nikki's opinion, only the Contessa de Silva was truly glamorous. With her natural charm and exotic, delicate beauty, she was a pleasure to be with, treating Nikki more as a friend than simply her beauty therapist.

A widow for many years, the Contessa still spoke to Nikki of her late husband, a man who it seemed had left her well provided for. With a mansion in Kensington, a flat in Rome and a yacht in the South of France, the Contessa had more homes and more money than she would ever need. Yet she still retained an enthusiasm for life and an almost childlike innocence that so many of Nikki's more jaded and spoilt clients had lost altogether.

Though part of the beauty therapist's creed is to allow clients to talk about themselves without doing likewise, over the months Nikki and the Contessa de Silva had come to know each other well. The Contessa had taken a real interest in Nikki, listening intently as she'd talked about Chris, their ambitions and their hopes for the future.

In recent weeks the Contessa had begun to confide in Nikki about the new man in her life. Since the Count had died Nikki knew there had been no one else. But lately, hesitantly at first, the Contessa had dropped the name 'Pierre' into her conversation, telling Nikki more and more about this dark and glamorous young man who seemed to hold a place in her affections that not even the discreet Contessa could hope to conceal.

Nikki had always believed firmly in the power of beauty therapy. She knew that good diet and exercise and the right skin treatments really did help prevent signs of ageing. She also knew that being in love was the real elixir of youth. The Contessa herself was living proof.

Nikki arrived at the Maison Naturelle with ten minutes to spare. She opened the front door, feeling the sumptuous carpets sink beneath her feet as she stepped over the threshold and the familiar smell of scented creams wafted towards her.

Another day had begun. And though she didn't know it, it was to be a day that would change her life forever.

'What a difference an hour makes,' thought Chris as he pushed his way through the heavy revolving doors of the Carter Taylor advertising agency and out into the lunchtime bustle of the Fulham Road.

He'd been a fashion photographer for eight years, but today he felt like he'd felt on the day he got his first assignment, a deep feeling of pride and achievement and a mounting excitement at the thought of what lay ahead.

He smiled at the memory. It had been a simple brochure for a High Street bank. And here he was, thousands of rolls of film later, being asked to work not only with the House of Labouchon, the world's most glamorous cosmetics and perfume house, but with Irana Petrovka, hottest supermodel on the catwalk and darling of the glitterati from London to New York, Paris to St Petersburg.

Like all photographers, Chris had known what it was to

work with clients whose vision was limited to the figures on a balance sheet. Now he need worry only about the pursuit of perfection.

It had all been so easy. The ad agency had welcomed him like an old friend, fired him with their own enthusiasm for the new House of Labouchon perfume 'Erotique', and appointed him on the spot.

But apart from the sheer prestige of the job, it was the concept which had excited him the most.

'Erotique. Let your spirit free' was the tag line – and it was Chris's job, along with the agency's art director, to make the idea come to life.

Within reason, they'd given him all the money he needed. What's more, he even liked the perfume. They'd handed him a sample bottle which he intended, that night, to present to Nikki along with news of his triumph.

Nikki's back and shoulders were aching as she sat in the small rest room adjoining the beauty room in which she worked. It was only one o'clock but already she'd given two complete body massages, three half leg waxes and pedicured Lady Olga Merchant's long, bony feet while hearing every last detail of Lady Olga's daughter's wedding. She'd heard about the pink and white silk ruched marquee, the ice sculpture of a swan on a lake of flowers which had taken pride of place on the top table, how gorgeous her daughter had looked and how absolutely everyone had said it was the best wedding ever.

It wasn't that Nikki was bored by Lady Olga. On the contrary, she was no more nor less self-centred than most of the clientele upon whose less-than-perfect faces and bodies Nikki lavished her skill and attention.

No. It was simply that Nikki received a very small wage for her pains and that, though she worked for Mayfair's most prestigious beauty salon, her pay at the Maison Naturelle was simply not enough.

Traditionally, beauty therapists had been girls who really didn't need the money. Many of the 'old school' salons paid a pittance or sometimes nothing at all, regarding the training and experience they offered young therapists to be payment enough. But though the old days were over, poor salaries lingered on.

Leaning back in her chair and looking up at the fern which moved gently in the breeze from the overhead fan, Nikki considered for the hundredth time how long it would take her to save the money she needed to open her own salon.

When her father had died when Nikki was sixteen, leaving her an orphan, she knew that she would have to make her own way in the world and that now there was no one to help her.

Her ambition was to be far more than merely comfortable. She wanted to be the best – and she wanted all that went with it. But how?

Nikki glanced at her watch. In a couple of minutes the Contessa de Silva would arrive for her weekly facial. She was the only one of her clients that Nikki liked unreservedly. She was also a pleasure to work with and Nikki looked forward to pampering the Contessa's exquisite skin – porcelain white and, for a woman in her early forties, surprisingly free of even the finest lines.

Nikki sipped thoughtfully at her coffee and thought, for the first time during her busy morning, about the disturbing dream she'd had last night. It wasn't the first of its kind and, while such erotic dreams were undeniably pleasurable, she did not understand why they invaded her nights with such frequency, such urgency . . . and always, always the same man.

And he did such things to her! Things that she'd never done with Chris, yet which she knew in her heart she enjoyed . . . In her dreams, this strange man dominated her totally, treating her as little more than a body to be used, an object for his own satisfaction.

She'd dreamt of him walking into her room one night, his slim body encased in jodhpurs, his long legs in high black leather boots. He'd carried a riding crop in his hand. She'd noticed his fierce, cruel prick bulging against his tight clothing, hard and long and ready to punish her, ready to ram its way into her as he held her down, kicking and screaming and begging for mercy.

In this particular dream he'd ordered her out of bed, commanding her to kneel at his feet and lick his boots. She remembered the taste of the leather, she remembered her fear as she crouched before him, her naked body cowering as he stood over her, stroking his crop against the side of his boot. He'd murmured his commands in a voice that was quiet yet full of menace. And then he'd beaten her . . . Hard, burning slaps across her buttocks with his crop, the blows raining down as, naked and defenceless, she'd clung to his leather-clad leg, imploring him to stop, the tears running down her face. Yet though the blows cut into her skin they brought with them a strange pleasure, arousing her senses, stinging her body into a state of voluptuous awareness that only this dark man could satisfy.

Lifting her from the ground, he'd laid her face down on the bed, tying her wrists to the bedstead and pinning her legs wide apart. Not bothering to undress, simply unzipping his jodhpurs and releasing a prick that slid out of its confinement fully engorged, he spread her buttocks and rammed himself into her. His hard, relentless thrusts had caused Nikki to cry out as he grabbed her by the hair, wrenching her head back to turn her face towards him, sliding his tongue between her lips and biting at the corners of her mouth.

His thick, hard prick plundered her for his pleasure alone. Deaf to her pleading, he had his way, driven only by his need to dominate her, to fuck her and fill her with his hot, wet juices. Flooding her bruised body, he came in a frenzy of wild pumping. His raw lust carried Nikki with him on a flood of strange sensation in which pleasure and pain were indistinguishable, reality was blurred and all that mattered was to feel him inside her, to obey and to do his bidding.

At other times he wouldn't tie her up. He would come to her in her dreams and she would find him standing over her, silent, menacing, a shadow in the darkness. He would grab her then, holding her wrists as she squirmed and hissed like an alley cat, pinning her down, stretching her body with his fierce manhood, silencing her protests.

He was a strange and evil image, a nightmare, yet part of Nikki knew that she adored him. To be there to obey and please him was all that mattered. No mind of her own, no life of her own, a body to do with as he pleased. Sometimes at night this was all she desired.

This dark man of her dreams satisfied her completely. While he took his pleasure she discovered her own. Deep, rich waves of orgasm swept through her body as she crouched before him. The touch of his fingers, the sting of his crop, even the taste of his leather boots lingering on her lips, precipitated a deep and thrilling pleasure of a kind she'd never known.

Used, bruised and utterly humiliated, she knew in her dreams she would always come crawling back for more.

Yet when she awoke it was with a sense of shame and confusion that such dark ideas could find their way into her thoughts.

Unreal and yet more real than she cared to think about, Nikki longed for these strange dreams to leave her. But why? Because she liked them too much? Nikki frowned to herself. Was she *that* dissatisfied? It wasn't a question she liked to think about. Besides, the Contessa was due at any moment.

Nikki got to her feet, put her coffee cup down and reached for a hairbrush, quickly smoothing her rich mane of blonde hair and twisting it back into a neat coil.

Smoothing her white uniform over her hips she stepped out into the glittering reception area of the salon to greet her client who, though Nikki was perfectly on time, was already waiting.

One glance at the Contessa's excited face and sparkling eyes told Nikki that this was to be more than a routine appointment.

'I've something to ask you, my dear,' said the Contessa as Nikki led her client to the beauty room, gesturing the Contessa towards the white beauty couch, urging her to relax.

But the Contessa remained absolutely upright, a smile playing around her lips.

'Nikki,' she said. 'Listen. I have a proposition. I intend to spend the summer on my yacht in the South of France and I want you to come with me. I want you to be my own personal beauty therapist for the next three months and, in return, I will pay you ten thousand pounds.'

Seeing the startled expression on Nikki's face, the Contessa looked concerned.

'Nikki,' she said, gently, 'I've thought this through carefully and I know I'm expecting a lot. I'm asking you to give up your job. I realise this. Would twelve thousand make a difference?'

Nikki's heart was thumping wildly in her chest as she thought of what such an amount of money would mean to her. With the savings she scraped together plus a bank loan . . . She felt her face flush at the thought. Maybe the idea of being her own boss wasn't such a pipe dream after all.

'Will you consider it, my dear?' continued the Contessa, softly. 'Will you at least promise to think about it?'

Chapter 2

Although it was only May, it was already hot in the South of France. The searing, bleaching heat of high summer was still weeks away and for now there remained a freshness and lushness that had yet to succumb to the relentless Mediterranean glare.

The market at Antibes was heavy with sun-warmed scents. Flowers in a riot of carnival colours poured onto the pavements. Huge strawberries, cascading mountains of cherries and fat, ripe peaches spilled forth from stall after stall. The fresh scents of fruit mingled with the richer aromas of ground spices, charcuterie and coffee wafting from the pavement shops and cafés which lined the ancient village street along which the colour and bustle of the market ran like a multicoloured ribbon, spilling down towards the sea.

It was Saturday morning. In the harbour, just a minute's walk from the market itself, some of the world's most beautiful yachts stood sleepily at anchor, gleaming in the sun-dappled water which danced with a thousand little shooting darts of bright light.

A gentle breeze teased the masts of the gigantic floating palaces, causing them to move with a lazy slapping sound heard only in the richest corners of the earth.

All along the quay, white-uniformed crews could be seen loading and unloading supplies, carrying floral arrangements into the inner stillness of sumptuous air-conditioned cabins and hosing the decks.

Though mooring fees alone for many of the yachts ran to hundreds of thousands of pounds, many stood empty. Flying the flags of the tax havens in which they were registered, they waited for their owners, silent in the sun save for the tinkling of masts.

Cherry de Silva had a terrible hangover. Despite a large espresso, two cigarettes and three aspirin at the little café opposite the boulangerie in the market, her head was still splitting and her mood less than sanguine.

Cherry felt her temper rise and her irritation mount. She'd asked that stupid bastard of a steward for a bottle of *eau minerale* at least five minutes ago and still it hadn't arrived.

Stretched out in the sun, she thought of her stepmother and how she hated her, hated the thought of her imminent arrival. Without that soft-spoken bitch, all this would be hers. She could sack the whole damn crew and start again.

Despite her discomfort, Cherry got to her feet and screamed. 'Jules! Get here!'

As if by magic a tray appeared – ice bucket, tongs, chilled water, glass. 'I'm not going to make myself hoarse yelling for you,' said Cherry. 'Next time, get off your arse when I tell you.'

With the utmost solicitude, Jules placed the contents of the tray on a small table which stood next to Cherry's sun lounger. He looked at the woman who once again had stretched herself out, ignoring him now he had served his purpose. Long, bronzed legs, long black hair and a gold bikini which made little attempt to cover even the most intimate parts of her body.

Jules was tired. Just four hours before he'd been roused from his sleep to half drag, half carry her up the gangway – drunk, dishevelled and smelling of the kind of rough sex only to be found in the seedier backstreet bars and discos of which respectable people were unaware. The sort of places where 'Madame' usually ended her evenings.

Jules looked with contempt upon the woman whose every whim he was obliged to indulge. The Contessa de Silva did not deserve this kind of a stepdaughter. 'Without her dear father's money she would be in the gutter,' he thought. 'Where she belongs.'

Cherry drank her mineral water and began to feel slightly better. Turning sleepily on her deck lounger and adjusting the cushion behind her head, Cherry lay quite still. She wanted to feel better. Her plans for tonight didn't include sleeping alone.

At last, the throbbing in her temples was beginning to subside. She wouldn't need to spend the morning in her cabin after all. Cherry smiled wryly to herself. Another day of basking in the sun, a long, relaxing shower and then . . . who knows?

By mid-afternoon Cherry was beginning to get bored. Jules had served her lunch of salad niçoise and cold white wine and she had read, dozed and swam but now, with her headache gone, Cherry was restless and impatient.

By seven p.m. she was made up, perfumed and dressed and had caught a taxi to the Provençal Hotel, one of the many smart hotels which lay back from the promenade at Juan les Pins, back from the shops and bars which viye with each other for attention, each out-glittering the next like the hundreds of hard and beautiful starlets who stretch themselves out on the sands in the weeks before the Cannes Film Festival, topping up their tans ready to be spotted, ready to be discovered, ready for anything.

Cherry had arranged to meet Solange at seven–thirty but though half an hour early, already she was getting impatient. She sucked greedily on her cigarette and ordered another drink. She sipped slowly this time. There was a long night ahead.

Despite her current irritation, Cherry enjoyed her evenings with Solange. She enjoyed the feeling of power that came from paying for the little shop girl to get drunk on champagne, but most of all she enjoyed the fact that she, Cherry, had been responsible for the girl's corruption.

Cherry had first spotted Solange working in a *parfumerie* in Cannes and had befriended her, listening to tales of her family: her papa, her three brothers and sisters. Lunch invitations had led to dinner on the yacht, by which time Cherry had been fully aware that the seventeen-year-old shopgirl not only had a crush on her but was totally seduced by all that she saw, from Cherry's extravagant and breathtaking wardrobe to the Mercedes convertible that Cherry drove so mercilessly along the Grande Corniche.

Feeding the girl's taste for good booze and good living, Cherry had persuaded her to come one night to the Blue Parrot, a notorious nightclub and pick-up joint where the only thing 'pure' to be had was the heroin. Leaving the club at four a.m. in the company of two men whom Cherry had agreed could 'see them home', Solange had lost her virginity in a back alley, crouched on her hands and knees and taken by each of the men in turn.

Her friend had comforted the distraught Solange, claiming that the men had held and gagged her, making it impossible for her to come to Solange's aid. Taking her back to the yacht and into her bed, Cherry had comforted the shaken and weeping girl, by morning turning her sobs of misery to those of pleasure.

The rest had been easy. In the weeks that followed, Cherry had convinced Solange that all men were bastards, her papa excepted of course, and were there to be used. Her protégée learned quickly and proved an apt and willing pupil.

Night after night they would set out together, trawling the clubs and bars in a relentless search for greater and greater kicks.

Cherry looked up as Solange walked into the bar. As usual, the girl looked fresh and pretty. Cherry was slightly taken aback that all the excesses of the past few weeks had made no impression on Solange's natural beauty. Fascinated and at the same time resentful, Cherry decided that the time had come to wean the girl off champagne and onto hard liquor.

'If she's going to live like a tart at my expense,' thought Cherry, 'she may as well end up looking like one.' But for now, Solange appeared as unsullied as the flowers in the market at Antibes. She was useful, too. Being out with her made it easy to pick up men.

Cherry smiled warmly as the younger girl approached, kissing her on both cheeks. As usual, Solange blushed slightly and, though she was perfectly on time, said she hoped she wasn't late.

As the soft evening breeze wafted in through the open doors of the hotel bar, Cherry felt a pleasant glow from her freshly suntanned skin and, as she looked into the sparkling eyes of her pretty little companion, she experienced the satisfying sense of invulnerability that came from living life entirely on her own terms.

Looking up, she caught the eye of a man at the other end of the bar. Tall, in his early forties and wearing expensive, well-cut clothes, he looked at her from under heavily lidded, dark-lashed eyes . . . a quizzical expression, interested though unsure.

'He thinks we're dykes,' thought Cherry, smiling at him warmly to signal otherwise, though aware all the time that he was looking with most interest at Solange.

A smile led to drinks being sent across 'with the compliments of the gentleman in the corner'. He wandered across. Introduced himself. His name was Paulo and he was 'in property'.

He invited them to dine. 'Unless of course you are waiting for someone else,' he said. He was handsome in a swarthy kind of way, thought Cherry, though he seemed unable to take his eyes off Solange's tits, even for a moment. Two drinks later and Paulo was suggesting that their dinner should be room service. Out into the warm, fragrant evening they staggered, heading for his hotel which he said was just around the corner.

Cherry went ahead, alone, sweeping imperiously past the desk clerk and catching the lift to the fourth floor. With Solange on his arm, drunk and smiling vacantly, Paulo followed moments later. The desk clerk looked dubious but decided not to make a fuss.

They got into the lift. Fingers, tongues, grasping hot and urgent. Meeting Cherry at the fourth floor, Paulo opened the door to his room and ushered the giggling girls into the twilight interior with its cool verandah and lowered shutters.

The air was fragrant outside and the night full of magic. Nobody noticed. Paulo began to undress.

Would they strip for him? Would they make love to each other? With a knowing smile, Cherry slipped off her silk shift dress and beckoned Solange to her side.

Taking the young girl's hand in her own, Cherry guided it towards her right breast, a moan of pleasure escaping from Solange's lips as Cherry held her fingers and slid them beneath the fine black lace of her beautiful handmade bra, so delicate that at first Solange hesitated, afraid to damage such lingerie, more exquisite than anything she'd ever owned.

But lust took over, banishing all inhibition as Solange groped greedily for Cherry's firm, dark nipple, taut and hard and budding forth from her heavy golden breast.

Unhooking Cherry's bra in one deft movement, Solange's soft, lipsticked mouth closed over her lover's nipple, her hand reaching to toy with Cherry's other breast as her mouth kneaded, sucked and teased.

Cherry felt a slight pain mix with the pleasure of arousal as the girl's urgent lips and fingers squeezed nipples made already tender by the warm Mediterranean sun. But this slight discomfort only heightened her pleasure as she felt her juices begin to soak into her black silk panties, the lips of her vulva swelling and throbbing, ready to be touched with the expert strokes which to Solange were instinctive, and had not needed to be taught.

With a deep flush of arousal spreading down her neck, Solange slid to her knees before her mistress, opening Cherry like a ripened fig and dipping her tongue inside the soft folds of Cherry's pulsating womanhood. With a sigh of pleasure, Solange lapped her lover greedily, using her tongue to explore the tiny folds of Cherry's clitoris from its base to its swollen tip.

Stepping out of her simple cotton dress, Solange rubbed her body against Cherry's own, the two women falling onto the bed together, licking, sucking and teasing, fingers plunged deep into each other's wet and yielding bodies, tongues darting like little fish, each feeling the clitoris of the other move against her tongue as she explored its hidden secrets.

Cherry looked up when she heard a moan. Sitting naked on a chair nearby, the man had come while watching them, his thick penis spent and hanging limp like a rag. Cherry lay down beside him on the bed while Solange fell asleep.

Stroking him gently and teasing his nipples with her tongue, she felt the first tremor of arousal in him, watching his penis rise hard and firm as her own breathing mounted. She slid the tip of her tongue along the shaft of his prick, feeling its hardness as it responded, quiveringly, to her touch and his whole body tensed with pleasure.

Unable to resist the temptation any longer, she took the bulb of him in her mouth, running her tongue in circular movements around the very tip, teasing the slippery shaft to obey her every command.

She felt him begin to move inside her mouth, felt his penis rise and thicken even more as she took him deep in her throat.

Massaging his growing and hardening prick with her lips, she began to suck, the rhythm of his thrust becoming more urgent. 'Now,' she thought. 'Now he's ready for me,' and she went to move away, to climb on top, to take him deep inside her, riding him hard and firm, angling her body to feel every thrust as he stretched to fill her, rubbing hard against his thick, pumping prick till she felt the thrill begin deep inside her like a mounting tidal wave.

She went to move her head but he grabbed her by the hair, ramming harder, forcing his prick still deeper into the back of her throat.

Struggling to wrench her head away, Cherry took hold of his balls. When he cried out in pain, she realised she'd grabbed him harder than she'd intended.

'I'm sorry,' she muttered as his prick slid rapidly out of her mouth. 'It's just that . . . I wanted a piece of the action.'

'Oh, you did, did you?' he replied, a cold gleam in his eyes.

Cherry smiled what she hoped was her most tempting smile and spread her legs wide apart.

'Come get me,' she invited him, sliding one finger into her vulva and bringing it out, wet and glistening, holding it towards him and beckoning.

Paulo got up from the bed and disappeared into the bathroom, returning a minute later with two lengths of fine rope.

Before she'd had time to gather her thoughts let alone her clothes, he was kneeling astride her, tying her arms to the bedhead so tightly that every time she moved, the ropes cut into her wrists.

'So you want a piece of the action?' he repeated. 'You're going to get it.'

Cherry looked into his handsome face as he towered above her on the bed. With one violent jolt, she tried to pull her arms free from the ropes which bound them and as she moved he caught her, holding her down with the weight of his athletic body. He laughed as he sat astride her, pinning her legs with his own.

'So my little ball-squeezer wants a piece of the action.' He smiled menacingly. 'Greedy little girl.'

Despite her fear, despite the ropes that cut into her wrists, Cherry felt herself aroused by this man who had defiled and then overpowered her.

For once, the girl so used to getting her own way was entirely at the mercy of another. She felt his thighs gripping her legs like a vice. She felt his cock begin to harden and, as the first twitching tremors began to raise it from where it had lain against her own skin, Paulo leant forward. Covering her left breast with his mouth, the fingers of his left hand reached to stroke the nipple of her other breast. Her body responded instantly, sending waves of hot sensation direct to her swollen, wet clitoris, causing her to squirm with frustrated pleasure beneath his touch.

'Please,' she begged. 'Pinch me harder and fuck me.' Paulo continued to touch her gently, teasing her left nipple with the very tip of his tongue while his other hand barely brushed the nipple of Cherry's right breast. The lightness of his touch drove her crazy with need, her whole body crying out for the rough thrust of his thick, engorged prick which by now, she noticed hungrily, was huge and firm.

'Please,' she begged again as Paulo lifted her head and looked into her face. 'Fuck you,' he murmured softly.

'Oh yes . . . yes,' replied Cherry, panting deeply.

With a cruel smile, Paulo slid gently off her body and moved across to the still sleeping Solange. Stroking her hair and murmuring, he woke her. As her eyes opened, he kissed her tenderly and slowly, exploring her mouth with his expert tongue, awakening her lust as she yawned and stretched into consciousness.

Tied to the bed and able to raise her head only with the greatest effort, Cherry saw Paulo slip his beautiful prick into an eager Solange, watching the girl's legs wrap around his back as she took him deep inside.

Still drunk, Solange was oblivious to the presence of Cherry who felt that to cry out her hunger or to object would only add to her own humiliation.

Cherry felt the bed creak and move beneath her as their coupling built up to a rich crescendo.

She watched Solange's fingers gripping his hair as she saw the young girl's body strain to take him further and deeper inside. She watched as Solange's pleasure mounted and heard the deep and husky groan which escaped from the girl's lips as she began to come, Paulo's taut and muscular buttocks thrusting her towards a pleasure that, by rights, Cherry felt was hers and hers alone.

When Paulo began to move towards his own climax, gyrating his body in circular movements inside Solange, stretching her soft canal and leading her closer towards her own strong and thrilling orgasm, Cherry could bear to watch no longer.

Though able to close her eyes, she was unable to stop her ears and was forced to hear them both climax, coming within seconds of each other with loud animal cries that ripped Cherry apart with longing.

Cherry lay still for what seemed like hours, hot, furious tears coursing down her face through tightly closed eyes.

Eventually, she felt the ropes begin to loosen and, opening her eyes, saw that Solange was leaning over her.

'I fell asleep again,' said Solange dreamily. 'And woke up to find him gone.'

Cherry tried to smile.

'It was good for you, no?' said Solange. 'He came to you first, didn't he? While I was still sleeping?'

Mustering all her shattered dignity, Cherry confirmed that yes, she'd had a great time with Paulo.

'He wanted you first,' said Solange, rubbing her lover's reddened wrists to soothe them. 'He wanted you first because you are the most beautiful.'

Cherry got dressed and left, leaving Solange cross-legged and naked, sitting on the bed smoking a joint and giggling. She returned to the yacht lying silent in the moonlight. Should she masturbate tonight or call one of the crew?

Fuck the crew. Tonight she'd make do with a vibrator. Fuck all men, she hated them all.

She leant on the rail, watching the lights from the boats in the harbour as they sparkled in the inky black water. Cherry lit a cigarette and inhaled deeply. Two days' more peace then her stepmother would arrive. 'The Contessa de Silva,' thought Cherry with contempt, smiling a bitter smile.

Chapter 3

As he heard the key in the lock, Chris lit the candles. The glasses on the table shimmered in the light. Though they weren't crystal and the napkins were only paper, he knew that the room looked worthy of the excitement he felt, worthy of the news he had to tell Nikki.

As she walked in he was pouring a glass of her favourite Australian Chardonnay, chilled to perfection. Suddenly she remembered where Chris had been today. The carefully laid dining table told her there was something to celebrate.

'You got it, then?' she said.

He handed her the heady golden wine. 'Drink to tomorrow,' he said. 'And as we say at the House of Labouchon,' he added, smiling, 'let your spirit free.'

Nikki had not expected this. In truth, the Contessa's offer of a few hours before had driven everything else from her mind. Glass in hand, she sat down on the settee and looked at Chris as he chattered excitedly. He'd planned a big dinner to celebrate his triumph. How was she to break her news?

After her father died, Chris was the first man who'd ever made Nikki feel safe and cherished. What's more, the 'old' Chris had taken a real interest in her career as well as his own, making her feel that no ambition was impossible, no dream too bold to be realised. 'But not any more,' she thought sadly as she looked at him.

Chris was in full flow, talking about his plans for the House of Labouchon. Every now and then he'd dart in and out of the kitchen to check on the dinner and refill her glass. But he didn't notice how quiet she was. Didn't notice that she simply wasn't listening.

For the second time that day Nikki felt the unwelcome bitterness rise in her heart as he chattered on. She had some news, too. Something she needed to discuss. But these days any news she had was dwarfed in importance by his own.

Once it had seemed that the future belonged to them both, their destinies intertwined as inextricably as their bodies. But now she felt he could go it alone if he had to. He simply didn't need her any more.

Nikki sighed deeply, so unexpectedly that Chris looked up at her, taken aback. 'Are you all right?' he said, leaning across to look closely into her face.

'Of course,' she replied. 'Just a bit tired, that's all.'

Chris took her hand. 'This is as much for you as it is for me, you know,' he said, holding her gaze.

For the first time in her life she didn't believe him. 'Chris,' she replied, 'there's something I must talk to you about . . .'

'Later,' he said, kissing the tips of her fingers and, standing up, he pulled her to her feet beside him.

Leading her into the bedroom, his hands began to unhook the fasteners on her dress, his lips brushing her neck as he slid the flimsy material from her shoulders to land in a crumpled heap at her ankles.

He slid his hand into her panties till his fingers found the cleft within the silky, blonde cushion of hair and, with a soft growl of pleasure, he slipped two fingers straight up into her vagina, plunging them into her rhythmically in a simulation of intercourse.

Dutifully, Nikki began to unbutton his shirt. Feeling her juices begin to flow despite herself, she felt the swelling of his penis through his trousers as he continued to finger-fuck her.

When they were both naked, he led her to the bed and, laying her on her back, he entered her immediately, thrusting in long steady strokes while Nikki thrashed and moaned, trying for all she was worth to recapture the desire she'd once felt for him.

'Why am I doing this?' she asked herself as she continued to pretend. The answer was simple. She'd begun faking it when Chris had first started to become dejected, at that low point in his career, just over eighteen months ago, when the path to the top of his profession as a photographer had seemed too steep to climb.

As his confidence had diminished and their passion along with it, she'd faked it to bolster his ego, believing that his self-esteem was too fragile to weather being further diminished. And besides, how do you tell the man you love that he just doesn't satisfy you any more?

As had happened so many times in the recent past, Nikki's initial excitement faded and she faked it again, juddering and moaning in a ridiculous pantomime of pleasure.

When Chris slipped out of her and lay on his back, she propped herself up on one elbow and looked at him. For a split second, seeing the smile of contentment that played around his lips, she realised how much it had cost her to bolster his ego through the bad times, and how he wasn't even aware of her efforts. Yet now all his dreams were about to come true.

'Chris,' she began, for the second time that evening, 'I've got something to talk to you about.' His eyes were peacefully shut. 'Chris!' she yelled, all the pent-up emotion of the last few months bursting forth. He sat up with a start, suddenly awake.

What followed was the worst night Nikki could ever remember. She told him he was a self-centred bastard who thought about nothing but his own concerns. All in a rush, she told him she was leaving . . . going away for the summer to earn some money because he wasn't the only one who was ambitious. Without pausing for breath, she told him about the Contessa's offer and how she'd be a fool to refuse it. But still, despite her apparent confidence, deep down she knew she felt nervous. More than anything, she needed his reassurance. She needed Chris to tell her she was doing the right thing.

Chris appeared dumbstruck at first and then began to raise all sorts of objections. What did Nikki really know of this Contessa? What guarantee did she have that she'd get paid? She'd be giving up a secure job and, anyway, what about him? 'You'll be abroad yourself, you selfish bastard!' Nikki had screamed in reply.

'Only for a few weeks,' he'd whispered quietly and Nikki had hardly known how to contain her tears. She'd looked for his support. But it just wasn't there.

'I need you here,' he'd said. Nikki had ignored him. Coolly, she told him there'd be no further argument. She'd made up her mind. She was leaving.

They went to sleep locked in their own private worlds, Nikki torn between guilt at wrecking his special moment and her own need to make him listen to her. Falling into a fitful slumber, she began to dream of how things used to be. How it was when they'd first moved in together. Nikki's body had ceased to be her own in those far off, happy days.

Once, when she'd locked herself out of the flat by mistake and was standing on the fire escape, he'd climbed out of the window to 'rescue' her. They'd made love standing on the cold metal steps, his penis slipped in through a hole she had torn in her tights in order to take him there, where they stood, six floors above street level.

Oh, how good that had felt! Her tights ripped, her panties too (a new pair at that), she had groped inside his boxer shorts, easing his thick, warm prick out of its white cotton confinement and guiding it through her ragged underwear into her eager pussy. Pressing down on him, she'd felt the tip of his prick as it drove against her womb, the rhythmic plunges of its shaft massaging her hot and hungry clitoris till the orgasm built inside her. Nikki had thrust her pelvis backwards and forwards in deep, frantic thrusts as Chris had squirted inside her and she came, biting the back of her hand to muffle her moans of delight and prevent her from disturbing the neighbours.

It all came back to her in her dreams and she woke with a smile, roused by the sound of the rain lashing against the window outside. It was still pitch dark and as she floated into consciousness, the misery of the night before hit her like a slap in the face.

She could still see the hurt look in Chris's eyes as she'd called him names. She thought of the dinner that they hadn't eaten. The lavish, extravagant dinner over which Chris had laboured all afternoon.

As Nikki lay in the darkness listening to the rain, she felt the tears trickle down her face and, getting out of bed, she moved across to the window.

The world looked cold and shiny-black under the merciless onslaught of the torrential downpour. What should she do? Her mind was in turmoil.

Shivering, she went back to bed. She'd try to sleep. She'd think it all out tomorrow.

It was raining in Milan that morning as well as in London and though Pierre Valbon had managed to catch his plane, it had been a close thing.

Why, he wondered, did rain always slow traffic down so dramatically?

Leaving home late, he'd gambled on his taxi driver knowing the short cuts and had arrived at the airport with just a few minutes to spare. He'd done it, though, and that was all that counted. In Pierre's world, winning was everything and the shorter the odds, the more exciting.

Pierre Valbon had always been a gambler, his motto being 'chicken today, feathers tomorrow'. But there never were any days of hardship. When his luck at the tables ran out, as it frequently did, Pierre was always pretty sure that there would be a woman around to put him back on his feet.

His speciality was rich widows whose fortunes were more accessible than those of married women whose husbands, so experience had taught him, were as shrewd as their wives were silly.

In all his thirty-five years, neither his luck nor his looks had deserted him. Women had fallen at his feet; quite literally in the case of the Princess Mathilde de Coruna. She remained in his memory as a sobbing, supplicating heap of misery, the recollection of whose distasteful performances was made all the more irksome by the fact that her reputed three-million pound fortune proved to be less than a quarter of that amount.

Pierre leaned back in his seat and glanced at his watch. He could relax. There was a good hour before the plane landed. Plenty of time to formulate his plan of action.

The Contessa de Silva, he felt, would be one of his more pleasurable assignments and the days to come no hardship at all. Pretty, charming and unusually well preserved, he looked forward not only to seeing her country home but to accepting, after a respectable amount of 'consideration', the invitation to spend the summer on her yacht in the South of France which she'd so delicately hinted at only the week before.

Pierre was more than proud of his success with women. With an insight as uncanny as it was ruthless, he never failed to isolate their areas of greatest vulnerability and offer solace.

He'd known from the start that the Contessa had a dark secret. His intuition and cunning had led him to talk about his own unhappy childhood, hinting at violence and watching her carefully as he spoke. Sure enough, her eyes had filled with tears of sympathy as he recounted his tale of woe. Maybe her father had beaten or abused her? He wouldn't ask. He'd wait till she told.

By their third encounter, Pierre knew he held her spellbound and though as yet he had resisted the impulse to seduce her, it was only a matter of time.

Pierre sipped his drink and watched the air hostesses as

they trotted up and down the aircraft, dispensing their saccharine sweetness along with the booze and cabin food. Two out of the three were definitely fuckable and he thought he'd have a bet with himself. Before the plane landed he would get the phone numbers of each of them. When he returned to Milan at the end of the summer, he would have them both. At the same time. In the airport hotel.

Would they do it? Ah, that was the challenge. Their body language told him that each of the girls would be happy to screw him. But together? That might be more difficult.

Pierre's glass was empty and, smiling his most seductive smile, he gestured to one of the two hostesses. She was by his side in an instant. He could smell the faintest trace of her arousal as he looked into her eyes. 'I've been watching you,' he said. 'It's difficult not to.' He saw the flush that his words brought to her cheeks and smiled again. 'Home and dry,' he thought to himself with satisfaction.

The Contessa de Silva had decided to meet Pierre at the airport in the Corniche. Though having Villiers drive her there was less intimate than meeting him alone in her ten-year-old Aston Martin 'runaround', she was anxious to impress.

Yes, Corniche plus chauffeur would be better. More formal, perhaps, but she wanted him to feel assured, relaxed and above all, wanted.

The Contessa de Silva looked at herself in the full-length mirror that stood close by the open French windows of her dressing room.

She liked to see herself in natural daylight, examining her appearance from every angle, hypercritical of every detail that failed to live up to her own impeccable standards.

Naturally slim, in the past few weeks excitement and anticipation had caused her to lose even more weight, recapturing, she'd noticed to her satisfaction, the girlish figure of her youth.

Rich auburn hair in exuberant waves framed a pale, delicately featured face. Her skin was smooth, her expressive green eyes sparkling and her generous mouth always ready to break into a smile which lit up her whole face, a face which betrayed not a trace of the sadness that had haunted her heart since the death of her beloved Dimitri.

A former ballerina with the Russian Ballet, as plain Marianna Ivovich, the Contessa had married Count Dimitri de Silva, forty-five years old to her eighteen and a man of the world.

Though captivated by her beauty, he saw through his young bride's natural charm to the frightened little peasant girl to whom fame and fortune lent only the thinnest veneer of confidence.

Orphaned at the age of fourteen, the Contessa's early life had contained moments of tragedy worthy of the pen of any of the great Russian novelists.

Following an accident at work and a blow to the head, her once kind and placid father had taken to beating her mother for the slightest misdemeanour, real or imagined. Yet when he deserted her, wandering off into the Moscow night crazed with vodka, her mother had never ceased to mourn him or to pray for his return. Each night on the dot of seven she laid his supper out for him and each morning she removed the now spoiled and barely afforded food in silence.

Working in a laundry to support her daughter and her remarkable talent for dance, Marianna's mother had often gone without her own supper to leave food for her absent husband, always believing that one day he would return.

Marianna was at her exercise class when it happened. Taking the usual tram ride back from work, tired and dispirited, Marianna's mother had spotted her husband going into a shabby apartment on the other side of the city.

Waiting and watching outside the apartment, she saw a woman enter, saw through the open window as her husband approached and wrapped his arms around the woman's waist in a gesture of tenderness that Marianna's mother could only stare at in silence. Creeping closer, drawn like a moth to a flame, she had stared through the dirty window, watching as her husband led this woman to a shabby bed in the corner of the shabby room, unfastening his coarse working trousers at the front and pulling up the woman's skirts, pushing his prick into her without preamble or finesse.

Yet how they clung to each other! How the woman moaned and writhed, crying out in an ecstasy that Marianna's mother had all but forgotten, the woman's moans tearing at her heart, blinding her eyes with tears.

She'd watched as her husband had pumped inside this woman, thrusting deep then deeper still. She'd watched as the woman lifted her legs and wrapped herself around his waist, her body hungry for his own as his cock filled her and she buried her face in the collar of his grimy jacket.

Watching them, Marianna's mother had felt her own arousal. She'd felt the lips of her vulva swell and throb and the moistness trickle down into her coarse undergarments. Instantly ashamed, she had turned her eyes away, only to find that she couldn't resist the temptation to look again, remembering what it felt like to take this man inside her own warm and slippery chasm.

Marianna's mother hadn't bought her husband's supper that night. Calmly, she had gathered up her pitiful pay and used it to buy herself a knife. Equally calm, she had returned to the apartment and knocked on the door. As her husband opened it, she stabbed him through the heart.

Dragging the body into the apartment, past the screaming and hysterical woman, she had lain the body tenderly, propping its head with a cushion. Then, lying with her own head on her dead husband's chest, she had opened the veins in both wrists.

It had taken the Count over six months to coax the story from Marianna and when he had, he had devoted his life to restoring her shattered self-esteem. Marianna had grown beautiful, wrapped in the warmth of his love. But then, at the age of sixty-eight, he had died, leaving her all alone.

There was a gentle knock at the door and Silvie, the maid, entered softly, walking across to where her mistress stood, lost in reverie. 'Madame,' she whispered. 'The car is ready.'

With a final glance in the mirror, Marianna swept out of the room, down the carved oak staircase and across the great hall of the palatial country house that for the last two decades she had called home.

Chapter 4

Irana Petrovka was not only a supermodel, she was also a superbitch. Though as Chris looked at her draped across the comfortable old chaise longue in the corner of his studio, he thought she was quite the most exquisite-looking bitch he'd ever seen.

The day had started disastrously. The art director from the Taylor Carter advertising agency had turned up on time that morning. The outfits selected for Irana had arrived minutes later. Her hairdresser, make-up artist and stylist had all shown up at the appointed hour, but Irana herself had not put in an appearance until nine-thirty. It had been 'impossible' to find Chris's studio, she insisted, despite the map faxed to her agency, Models First, the clear instructions handed to her chauffeur and the assurance from Irana herself, given only the day before, that yes, she would arrive at eight-thirty a.m. sharp.

Haughty and imperious, Irana had swept into Chris's studio demanding to see 'the man who will be taking me'. It was obvious that Chris's work had better be to her satisfaction or she would withdraw her cooperation.

A covert reference to her poor timekeeping had sent Irana into a blinding temper which she then claimed had caused a migraine, alleviated only when her personal assistant-come-bodyguard had been summoned to give her a shoulder massage.

Chris was astonished. Though he'd never photographed a

supermodel before, he'd believed them to be, at the very least, professional. This woman was the exception. But, undeniably, also the most beautiful woman he'd ever set eyes on.

Attending to her hair and make-up had eventually started at about ten-thirty. By twelve, a very nervous stylist had begun selecting outfits and accessories for the trial shots that were planned for that day. Late though it was, as soon as Chris got behind the camera he understood why this woman could command such breathtaking fees and why 'super-model' was the only possible label that could be applied to a creature so beautiful as to be almost ethereal.

The shots were magic. And now here she was, stretched out like an exotic panther, smoking a slim cigar, while all around her, everyone from the hairdresser to Chris's cleaning lady – who was waiting patiently to begin her evening's work – was a mass of frazzled nerves and frustrations.

Irana herself appeared entirely relaxed. With her soft, chestnut hair spread out like a halo of dark silk, she smiled gently to herself. She watched the stylist pick up outfit after outfit from where she had stepped out of them. She watched the make-up artist sorting her brushes. She stared languidly at Chris and his assistant as they packed away their cameras and switched off the hot, bright lights which had so accentuated her beauty.

Irana had a love affair with the camera. Not only did she respond to its gaze, she appeared to become aroused by its attention. A curious, physical transformation took place, Chris thought, as though she'd been touched by a man.

Having just despatched her bodyguard for pizza, Irana sat up and, oblivious to the fact that he was busy, called Chris to her side. She'd seen the first of his test shots a few hours earlier and her temper had turned to charm. From the middle of the afternoon onwards, Chris had been treated like a long-lost friend or confidante. But now her shoulders were hurting again.

'Christopher, angel,' said Irana, turning her turquoise gaze in his direction, 'please . . . to rub my back.' Embarrassed, though reassured by the fact that they were in full view of the rest of the studio, Chris dutifully put his hands on Irana's shoulders. 'It is no good like this,' she said as his hands touched the silk of her dressing robe and, with one deft movement, she let it slip off her shoulders to leave her naked, except for a pair of ivory silk French knickers.

Despite his many years as a fashion photographer, Chris was entirely at a loss. 'My shoulders,' said Irana. 'Please. They are aching me.'

Chris's hands moved down to meet her naked flesh as the studio looked on in silence. As he massaged her shoulders, her small, firm breasts moved in rhythm with his stroke, and a gentle murmuring started up in her throat.

Near enough to be seen, though too far away to be heard by others, Irana began whispering to Chris as he rubbed her neck. 'Are you hot for me, my beautiful blond boy?' she purred. 'Does the touch of Irana's skin make you want to love her?'

Chris felt himself getting decidedly uncomfortable and though he went to move his hands away, she reached up and held them tight. 'Just one minute more, my genius photographer,' she whispered. 'Your fingers make me melt for you inside, make me want to open my legs for you, like naughty girl.'

Irana took slow, measured breaths, smiling up at him wickedly. 'Mmm,' she moaned, stretching her neck and sighing.

As the door opened and Irana's bodyguard walked in carrying her favourite American Hot pizza, Chris saw his chance to move away. Shaken, and with a cock like a broom handle, he walked back towards the studio lights, glancing over his shoulder to see Irana, still naked to the waist, lifting a triangle of pizza to her mouth, strands of melted cheese hanging off each side, brushing her breasts.

Chris now dreaded the thought of spending a month with this vixen. The advertising agency still hadn't given approval to any of the locations he had suggested for the shoot though they'd definitely be working abroad – his idea of shooting the campaign at an English stately home having met with a thumbs down.

A month away with this woman! And now, no Nikki to come home to.

Chris hadn't realised that Nikki was so unhappy until last night. She'd broken the news of the Contessa de Silva's offer in a furious and totally unexpected tirade. And the more he'd voiced his objections and concerns, the more Nikki had refuted them, unleashing a torrent of abuse, calling him selfish and, most hurtful of all, jealous.

He'd been totally confused by her sudden outburst and quite taken aback. He'd tried to reason with her but she just hadn't listened. Now his career was taking off, he'd told her, he'd soon be able to help her financially himself. Not for a while maybe but couldn't she be patient? Couldn't she just wait?

This had made no difference. She hadn't even considered it. She'd had this 'chance of a lifetime' offer and she was determined to take it.

Chris had known he was being unreasonable when he'd objected so strongly. He'd been fully aware that part of his motive for wanting her to stay had been purely selfish. But not entirely. After all, what did Nikki really know of this Contessa?

The stiff rod in his pants showed no sign of diminishing and, though he knew it wasn't visible through the heavy black linen of his trousers, he felt sure Irana Petrovka, smiling at him over her third slice of pizza and looking totally at ease with her nakedness, understood exactly what state he was in. 'Bitch,' thought Chris as he continued to pack up ready to go back home to an uncommunicative Nikki. 'Bitch.'

* * *

Irana Petrovka was fascinated. Teasing Chris that afternoon she'd sensed his genuine embarrassment. And while instinct and experience told her that he would prove a memorable lover, there was an essential shyness about him that she found irresistible.

It was early evening. Irana Petrovka had left the studio two hours earlier, commanding her chauffeur to drive her to the exclusive Total Therapy Clinic just off the Brompton Road. Now she was having an aromatherapy massage, her regular daily ritual to remove the toxins and pollutants of the London air from her skin and restore its freshness and bloom.

Closing her eyes, she breathed in the blended and heady aroma of chamomile, lavender and rosewood oils, her senses soothed by the steady, rhythmic kneading.

Tonight she would be dining at Al Fresco, the fashionable new Soho restaurant designed to look like a lush Victorian conservatory, after which she intended to finish the evening at one of the many transvestite clubs of which Soho could offer an interesting 'cross-section'.

She knew that her companion, Guy Linkforth, would be deeply uncomfortable in any of these establishments. This only added to her pleasure. Ludicrously rich and as malleable as a lump of dough, Irana would phone Guy whenever she was in London, keeping him on stand-by to fill those evenings when all she required was an escort, and someone to pick up the tab.

One of the chinless wonder brigade of English aristocracy for whom Irana had nothing but contempt, Guy would put up with anything, take any amount of humiliation, simply to be seen out with a supermodel.

On many occasions Irana had arrived at a restaurant or party with Guy, only to leave with someone else. His role was clearly understood. He was there to pay, to keep quiet and to disappear when required to do so. It was a rotten deal, but one which Guy embraced with all the enthusiasm of a natural born fool.

Irana relaxed as the *effleurage* strokes to her back and shoulders worked their magic. Again, she thought about Chris and the events of the day. A smile played around her lips and she remembered his touch as he rubbed her shoulders. He'd had an erection then, of that she had no doubt.

Lying comfortably on her stomach, she ran the afternoon back through her mind, like rewinding an old film. How deliciously she could have rewritten their scenes together!

Irana sank into her daydream, imagining herself dismissing the photographic crew, leaving the huge expanse of the studio empty but for herself and Chris, who would still be massaging her.

She would guide his hands from her shoulders down to her breasts, moving his sensitive, artistic fingers to cover each nipple, feeling him stroke and massage each deep-red bud into the hardness of complete arousal.

His mouth would come down to kiss her throat then, and soon he would be kneeling before her where she sat on the chaise longue, her robe about her waist, her eyes half closed with desire.

She thought of him undoing the tie of her dressing robe and pushing her gently down till she was lying on her back. She felt his mouth cover her in kisses. She felt his hands as they opened her legs, one hand resting on her knee while the other moved slowly up her thigh and Chris slid his fingers into her soft, wet vulva. She imagined him stroking her clitoris in steady circular movements, varying the pressure from the slightest whisper of a touch to a firmer stroke, squashing the soft folds of flesh against the bone behind. Yes, he'd know just how to touch her, building up the rich, wild waves of pleasure that only his cock could send crashing onto the rocks of orgasm.

She pictured his mouth on her breasts, that serious mouth from which issued only the most sensible, work-related comments. She longed to feel his lips sucking her small, cherry-coloured nipples. She wanted to feel his tongue flicking each little pointed button of flesh while his fingers moved between her legs, exploring the dark wet cavern which waited for him.

In her mind, she felt him enter her. She knew what he would be like, how deeply he would penetrate, how perfectly they would fit together. He would ride her, masterfully and expertly, leading her over the edge of control and into delicious oblivion.

He was thick-set and stocky and he knew that to lie on top of her would bruise her delicate ribs. She saw him making love to her as if from above, the muscles in his back and his small, neat buttocks thrusting while her legs spread out on each side of him like the delicate wings of a pinned butterfly.

He would take his time, she knew that. Long, deep thrusts would give way to burst of hard pumping, his fingers all the while stroking and massaging her clitoris.

He would be alive to her needs, of that she was convinced. His body was as sensitive as it was sensual, his mind even more so. Lost in her reverie she could almost smell the faint odour of his fresh sweat as he thrust inside her, pinning her beneath his stocky body, filling her full of his thick, pulsating cock. Yes, he'd be a world-class fuck. Just the touch of his hands had told her. But could she seduce him?

Irana sighed with confident contentment. She turned onto her back and closed her eyes, feeling the pleasing sensation of her toes being manipulated each in turn, and the soles of her feet stimulated by the deep, probing movements of a practised thumb.

As Chris was leaving the studio and heading for home, Nikki was just beginning to enjoy herself. And she felt entitled. After all, the day had begun miserably enough.

She had woken with a headache that morning to find that Chris had already left the flat, the evidence of last night's abandoned meal still on the table.

Showering quickly, Nikki had cleared up as best she could in the time she had available, arriving at work breathless and tense.

With a sinking heart, she had remembered that the Contessa de Silva was due to phone that afternoon, hoping for a serious answer to her proposal, a genuine commitment to her offer.

But what was Nikki to say? Though she'd told Chris she was definitely going, she still had doubts.

She knew that if she went with the Contessa she might be unhappy. On the other hand, if she stayed in England to please Chris, she would never forgive herself. He'd said he'd soon have the money to help her if she wanted her own business. But she didn't want his money. She wanted her own.

The day had passed slowly. For the first time ever, Nikki had felt that her beauty treatments had a mechanical quality about them. Though her clients seemed perfectly happy, Nikki was not. By four o'clock she was in the small rest room, drinking coffee, when the door opened and Madame Etoile entered, smiling broadly and carrying a large bouquet of flowers with an envelope attached.

'From your young man, I think?' she said inquisitively.

Flustered, Nikki murmured, 'I think so . . . we had a row last night,' at which Madame Etoile made sympathetic clucking noises. Handing over the flowers, she said not to worry, it would now be better.

'If only it were that simple,' thought Nikki as Madame Etoile left the room, patting Nikki's hand as she went.

Opening the envelope, Nikki realised with a shock that the flowers weren't from Chris. There was a simple note saying, 'I will phone you at five. Please say yes. And buy what you need for the trip.' Inside the envelope, accompanying the note, was a large bundle of cash. Counting the crisp notes carefully, Nikki found, to her astonishment, that she had been given a thousand pounds.

'Buy what you need for the trip,' she read again and, suddenly, there was no longer any doubt in her mind.

If Chris was jealous, so be it. He didn't need her around anyway, so what did he have to be resentful about? A more exciting life was beckoning her, daring her to take a chance. She would go late-night shopping at Harrods, finding the perfect bikinis and sunscreens and deck shoes and costume jewellery and everything she wanted.

The Contessa's generous gesture had finally made up her mind. There was no going back.

The Contessa phoned on the dot of five. Nikki told her that yes, she would accept the offer. Sensing that Madame Etoile was in a sympathetic mood, Nikki asked if she might leave a little early and by five-fifteen she was making her way past the green-liveried doorman and into her favourite shop.

Walking into the marble-floored perfume hall on the ground floor, Nikki felt her lingering doubts evaporate completely and a new confidence flood through her mind as she surveyed this busy and exciting temple to the pleasure of luxury, this glorious, glamorous store which she loved so well.

In five years of working on its doorstep, Nikki had never tired of Harrods. From the mixed aromas and bustle of the grand, high-ceilinged food hall to the opulence that lulled her as she strolled through room after room of designer clothes, exquisite crystal, rich furnishings and elaborate antiques, Nikki felt today as she always felt – that one day she would shop here regularly and by rights. There would come a time when she would no longer be in awe of this beautiful store, but as comfortable and relaxed with a Harrods account as she currently was with her Post Office Savings book!

She spent the entire thousand pounds in just over two hours, emerging from the store loaded with parcels.

The thought of going home to face Chris depressed her. The prospect of facing Madame Etoile the next day to tell her she would be leaving depressed her even more.

No matter. Soon she'd be miles away, under a Mediterranean sun. Strengthened by the thought, she hailed a cab and headed back to the flat.

Chapter 5

Pierre was impressed. Though no stranger to elegant surroundings, he found Netherby Hall, the Contessa de Silva's country residence in Hampshire, much to his liking.

The sixteenth-century manor house was decorated in impeccable taste. He approved of everything from the original beams and open fireplaces to the pure linen sheets on his bed – starched and ironed to perfection beneath soft woollen blankets and a heavy brocade counterpane. Shaving requisites stood ready for him in his bathroom. The finest sable-hair shaving brush, a large pot of shaving soap and a traditional cutthroat razor of the kind used in old-fashioned barber's shops. He looked around him with pleasure.

Surveying the room with its small bowl of freshly cut garden flowers on his bedside table, Pierre sighed and realised how much he had missed the subtle pleasures of England. 'I've been in America too long,' he thought. 'Much too long.'

There was a gentle knock at his door and at his command to 'come in' a uniformed maid stepped tentatively into the room. 'May I help you unpack, sir?' she enquired.

Pierre smiled and shook his head. 'I'm fine, thank you,' he replied.

'In which case, sir, the Contessa would be very happy if you would join her in the drawing room for an aperitif at eight p.m.'

The girl left as quietly as she had entered and, slipping out of his clothes and lying naked on top of the bed, Pierre decided to rest for a while. After all, it could be a long night.

The Contessa de Silva had tried to rest since returning from the airport. Her conversation with Pierre during the drive back had been light and full of laughter, and when they had parted downstairs in the hall, agreeing to freshen up and meet for dinner, she had kissed him on the cheek as she would an old friend and had strolled to her room as though about to write a few letters or listen to a play on the radio.

But Marianna was in no mood to relax. Disturbed, she paced her room, unable to rest or even to sit. Never before had she felt this hungry desire for a man, not even her dear Dimitri. Marianna de Silva was consumed with longing for this young man who, she had been deluding herself, was just 'a friend'.

Confused and alarmed, for the first time in years, Marianna felt her poise and natural self-control desert her. If he so much as touched her tonight she knew she would be his. And if he did not, she felt she would die.

Pierre knew exactly how to time his entrance. Hurrying into the drawing room at ten past eight, full of profuse apologies, he saw the high flush of anxiety on Marianna's cheeks and knew that his slight lateness had had the desired effect. 'She's like a bitch on heat,' he thought, 'and every bit as desperate as I could possibly wish.'

Their conversation throughout the meal was pleasant and non-committal. Had Pierre had a good rest after his flight? Was his room comfortable? Pierre showed the required degree of enthusiasm and declared himself fully refreshed and delighted with everything.

Complimenting the Contessa on her home, her garden and, as each course was served, the deliciousness of the food they were eating, Pierre epitomised the gracious house guest.

The little maid who had come to Pierre's room earlier in

the day served the vichysoisse, followed by monkfish, cooked to perfection and presented with a selection of vegetables from the Contessa's garden. When the fine bone china plates had been cleared away and the girl appeared with an exquisitely delicate lime sorbet, Pierre told her that that would be all. Should they wish for coffee, they would ring.

As the girl left the room, Pierre rose to his feet at the end of the long mahogany table and walked towards the Contessa. Kneeling by her side, he held her hands in his own. 'Forgive me for giving instructions to your staff,' he said. 'But I needed to make sure that we would be left alone. Sitting at the other end of the table from you has been torture. This meal has been the most delicious torture I have ever endured.'

Pierre stared up at the Contessa, his eyes awash with emotion. Freeing her hands from his, she placed them on either side of his head, closing her eyes to bury her face in his hair. She kissed him on the head, the forehead, the corners of his eyes, forgetting everything but the touch of his skin beneath her lips. Drinking in the taste of him she sank deep into this moment that was the culmination of her dreams, the end of lonely years of widowhood, longing and iron self-control. 'Marianna,' he murmured. 'Marianna, my darling . . . my only love . . .'

Covering her in kisses he felt her tremble. The slightest touch from his fingertips against her skin set up a shivering which spread throughout her body, shattering the composure he'd come to believe was as much a part of her as the colour of her hair.

He lifted her gently to her feet and led her from the dining room. Hand in hand they crossed the empty, high-ceilinged hall which echoed beneath their footsteps, and on up the huge sweep of staircase which led to his room.

Pushing open the door, Pierre led Marianna into the oak-panelled sanctuary before them and closed the door. 'This is a beautiful room,' he said. 'I lay on the bed earlier and listened to the wind in the trees outside. It's the most peaceful room I've ever been in.'

Marianna smiled up at him in pleasure. Pierre lifted his hand gently to stroke a strand of hair away from her eyes. Guiding her towards the bed he sat her down and, on his hands and knees before her, removed her shoes. Like an obedient child, Marianna sat dutifully while he slowly undressed her, unzipping her dress, removing her slip, easing her panties away from her hips until she lay, naked and breathing deeply, before him on the bed.

Pierre lifted his right hand and carefully traced the curve of Marianna's shape. His fingers trailed from just beneath her left breast to follow the contours of her waist, coming to rest at the top of her thigh.

'Oh, Pierre,' murmured Marianna, her eyes half closing.

'Not so soon, pretty lady,' he replied. 'Not so soon.' The hand that had been stroking her suddenly stiffened. His fingers grabbed her body, dragging her over from her back to lie face down across his knees, her head dangling towards the floor, the rounded pink cheeks of her buttocks up in the air. With a sudden, total shock, Marianna felt a sharp stinging on her backside and, with a mixture of incredulity and fear, realised she was being spanked.

'No,' she cried. 'Pierre, please!' But still the slaps continued.

'You are going to be punished,' she heard him say coldly as the sharp slaps rained down, making her gasp and plead as her buttocks began to burn.

Struggling and squirming, she tried to get up but he held her, pinned across his knee. All of a sudden, the more she struggled the more she became aware of a sudden rising sensation of pleasure which grew with each stinging slap. It was a mixture of fear and arousal that was totally unfamiliar, a longing both to get away from the bee-sting pain and, at the same time, the strange thrill of knowing that there was no escape. She was trapped, pinned and totally at his mercy.

Burning deeply from the blows, Marianna felt herself dragged upwards and pushed face forward onto the bed. Unable to turn round or look up she felt her buttocks being prised apart.

Pierre's fingers reached from behind for her clitoris, rubbing and stroking its slippery little tip as she lay on her stomach, pinioned and unable to move. She felt a deep, hot thrill pour through her body as his fingers explored through the wetness to find the most sensitive folds of her inner lips, touching her gently one minute and scratching her with the points of his nails the next.

He seemed to know her body as well as she knew it herself. Marianna closed her eyes, lost in the waves of pleasure that his hands alone had caused to sweep over her. His fingers moved away and suddenly she felt his cock force its way inside her. Thrusting at her from behind, he turned the burning pain of her buttocks into a deeper and more urgent burning inside as he slid rhythmically in and out, in and out. At each thrust he almost left her body, only to plunge himself back again more deeply into the slippery shaft that tightened and throbbed around him.

With each plunge of his cock, his hunger seemed to grow as he reached deeper into her. Pierre was fucking her as if his life depended upon it, his thrusts causing her to moan as he stretched the sides of her soft canal, which for so long had remained unexplored.

Her juices flowed, coating Pierre in a slippery film despite which she still felt the friction of each deep penetration. As his huge cock filled her, he slid his arms around the front of her belly, his fingers buried in the wet and swollen lips that hid inside the triangle of dark hair between her legs. Closing her eyes more tightly, she gave herself up to the overpowering pleasure of each sensation. Never, never had she imagined it could be like this. Deep inside, at the very top of her velvet passage, she felt it begin . . . the unfamiliar, thrilling wave of deep throbbing at which the entrance to her womb opened wide while the muscles around Pierre's cock began to contract and relax in slow, pulsating spasms over which she had no control.

As Pierre thrust harder still, the sensations grew more intense. Each spasm flooded the length of her from where the top of Pierre's penis trespassed deep inside to the very tip of her clitoris. As he moved within her, she felt her womanhood being thrust towards an unknown joy – a rich, earth-shattering pleasure that made her bear down on his fingers, wriggling her body to make him rub her harder, at the same time pushing her ravenous pussy hard onto his cock, greedily swallowing every bit of him, pumping against him as hard as he pumped inside her.

She heard him pant, his hot breath on her neck as he fucked her from behind like a dog. And she didn't care. This was all she wanted. To be taken by this young man in any way he wished, because she knew, as she felt the orgasm begin, that he'd lead her towards a kind of pleasure she'd only ever imagined.

Marianna awoke to feel the sun on her face. Slipping out of bed like a naughty schoolgirl, she felt the sticky essences of her now sleeping lover cascade down her thighs; the warm, masculine smell of him clinging to her hair, her breasts, her womanhood.

She leant across the bed and touched him gently, her fingers enjoying the silken texture of his thick, black hair yet at the same time afraid lest she wake him.

Marianna crept back to her own room and climbed gratefully into her bed. In a deep, dreamless sleep, she lay cocooned in the softness of her pillows, succumbing to the blissful comfort of her eider-duck duvet billowing inside its fresh white cotton cover, cool to the touch on her burning skin, soothing her exhausted body.

Down in the morning room a freshly cooked breakfast waited forlornly in its silver dishes; eggs, bacon, sausages, mushrooms, kidneys and tomatoes were eventually cleared away and the table relaid for luncheon.

By eleven-fifteen, Silvie, Marianna's personal maid, was becoming anxious. Knocking gently on her mistress's door then entering the room, she found Marianna's bed empty, though steam was pouring forth from the bathroom which led off Marianna's bedchamber.

'Contessa?' murmured Silvie anxiously. 'Are you all right?'

'In here, Silvie,' came the Contessa's reply and, approaching gingerly, Silvie stepped into a scented cloud of perfumed bath essence to find her mistress up to her neck in bubbles.

'Madame,' said Silvie, 'forgive my intrusion, but I was worried. You so rarely sleep this late . . . I was . . .' Blushing and full of confusion, Silvie shrugged her shoulders, both women conscious of the reason for the Contessa's fatigue and both avoiding the subject with as much delicacy as possible.

'I'm fine, my dear,' replied the Contessa, smiling gently at her faithful servant and friend. 'It was a long day, that's all.'

Silvie smiled at her mistress, relieved that they'd both agreed on an unspoken alibi to avoid any further awkwardness.

Laying back in her bath, the Contessa blushed deeply, raising her hand to her face as if to scratch her nose, in order to cover her confusion. Thanking and then dismissing Silvie, she relaxed in the bubbles, wondering why she felt such shyness about what was essentially her own business and nobody else's.

So. He was her lover and he was years younger. Who cares? As the water lapped over her aching limbs, the Contessa thought of the days to come. She had never known such excitement.

She would take him to the yacht, she would lay the whole of the sparkling, shimmering Côte d'Azur at his feet, she would wrap him in a web of love and luxury that he would never wish to escape.

Marianna lifted her hands to her breasts, slippery with

bath oils, and stroked her nipples. At the slightest touch she felt the throbbing in her vulva begin and her weary body longed once again to be coupled with that of Pierre.

She knew that she was his slave, yet the thought did not frighten her. Smiling, she let the water caress her, dreaming of the days and nights to come.

Chapter 6

Nikki watched her suitcase emerge from behind the rubber curtain and head towards her on the packed carousel.

She hadn't wanted flight EA 127 to Nice to ever end. Gliding above banks of white fluffy clouds suspended in the endless blue sky, she'd felt safe, her old life left behind, the new one not yet arrived at. But now she was on the ground among the rush and bustle of the airport.

Though it was only ten a.m. the day was already warm. Golden-brown, happy-looking people chattered animatedly, the women with their glossy, sun-streaked hair, their cool, linen-clad menfolk pushing trollies laden with perfectly matching suitcases. Nikki was suddenly very grateful for the thousand pounds the Contessa had given her. Dressed expensively in a simple cream linen shift dress and clutching her 'good' sunglasses, she didn't feel out of place in this airport of the rich. This warm and scented gateway to one of the world's most glamorous playgrounds.

Nikki knew that she'd have to wait at the airport for a while. Speaking to her new employer on the phone the night before, the Contessa had arranged to pick her up at Nice airport at eleven-fifteen, telling her to have a coffee and a stroll in the meantime.

Nikki suspected that the Contessa was reluctant to disturb Pierre too early. Left to her own devices, Nikki knew the Contessa well enough to believe she would have been there on the dot to meet the plane. Nikki didn't mind. She remembered what it had been like to be newly in love.

Customs cleared, passport inspected, baggage collected, she found a coffee shop and took her seat, surveying the world over a huge cup of frothy cappucino and a chocolate croissant.

In the short time since she'd left England, it had all become like a dream. Since the night she had told Chris of her plans, their relationship had gone rapidly downhill. Both had hidden behind their work as a means of protection, shielding them from the need to communicate, to discuss, to explain, to justify.

Though Nikki hadn't wanted to consider it, as she sat in Nice airport feeling the tension drain from her, she began to face the fact that her relationship with Chris was probably over.

Chris was so wrapped up in his 'big break' that there was no longer any room for her. Maybe their love had been destined to survive only while they were both struggling.

But did she still love him? Yes. That could not be denied. But they'd grown apart, and as Nikki wiped the croissant crumbs from her lips and re-applied her lip gloss, she felt there was no going back.

They hadn't made love since that night three weeks ago. And though he'd driven her to the airport just hours before, his farewell had been bemused, awkward, brotherly almost. Still, he knew where she was, though soon he too would be flying away on the photographic shoot upon which he had pinned all his hopes for the future.

By eleven o'clock Nikki was waiting at the pre-arranged meeting place at the main entrance to the airport, drinking in the soft warmth of the day, feeling the Mediterranean air caress her skin as the sun beat down from a cloudless sky.

Cars came and went, collecting and disgorging their happy, sun-kissed occupants. They looked so relaxed, with the confidence that, so it seemed to Nikki, only money could buy.

At eleven-fifteen precisely, a pale blue Mercedes

convertible came gliding into view and she knew instinctively that this was the Contessa.

She'd been told that Pierre would be driving. That he was anxious to meet her. She doubted this very much, but knowing the Contessa to be always polite, she had accepted the compliment gracefully. What would he be like? She had only seconds to speculate one last time before the car glided to a halt in front of her.

Nikki was aware of the Contessa rushing towards her and kissing her on both cheeks. Overcome and slightly embarrassed by this effusive greeting, she nonetheless had time to notice how well the Contessa looked, how excited, how animated. 'It's good sex,' thought Nikki recognising the signs. She had always known when her clients were having good sex. It glowed from them as clearly as a beacon.

'Nikki,' said the Contessa, 'I want you to meet Pierre.' Standing aside proudly, she pushed a tall, dark man to the fore, a man who'd taken his time in getting out of the car, who'd strolled lazily towards the women, who'd stood quietly by, looking on in suppressed amusement.

'Pierre . . . Nikki,' said the Contessa and, as Nikki looked up at the man who'd extended his hand to take her own, she felt her whole world spin on its axis. She felt herself sinking into a confusion so deep it seemed she would never surface.

Panic set in. As he touched her hand, she felt her body turn to liquid, a jolt of sheer animal lust sending her senses reeling, the merest brush of his fingertips shooting a moist, throbbing spasm of arousal straight between her legs like a little dart of warm pleasure.

It was him. Standing before her she saw, to her fascinated horror, the man she had dreamed about for so long. The man of all those troubled and disturbing dreams stood before her. He really existed. He was here. And she was to spend the sun-kissed summer living next to him on her employer's yacht.

Nikki climbed into the back of the Mercedes as if in a

daze. Huge, white apartment blocks, palm trees, sparkling marinas harbouring millions of pounds worth of sleek white yachts, all flashed past as Pierre steered the car smoothly along the sun-baked coastal road, the smell of the car's soft leather upholstery mingling with waves of 'Chamade', the Contessa's favourite perfume.

Nikki sat quietly, answering the Contessa's questions with as much enthusiasm as she could muster. Yes, the flight had been fine. Yes, Madame Etoile had accepted her resignation regretfully, though without too much fuss. Yes, Chris was well and looking forward to the work he had planned for the summer. Yes, she had been sad to leave him. But had she?

Breathing deeply and slowly and trying to control her emotions, Nikki stared at the back of Pierre's head; jet-black, stylishly cut hair, past which she could catch the occasional glimpse of his fingers on the steering wheel.

How she longed to feel those fingers playing inside her pussy! In her mind's eye she saw him pull over to the side of the road and stop the car. Moving out of the driving seat, he got in the back beside her, lifting her skirt, dragging her panties down over her thighs and burying his face in her furry mound, teasing the soft and throbbing lips which even now were wet and swollen, her panties sticky between her legs. There on the side of the road, he would lick her till she squealed with delight. The tip of his tongue in her vagina, he would taste her till the trickle of her wetness became a torrent. Spreading her wide he would slide into her hot and throbbing pussy as he bit her breasts and she moaned among the soft leather, the sun beating down.

She closed her eyes and tried to banish such thoughts. By the time they arrived at Port Printemps where the boat was moored, Nikki had regained her composure. The Contessa de Silva was an employer not a friend, she'd reminded herself, she needed no excuse to keep a respectful distance from Pierre. She was not on holiday. All would be well. It must be so.

The yacht was more beautiful that she'd ever dreamed. A huge white floating palace lying at anchor in still, calm water in which it was reflected as if in a mirror. The Contessa herself showed Nikki to her cabin and told her to relax. Luncheon would be served at two.

Nikki flopped onto her bed and tried to compose her thoughts. The warm smell of the sea filled the quiet cabin with its freshness, the gentle rocking of the boat lulling her senses. Looking around at her simply furnished yet luxurious surroundings, she knew she had arrived in paradise. So why was her heart racing and her mind unable to rest?

She could not get the image of this man out of her mind. The feel of his fingers on her own when he had come forward to touch her hand. Lying on her bed, she again imagined those fingers reaching into her underwear, moving in circular movements inside her vagina. As she did so, she slipped her own fingers inside her panties, wet with her own juices. It felt good and slippery in there and Nikki began to play with herself, feeling the orgasm come in seconds, so close had she been!

Juddering to its climax, she felt the contractions of her body around her fingers and saw in her mind's eye the image of his beautiful face.

'No,' thought Nikki, getting up from the bed and reaching for her suitcase, ready to unpack. 'No. No. No!'

Marianna de Silva returned to her cabin and slipped out of her black cotton sundress. As she heard the gentle knock at her door, her mouth turned up in a smile and she whispered, 'Come in,' an excited tremor in her voice.

'I wanted you when we were in the car,' said Pierre, advancing towards her. 'Your legs were a little apart the whole way back and . . . and . . .'

'Hush,' she whispered. 'Hush, my darling.' Wrapping her arms around his neck, she gazed into his eyes. 'May I?' she said, smiling at him with her wickedest smile.

'Go on,' replied Pierre, and sinking to her knees she unzipped his trousers, lifting her hand to stroke the thick swelling at the front of his silk boxer shorts. Pierre sighed deeply as Marianna began to kiss him, her lips exploring every inch of his hard, flat stomach.

Easing the boxer shorts down, she stared in wonder at the huge smooth cock that rose from between his slim thighs, the heavy balls that nestled beneath, buried in the forest of his jet-black hair. She revelled in the sheer joy of touching him, tasting him, a voyage of discovery of which Marianna knew she would never tire.

She took his penis in her hand, feeling the hardness beneath the silky skin which seemed stretched almost to breaking point. She felt the throbbing pulse which caused it to give little jerks as it responded to her touch.

Moistening her lips, Marianna guided his cock towards her mouth. She slid her tongue between her teeth to touch its very tip, circling the tiny hole at its end, feeling her desire grow stronger as her tongue came in contact with the slippery white liquid that had escaped from him, lubricating the shaft that Marianna could no longer resist taking into her mouth. She massaged its whole length with gentle compressions of her lips as Pierre's fingers reached down to find their way to her nipples, kneading them between thumb and forefinger, each twist causing Marianna to suck more greedily upon this man as the juices ran from her body and she clenched her legs together to heighten the sensations of pleasure, the throbbing in her pussy which fuelled her own appetite.

With one firm movement, Pierre lifted Marianna under her elbows and placed her, face down, on the bed. Standing behind her, he pulled her backside towards him, causing her to kneel as he did so. Leaning across her, he positioned his hands so that he could reach both her breasts, leaving Marianna kneeling; her body wide apart, wet and welcoming.

He massaged her breasts, his hard cock pressed against her buttocks, thrusting his pelvis as he teased her, working her into a frenzy of desire.

Squeezing against him, she tried to coax him inside her but still he teased her. Burning with hunger, she tried her very hardest to manoeuvre his cock into her wet and craving shaft, rubbing her clitoris against his hard body to find relief from the exquisite torture he was putting her through.

Suddenly she felt his prick at the entrance to her passage and her body opened wide in anticipation. But he took it away again, holding it in his hand and guiding the tip along the length of her throbbing clitoris as she stood kneeling like a mongrel bitch, her body pleading with him to plunge into her, to satiate this terrible longing.

Circling her entrance once more and teasing her clitoris almost to the point of climax, with one great ramming thrust he was inside her. Each stroke of his manhood touched the tip of her womb, the angle of his cock as she knelt on all fours putting the most delicious pressure on her clitoris. She thrilled to every thrust, skin against skin, craving the hot and urgent friction that led to the only kind of pleasure that Marianna now needed from life.

Marianna bore down upon his cock, moving her pelvis in fast circular movements. She felt his thick prick strain at the walls of her yielding passage, filling her with spasms of thrilling sensation, its swollen head invading her very being.

Pierre's short gasps told her that soon he would squirt deep inside her, the shuddering moan of his climax speeding her own as they moved as one towards the moment of release.

With one final deep thrust against him, Marianna came in a flood of ecstasy. Pierre's measured thrusts built up in speed and urgency till he was fucking her hard and fast. Seconds later, a rich moan escaped from his throat as the juices shot out of him, the pleasurable pain of his final, vicious poking leaving Marianna bruised and exhausted.

They fell onto the bed and slept deeply. Out on the deck, shaded by a parasol, Nikki ate her lunch alone.

It was four o'clock. The sweat trickled down the front of her white therapist's gown and for the fourth time in an hour, Nikki reached for the water spray that stood on a table next to her deck chair. Her lunch had been delicious. Melon with parma ham, salad niçoise and a crème caramel had all been served with the utmost solicitousness by Jules. But now she was bored as well as restless. Would every day be like this, she wondered? As if in answer to her question she looked up to see the Contessa walking towards her, her slim body clad in an elegant one-piece citron yellow swimsuit which accentuated her figure to perfection.

'Nikki,' she cried in horror, advancing towards the startled girl. 'What are you doing?'

'Madame,' replied Nikki, flustered and jumping to her feet, 'I was only reading . . .'

'No,' replied the Contessa, 'I mean what are you doing all dressed up?' Seeing the confusion on Nikki's face, Marianna de Silva smiled kindly. 'Nikki. Let's get a few things straight,' she said, motioning for the girl to sit down. 'You are here as my beauty therapist. But unless I am calling you for treatments I want you to relax. I want you to swim and sunbathe and go about. Look around you! This is the most glorious place on earth and the summer is only just beginning. There will be as much play as work, my dear. Starting tonight when we will all go out to dinner together. Now. Go put on your bikini and start getting some colour in that pale complexion. Come to my cabin at six to give me a manicure. That will be all for today.'

Marianna touched Nikki's hand gently, then she was gone. A moment later, Nikki heard a splash. Looking over the gangrail, she saw her employer swimming determinedly towards a little rubber boat attached by a long rope to the back of the yacht – a small, bobbing craft in which Pierre was lazing in the sun, his long muscular legs dangling over the side, his toes dragging slowly backwards and forwards through the warm, fathomless ocean.

Jules stood in the galley chopping radishes. He had enjoyed waiting on the pale blonde girl who had sat in her white uniform, anxiously eating her lunch. He had been relieved when the Contessa had arrived earlier in the week, and though he had reservations about the young man who was accompanying her, he felt that at least the yacht was now in safe hands.

Mademoiselle Cherry had made herself very scarce since the arrival of the Contessa. However, she had summoned him earlier that day to tell him that the sink in her bathroom appeared to be blocked. He knew that soon she would call him again, impatient at being kept waiting, even for a moment.

Jules muttered to himself and chopped faster, an anxious frown furrowing his brow.

'What is it, Papa?' said a voice and, glancing up, Jules looked into the steady green eyes of his son who was standing by his side washing lettuce. Jacques was a good boy. On holiday from school, he had volunteered to give his old father a hand, knowing how busy he was now that the Contessa and her guests had arrived.

'It's nothing,' said Jules. 'Simply that Mademoiselle Cherry has trouble with the basin in her cabin. Well, she'll simply have to wait!'

Jacques had overheard his father talking about Mademoiselle Cherry in hushed and disapproving tones. He'd heard other members of the crew discussing her too – the younger carefree ones describing her in lascivious terms, the older married men voicing their disapproval.

His father had told him never to have anything to do with her. But his father needed help. He was overworked. 'And besides,' thought Jacques. 'I'm a man. What have I to fear?'

Slipping quietly out of the galley, Jacques climbed the steps to the upper deck and the cabin which he knew was strictly out of bounds. With luck she would be off somewhere. He could inspect the problem and hopefully fix it. That would impress his papa.

Knocking gently on Cherry's cabin door, Jacques was commanded to 'enter'. The cabin was cool and the shutters half closed. Sitting at a desk, writing, was the woman he'd been warned about, wearing a simple shirt and culottes.

Explaining the purpose of his visit, he walked past Cherry and into her bathroom, his brow furrowed into a frown much like his father's as he crouched to fiddle with the pipes beneath the sink.

Conscious of the fact that Cherry had got to her feet and was standing in the doorway watching him, Jacques tried to adopt an air of authority and experience way beyond his seventeen years.

'How are you doing?' said Cherry after a couple of awkward moments had passed, a note of mockery in her voice.

'There is a blockage,' replied Jacques, stating the obvious in a voice which he hoped conveyed his unquestionable command of the situation.

Twisting one of the valves beneath the sink with a firm jolt, a jet of water shot out and hit Jacques full in the face, soaking his white shirt and shorts, soaking his hair, leaving him dripping.

From her vantage point in the doorway, Cherry let out a loud shriek of laughter which, despite himself, Jacques found infectious. 'Quick!' she yelled. 'Turn it off . . . turn it OFF!' and falling onto her knees beside him, they wrestled with the water pipe, the relentless jet soaking them both before they managed to stop the gush.

'Oh, Mademoiselle,' said Jacques, blushing deeply. Looking up at the girl whom he'd been told was an ogre, he saw that she was still laughing delightedly.

Jacques continued to look at her, his curiosity aroused by her reaction. She was very pretty in a sultry kind of way. Not fresh-looking like his sisters or mama, but pretty enough just the same. And disturbing.

'You can't go back like that,' she said. 'They'd all laugh. Stay here till you dry off. It's only water. It won't take long.' Ignoring his protests, Cherry ordered the young boy to take off his shirt, draping it across the towel rail in her bathroom.

Pouring them both a glass of rosé wine from the fridge by the bed and bringing the glasses over to where he stood, she told him to take a seat. Despite his ever-cautious papa's dire warning, he felt his faux pas might go unpunished. Or would it?

Cherry asked Jacques how old he was and what his plans were for when he left school. Surprisingly, she seemed genuinely interested and he found himself telling her of his ambition to become an architect, his plans to build an entirely new style of hotel along the Côte d'Azur, his determination to succeed against all odds.

'You are a clever and a wise young man,' she said, smiling up at him from where she had positioned herself on the carpet in front of him. 'Wise enough to know that you must pay for your mistakes.'

Jacques looked closely at Mademoiselle Cherry. She didn't mean to tell his papa of his foolishness. His 'payment' would be something else. He knew exactly what she meant.

She was beautiful. Of that there was no doubt. Beautiful and dangerous. But though entirely inexperienced in love, Jacques lacked the cautious nature of his father. The recklessness that he'd always been encouraged to suppress came to the surface, fuelled by the wine and the intoxicating presence of this woman, so close . . .

Smiling, her eyes half shut, Cherry moved towards him on her knees. He felt her lips on his chest, aware that his penis was swelling uncontrollably inside shorts that were still wet from the earlier soaking.

body on a voyage of fascinated exploration.

Pulling his fingers out of her wet pussy, she told him, 'Now you will fuck me,' and as the colour rose in his cheeks she positioned herself over him on the bed. She lowered her body down upon his fresh young cock, watching his face contort in ecstasy as he felt, for the first time, the pleasure of being inside a woman.

Thrusting tentatively, suddenly his newly liberated lust took over and, unable to control himself, he pumped recklessly, coming with a yelp just moment later. Rolling off him, Cherry felt his juices pour out of her body and was surprised at the intensity of his youthful orgasm. 'I will teach you how to make love slowly, how to satisfy a woman,' said Cherry. 'Now go. And . . .' she added, watching him struggle back into his shorts, 'tell anyone about this and your father will be sacked.'

Chapter 7

Chris hated doing the weekend shopping. Dragging dejectedly around the supermarket, he loaded his trolley with anything that came to hand. If Nikki had been here she would have been lecturing him about getting a balanced diet. He'd always tell her not to nag. But now he wished she was here and nagging him rotten.

It had been a week since she'd left. Seven days since that miserable morning he'd driven her to the airport, not knowing what to say or how to cross the great divide that had opened up between them – a chasm of resentment and misunderstanding so deep that he hadn't known where to begin to try and bridge it.

Chris picked up packet after packet of processed food, stuffed with chemicals, artificial colourants and preservatives. Nikki would have a fit if she saw how he was living. But what did it matter? One more week and then he, too, would be on his way. But try as he might, Chris could no longer muster the enthusiasm he'd felt such a short time ago for this, the assignment of a lifetime.

Irana Petrovka had phoned last night, inviting him to a dinner she was giving at Nikita in Elystan Crescent. Two weeks ago an invitation to be part of a supermodel's entourage would have been a prospect he'd have jumped at. But Chris had declined, pleading a prior and unbreakable engagement. His 'engagement' had been with a pizza and a bottle of wine in front of the TV.

What was happening to him, he wondered, as he stared blankly at row upon row of breakfast cereals. This was his big chance. What was going on?

Next week, surely, it would all be different. On Friday they would fly to Sicily and work would begin. After much consideration, they had finally agreed on a visual concept to express the mood of the new House of Labouchon perfume.

Instead of glamorous locations and be-jewelled images, 'Let your spirit free' was to be given a simple, back-to-nature interpretation, contrasting effectively with the polished and glitzy images usually found in the upmarket, glossy magazines in which the new perfume was to be launched. Well, that was the theory, anyway.

On parched and sun-bleached hillsides, against a backdrop of simple peasant dwellings, Chris would photograph Irana as she'd never been seen before, capturing the erotic essence of both woman and perfume in a way that would best express the agency's idea.

Irana in specially designed simple 'peasant' clothes, gambolling about the beautiful and wild Sicilian countryside. He smiled at the thought. Yet he knew that her beauty would shine out, that the end result would be something very special and quite unique. The next few weeks would make his reputation. So why was he so gloomy?

Chris picked up a giant bag of tortilla chips and, with a sigh, headed for the checkout.

Irana Petrovka was still lying in bed though it was three in the afternoon. Next to her, breathing peacefully, lay Marco Lazalle. Darling of the international tennis circuit, he was, according to the media, the lover of Kiki Angelis, Hollywood's hottest female star and the human embodiment of those traditional, wholesome American values that Hollywood strove so anxiously to promote.

Everyone expected Marco and Kiki to marry. Few knew that Kiki was a lesbian with a predilection for sadomasochistic practices. She also had an ex-girlfriend with permanent brain damage, caused when one of their little sessions of auto-erotic asphyxiation had gone badly wrong. But no one talked about that side of Kiki, least of all Marco.

Irana, though, was someone in whom he could confide. They'd known each other when both were struggling. Each knew secrets about the other that neither would divulge.

Irana felt Marco stir in his sleep and licked her lips in anticipation. It had been fun last night, bumping into him unexpectedly at Nikita's. Poor old Guy Linkforth had ended up like a spare prick at a wedding. But that was his lookout. He knew the score.

As Marco began to surface from sleep, Irana sat up, turned over and climbed across him, straddling his body as his eyes opened to stare up at her, beautiful and predatory as a panther. 'You want more?' he said with amusement, at which Irana pulled herself farther up the bed until her pussy was level with his head, her legs spread wide apart.

'Well, I suppose someone's got to do it,' he said as he brought his face up to her furry mound, his tongue reaching out to touch the tip of her clitoris which hardened in response.

His hunger aroused, he buried his face deeply in the dark softness that yielded to him. As he licked her slowly and firmly, Irana moaned and sighed, bearing down as his tongue slid into her wet canal, shivering with pleasure as he stroked the throbbing folds that met his tongue.

Taking his face away from her pussy and pulling her down the length of his body, he turned her on her back, his mouth still wet with her musky juice. He moved across to suck her breasts, first one and then the other, with the same slow, measured determination that had taken him from number ten in the world's international tennis ratings to become the favourite to take this year's Wimbledon title.

His gentle sucking movements turned to hard pinches and he clasped her nipples with his lips. Marco felt Irana lift her pelvis up to meet him and, spreading the folds of her vulva wide apart with his fingers, he slipped his prick deep inside.

Feeling her excitement mount, Irana slid her hand down gently to the base of his penis, squeezing it with the lightest touch in an effort to slow his ardour and her own.

'I want to take a shower,' she said.

'What, now?' replied Marco incredulously.

Irana moved out from under him, climbing off the bed and heading for the bathroom. Turning on the water, she stepped into the shower cubicle, reaching for the soap with which to massage her tingling breasts. Washing between her legs, she slid her fingers between the swollen lips of her pussy which cried out for the man who lay on his back in the other room, stroking his penis as Irana caressed her own body in the bathroom beyond.

To the amazement of the agent who had arranged for Irana to rent the sumptuous apartment she now occupied in Northcliffe Square, the supermodel had asked for a cheap plastic shower curtain to be hung up in the elegant, marble-floored shower cubicle in which she now stood.

Moving towards this curtain, she felt its wet folds cling to her body. In a voice thick with longing she called out to Marco. Handing him the soap as he came towards her, she asked him to wash her through the flimsy shower curtain, her pleasure enhanced by the feel of the plastic folds clinging to her breasts as the foam slithered over her. As Marco's expert fingers massaged and pinched her in all the ways he knew she loved, she could feel his cock against her. The layer of plastic film between them heightened each sensation, the touch of Marco's lips on her plastic-covered, soapy nipples made her pussy throb and her juices run free. Suddenly she could stand it no more. Ripping the curtain away, her mouth sought hungrily for his, her legs opening as he pressed against her, her pussy tickled by the water that poured down their hot and hungry bodies as they stood clasped in each other's embrace.

With the strength and ease of an athlete, Marco lifted Irana from the ground. He wrapped her legs around his waist and, supporting her under her small, silky buttocks, slid his prick inside her. She gasped, her mouth filling with water as she threw her head back and moaned out her pleasure.

Rammed against the glass wall of the shower, her hands around his neck, he fucked her like the champion he was. The water poured down their bodies and as the steam rose she came in a rush of intense and throbbing pleasure, gyrating her body wildly, squeezing against his cock with a hoarse cry as the spasms of orgasm broke deep inside her.

When they were both exhausted and spent, he wrapped her in a thick white towel and carried her back to the bed. He placed her tired body carefully on the already crumpled sheets. 'Game, set and match, I'd say,' said Irana happily. 'I'm famished. Let's order some lunch.'

Chapter 8

Pierre had been prepared to be a little bored this summer. It didn't matter who the woman was. There always came a time in each assignment when his 'duties' became slightly tedious.

As he sat on the upper deck of the yacht, sipping a kir and idly eating olives, Pierre realised that he wasn't bored at all. For once in his life, he felt strangely elated and happy with his lot.

Firstly, there was the Contessa herself who, much to Pierre's surprise, had proved to be a real 'original'. A middle-aged woman who possessed a degree of genuine modesty that most women of Pierre's acquaintance had shed along with their puppy fat.

Marianna had shown a genuine wonder when introduced to the more adventurous areas of lovemaking. There was much he still had to teach her. Much that she was eager to learn.

The unexpected pleasure of screwing the Contessa was undeniably a bonus, though there were also a number of other, equally unexpected treats.

Rubbing suntan oil into his gleaming upper torso, Pierre mused upon the relationship between the Contessa and her stepdaughter Cherry, a type of woman whom Pierre recognised at once. Greedy, oversexed and overblown, she was destined to make the lives of all around her as unhappy as her own. He knew the type well. He'd seen her face all round the world, staring out at him from a thousand 'society' newspaper columns. Petulant, spoilt and eternally dissatisfied, sucking up each new sensation, each new fashion, each new man who came her way, growing bored and restless as everything she tried failed to offer her the satisfaction she sought.

She was a looker, yes. But too obvious to be really attractive. A woman with too much money and no class who recognised all that she lacked embodied in the elegant person of her stepmother, her hatred for whom was almost tangible, an obsession to the point of sickness. That was an interesting relationship to watch, thought Pierre.

And then there was the little beauty therapist whom Pierre had kept his eye on from the day she arrived. Pale at first, her skin was now the colour of honey, her smooth limbs and small breasts enticing him every time she walked his way.

Unlike most other women along this coastline of decadence and delight, the little beautician never removed her bikini top. Before he left the yacht he determined to see her breasts, to suck them, to discover whatever secret it was that caused her to treat him with such cool civility. For she was not a 'cool' girl, of that he had no doubt.

Nikki, he felt, would be a not-to-be-forgotten fuck. He determined to have her before the summer was out. But not yet. Not now.

Pierre leaned back on his sun lounger with a contented sigh. Another hour to go and then he'd dress for dinner. Where to tonight, he wondered? What little treat did Marianna have planned?

The beauty room on the lower deck smelt pleasantly of herbs, Nikki having crushed some fresh sage and rosemary and mixed them with milk and witch hazel in a refined clay base to make one of the many organic face masks that were part of her beauty therapist's repertoire.

Though she had expected only the most basic equipment, Nikki had been amazed to find that the Contessa had equipped the beauty cabin as lavishly as any salon.

There was everything from a steam cabinet and massage couch to tubs of the latest organic depilatory wax, a whole range of seaweed-based body treatments and mud masks and every possible aromatherapy oil from coconut and jojoba carrier oils through to ylang ylang, sandalwood, patchouli and her favourite tea tree oil.

Like a child in a sweetshop, Nikki had explored the exquisite *maquillage*, the soft towels, the layout of this perfect little working environment in which she felt completely at home.

For the first few days on board the yacht, Nikki had attended only to the Contessa. Her working day had been laughably short. Most of her time had been spent in the sun, a gentle breeze in her hair as she sat on the top deck and the yacht sped out to sea. Each night they moored at a different port along the coast, dropping anchor in the late afternoon to leave time to stroll and explore and to work up an appetite for dinner.

Last night they had stayed at Port Colombe, an enchanting little port with its shops, boutiques and restaurants set against a backdrop of quaint buildings, all of which looked extremely old. It had appeared to be an ancient fishing port. Nikki was surprised when the Contessa told her that the port was in fact quite modern and had been built to resemble something from a more appealing, bygone age. 'Like a film set,' Nikki had thought at the time. 'Like a pretty dream.'

Carefully wiping the white working surfaces of her little salon and placing her brushes in the steriliser, Nikki thought how pleasant it would have been if her duties were confined to caring only for the Contessa. But since last week, Nikki's services had also been called upon by Cherry, the Contessa's stepdaughter, whose coarser complexion and arrogant manner made her visits arduous and unpleasant.

Still, she didn't ask for an appointment too often, at least not so far, preferring to spend her days lolling on deck reading trashy magazines and drinking Pernod.

Nikki surveyed her small kingdom with satisfaction and thought of the evening ahead. The Contessa had been most generous with her invitations, leaving Nikki to eat her dinner alone on very few occasions. Nine times out of ten she was included in the party which left each evening to discover yet another hidden treasure of a restaurant, to eat, drink and laugh among the pretty pink tablecloths and the crystal, succumbing to the seductive pleasures of good food and fine Provençal wines as the sea sucked and spat along the shoreline, wrapping the black night in its warm embrace.

Nikki was excited about tonight. The Contessa had told her they were to dine at the Hotel du Roi near Cap Ferrat. She'd heard much of this magical place. And though she wouldn't admit it even to herself, Nikki was excited at the prospect of spending another evening with Pierre.

The Contessa had invited her old friend Charles, who lived along this part of the coast, to accompany them. A retired English banker, he lived eight months of the year in the small village of Eze, just a few kilometres from where they were moored.

Nikki walked back to her cabin and turned on the shower, moving across to her small wardrobe to select something special for tonight. The red silk. Dramatic yet simple. Yes, that would be perfect.

It was so kind of the Contessa to include her. Kind and generous. She must be truly in love, thought Nikki as a picture of Pierre's face came unbidden into her mind.

They'd been living in close proximity for over three weeks now, yet he still disturbed her as he'd done on the day she first saw him at the airport. He watched her, she knew, and though his manner towards her was very polite, she sensed an undercurrent of meaning in his every remark. Or was she imagining things?

The shower was pleasantly cool and she lathered herself

carefully, feeling tremors of pleasure as her hands caressed her body, the smell of carnations drifting towards her from the soap she had bought in Grasse the week before.

Pierre would not leave her mind. Even as she stepped out of the shower and dried herself, the smooth touch of the towel upon her suntanned skin aroused her, setting her pulses racing, the throbbing between her legs somehow too insistent to be ignored.

Nikki sat on the bed wrapped in her towel and slid the tips of two fingers into her womanhood. Surprised to find how wet she was and, excited by her own arousal, she began to play with herself. She rocked back against her fingers, feeling the pleasure increase as she moved them in and out of her body, at the same time pressing upon her clitoris with her thumb.

She tried to think of Chris but could think only of Pierre. Her dark dreams flooded back to her and the throbbing in her pussy intensified.

As the warm breeze brought the waves slapping against the hull of the yacht and the seabirds dived and called, Nikki lay on her cool cotton sheets, luxuriating in the sensations of her own body. She closed her eyes and imagined that her fingers were Pierre's tongue and that any moment she would feel his chest crushing against her breasts, his thick cock probing between her legs as he screwed her in the heat of the afternoon.

But her fingers just weren't enough! A puny, pathetic substitute for a man.

Moving off the bed and opening the drawer of her bureau, Nikki removed a package which lay hidden beneath her underwear. She'd bought it before she left England. Covered with embarrassment, she'd gone one afternoon into a sex shop, emerging ten minutes later with her shamefaced purchase. She would be away from Chris for months, she'd reasoned, and even before she left she was frustrated. It would help her cope. That was why she'd bought it, though she'd fought steadfastly against the desire to use it. But she could stand this need no longer.

Returning to the bed, Nikki switched the vibrator on and slid the strange object slowly between the lips of her vulva. It whirred against her clitoris, its thick tip wet with her juices as she moved it back and forth, brushing her inner lips. Oh, it felt so good! Pinching her breasts with one hand she manoeuvred it inside her with careful sliding thrusts, the vibrations of her new and thrilling toy leading her towards a deep and satisfying orgasm which she knew she'd have to bite her lip to silence.

Lying on top of the vibrator she opened her wet pussy wide to take the full length of it deep inside her. Moving it up and down slowly, controlling each thrust, Nikki felt her orgasm begin to build. She tried to delay the moment but it was no use. She came in one great shuddering spasm of contractions, her body gripping the vibrator as she pressed it hard against the walls of her glistening channel, her pleasure throbbing through her clitoris and up into the depths of her belly.

Sliding it out of her body, she looked at the vibrator sadly. She had come, but what difference had it made? All the mechanical objects in the world could not satisfy this longing. With a thrill of horror she realised that all she wanted was Pierre.

The restaurant was as fabulous as Nikki had imagined it would be, set upon a verdant hillside with views across the ocean.

While enjoying the driest of martinis, Nikki studied the menu, which Charles was happy to translate for her.

The evening passed in pleasant, civilised conversation. Charles was a good listener and Nikki found herself chatting easily to this tall, distinguished gentleman.

Pierre was charming and very amusing and, Nikki discovered, very well connected. His tales of the scandals and misfortunes that beset those members of the glitterati she'd only ever read about in magazines held her enrapt, his confidential tone and gleeful indiscretions keeping the whole table entertained and enthralled.

After the main course came a delicious champagne sorbet to cleanse the palate, at which point Charles asked his 'charming hostess' if he might have the pleasure of a dance.

The Contessa got to her feet and, resting a fleeting hand on Pierre's shoulder, she was led to the dance floor, disappearing into a melee of chic couples dancing through the warm night to a medley of classic and timeless songs.

Pierre looked across the table and smiled at Nikki. 'You'd rather be in a disco in Cannes right now, wouldn't you?' he enquired. 'If we were there together, just think . . .'

Emboldened by the heady wine coursing through her veins, Nikki looked across at him. 'There's nowhere in the world that I'd rather be than right here, right now,' she replied, trying to show him that, contrary to her instinct, contrary to her body language, contrary to the message in her eyes, she had no interest in anything but what was on offer. But it came out all wrong, her declaration of contentment with her surroundings betrayed by her voice.

'You want to be right here, right now,' he said. 'With me, then. You want to be with me . . .'

Confused and awkward, Nikki was glad to see the Contessa and Charles heading back towards the table. 'Now it is my turn,' said Pierre, getting to his feet and taking the Contessa's hand.

'Oh my dear,' she said, 'let me recover my composure. It is too long since I danced! I am getting lazy.'

'Then I will dance with Nikki,' replied Pierre, 'until you are ready.'

The Contessa smiled across at her beauty therapist. 'Go on,' she said with a smile, 'keep him quiet.'

'Oh, Madame,' said Nikki, her confusion mounting, 'I'm a terrible dancer . . . no . . . it's very kind.'

'He'll teach you!' replied the Contessa, waving her hand dismissively. 'Go on . . . I want to talk to Charles . . .'

Like a woman being led to the gallows, Nikki got to her feet and, without looking at Pierre, walked across to the dance floor. The band struck up 'Lady in Red', at which point all the couples on the floor moved closer together.

Pierre came towards her, taking her hand gently in his own, his other hand on the small of her back, his body close to hers. As the music worked its magic, Nikki felt her body relax, though every instinct for survival told her to keep her distance.

He held her tight, the smell of his skin and hair familiar to her from her strange and tortured dreams. But she wasn't dreaming. He was here and he was real. His hand began to stroke her back, his fingertips moving slowly over her bare skin. As the song came to an end he took her hand, lifting it to his lips, kissing every fingertip in turn. As a parting gesture he slid her index finger between his lips and caressed it with his tongue.

Nikki could hardly stand, her panties soaked by the juices of desire, her legs weak and trembling.

'Thank you,' he said, leading her from the far side of the dance floor back to the table.

They made a night of it. It was two a.m. before they returned to the yacht, the Contessa leaning exhausted and happy on Pierre's arm, Charles escorting Nikki like the gentleman he was.

Nikki returned to her cabin, took off her red dress and lay on the bed. It was so hot! Despite the meal, the dancing and the lateness of the hour, she was wide awake and knew she would not sleep. She was also slightly drunk. Drunk and unsettled and far from home.

She glanced at her watch. Three o'clock. She could not rest. Getting up and walking across to her wardrobe, Nikki rummaged on the shelf till she found what she was looking for. Her black bikini. She would go for a swim.

Out onto the silent deck, Nikki made her way towards the steps at the back of the boat which led down to the sea.

Jules regularly forgot to bring the steps up at night and though his forgetfulness often worried her, tonight she was grateful.

Climbing carefully down, she felt the water come up to meet her, cooling her fevered senses as it soothed her tired body. Striking out into the warm, salty darkness, Nikki decided to swim for a few minutes then return, hoping that she would be able to sleep.

Yards from the boat she became conscious of an object in the water. A large object. She wondered at first if it was a buoy or even, illogically, an abandoned lobster pot. Then it began to move, coming towards her, and Nikki realised it was a head. A body. A man, swimming in her direction.

'Oh, no!' yelled Nikki, her heart beating and her pulse hammering in her throat. 'Please . . . no . . .'

'Shhh!' said a voice. 'Nikki! It's me . . . it's Pierre.' Her heart raced in the darkness as the body caught up with her and a hand reached out, resting on her arm in an attempt to calm her. 'Nikki, it's Pierre.'

Her breath coming in short gasps, Nikki began to shiver. Wrapping his arms around her, Pierre held her tight.

'Oh . . . oh . . .' she gasped. 'What are you doing here?'

'I might ask you the same question,' replied Pierre, a note of sardonic amusement in his voice.

'I . . . I couldn't sleep . . . I was hot,' she replied.

'Mmm,' said Pierre, 'in that red dress you had on tonight, I'd say that again.'

Even though she was hidden by darkness, Nikki felt herself blushing, her confusion, despair and arousal escaping from her lips in a little sigh, barely audible except in such silence.

'Hey,' said Pierre, holding her gently, 'I was only teasing you.'

Nikki knew it was hopeless to protest. He was her

employer's lover. He had no right to be holding her close in the middle of the night, in the middle of the ocean. Yet she knew that if she objected, her protestations would sound hollow and futile, because that is what they would be.

As if reading her thoughts, Pierre whispered quietly in her ear. 'Marianna is sleeping. She was very tired.'

'I must go back,' she replied, her one thought being to get back to the safety of her cabin. But where was safety? She'd paced her cabin for weeks, torn between regret at what had happened between her and Chris and longing for this man, this stranger of her dreams.

'What do you want?' she said.

'I want you just as you want me. I thought we might wait until later but I think that would be difficult for both of us, don't you? But we can both keep a secret. We both have too much to lose.'

Shocked by this spoken betrayal of the Contessa, yet feeling at the same time that here was the chance to get this madness out of her system without the world crashing about her ears, Nikki decided to fight her instinct no longer.

As if by telepathy Pierre knew the effect his words had had on her. Taking her hand, he swam with her back to the yacht. They stood on the deck, silent in the moonlight, the salt water running down their bodies.

Without a word, Pierre guided her towards the steps that led to the upper deck, the sundeck where nobody slept, where no one but the seabirds and the stars would share their secret.

Pierre looked at Nikki as if for the first time, his deep brown eyes boring into her own, holding her gaze. She was no longer afraid.

When his hands reached behind to unhook her bikini top, she held his gaze. When his tongue began to lick the salt from her body she sighed and touched his hair, pulling his head back, boldly seeking his mouth. Her own need banished all fear as her tongue found his own, her lips crushed against those of this man she had dreamed about for so long.

They moved towards one of the cushions strewn about the deck. Pierre sat Nikki down and slipped her damp bikini bottom over her slim, tanned legs, putting it carefully to one side with a meticulousness she found surprising. Laying her on her back, he began to lick her with light little brushings of his tongue, starting at her earlobe and working down past her throat and across to her breasts.

She could smell the sea on their damp bodies. She could feel the wetness between her legs. She longed for him to touch her but still he continued to tease her gently with his tongue, licking the salt from her breasts.

He looked up at her. 'This is all I am going to do to you. I'm not going to fuck you,' he whispered. She gazed down at his huge, erect penis, so hard it had pulled his bathing trunks away from his body. Its firmness had stretched the elastic at their waist to breaking point. And all he would do was lick her!

Tears of shame and frustration started up in her eyes. Nikki struggled free of him and, clambering to her feet, scooping up her bikini, she rushed towards the steps.

He was behind her in a flash, grabbing her arm. Wresting free of him she began to run, anywhere, anywhere to escape this cruel torturer, this man who mocked her. But each time she tried to escape he was behind her, ambushing her as she tried to evade him, laughing at her confusion. He was toying with her and she hated him. Really hated him.

With one huge effort she managed to get past him and place one foot on the top of the ladder. This time though he wasn't playing. Grabbing her, he dragged her back to the upper deck, carrying her towards the cushions laid out to greet the sun which soon would rise to give life to another perfect day. But now it was still dark. And Nikki was struggling.

'You won't scream though, will you?' said Pierre, ramming Nikki's face into one of the cushions and pulling her arms behind her back. She was conscious of her wrists being tied together and felt Pierre kneeling behind her, his muscular body intent on its work.

With a pain that took her breath away she felt his hand come down upon her arse, a stinging slap that brought the tears running from her eyes as one blow followed the next. Rolling her over onto her back, her tied hands squashed beneath her, Pierre spread her legs and began to bite the insides of her thighs. Nikki was alive with strange, unknown sensations, the fear of being tied up and beaten mixed with an unfamiliar arousal which his sharp nips only intensified. Suddenly, the sharpness of his teeth gave way to the soft rasp of his tongue. She felt him lapping the juices which had flowed from her body, soaking the hair between her legs, running down to cover the tops of her thighs where Pierre had been biting her. She felt his hands prising her legs apart as his tongue moved upwards, sliding at last into the burning mound of wet frustration that had waited for him for so long.

Nikki's body moved with pleasure as she felt his tongue touch the tip of her clitoris. At her slightest movement, she felt him grab her legs again.

'Don't move!' he commanded. 'Don't say a word.'

Pinning her legs wide apart he began to flick her slippery wet clitoris with the tip of his tongue. He thrilled her so much that sweat broke out on her forehead and she fought not to cry out.

Nikki was within seconds of orgasm when she felt him lift his head. As he knelt over her, she watched him remove his straining swimming trunks. He cock was far bigger than any she'd ever seen. For such a slim man his penis was, she felt, out of proportion; thrilling to look upon but huge, standing erect between two slim, almost boyish thighs.

Working his way up her body, one knee on either side of her, Pierre's cock came within inches of her face. With her hands pinned behind her, Nikki could neither object to nor control his actions. He began to trace the shape of her mouth with the tip of his penis, teasing her again, bringing it within licking distance then taking it away.

As he stroked her mouth with his prick, following the shape of her lips with its slippery, round knob, she managed to raise her head slightly and grab the skin that surrounded its tip. She pressed her mouth gently but firmly around him, sucking and licking as she felt the shaft slide into her mouth. Now she could smell and taste him. Closing her eyes with pleasure, she began to stroke him with her tongue, careful not to take him too deeply into her throat in case the huge size of him should cause her to choke.

Without warning, Pierre gave one huge thrust to the back of her throat and slid straight out of her mouth. He moved swiftly back down her body to grab her by the ankles. Trapped by the rope that bound her hands, she felt her legs being lifted and wrapped around his neck. She felt his penis at the entrance to her tingling pussy and the tip of him burrowing till he found her opening. In one long, smooth movement, he entered her upturned body. His prick sent a jolt of pleasure through her which she felt in every pore of her skin, from the tips of her fingers tied behind her back to her burning buttocks, a pleasure which coursed through her slithery labia and up into the dark passage which Pierre was pumping and stretching with the full force of his manhood.

As in her dreams, she wasn't allowed to cry out or moan as he fucked her. His huge balls squeezed against her upturned arse as his long fingers pinched her hard and tender nipples and her clitoris was dragged with the force of the friction he created inside her. He pumped and pumped till she felt she could take no more.

Never in her life had she been fucked like this. Instinctively, he knew everything about her. He knew when to pump hard, when to slow down and slide gently in and out. He knew exactly which angle to plunge from to create the maximum pressure which gave her most pleasure.

He knew when Nikki was close to orgasm, slowing his

pace to long, luxurious glides of smooth penetration. With each deep, slow thrust, his cock ran the length of her clitoris, pressing against it in a slow sweep that carried the throbbing up into her gaping womb.

As she came, Nikki could feel blood in her mouth. The spasm of pleasure gripped her so forcefully that she bit her lip to stop herself crying out.

She could feel the knob of his prick as her body closed around it and Pierre's own thrusts grew faster and deeper still. He came seconds later, as the sun began to break over the horizon.

Down in the galley below, Jules dragged himself sleepily towards the cappuccino machine to begin his preparations for another day.

Chapter 9

Nikki had not returned his calls. Though Chris had phoned her twice, leaving careful messages, he had been ignored and there was no point in denying it.

The first time he had kidded himself that maybe she hadn't got the message but when he called again, speaking a second time to Mademoiselle Cherry, she assured him that yes, Nikki had been told of his previous call and his message had been relayed to her, word for word.

Maybe it was Nikki's way of telling him it was all over. He was surprised though. Nikki had never been a coward. The least he would have expected was to hear it from her own lips.

But there was no point in brooding. He would think about what to do when he got back to England but, for now, he had to think only of the days ahead and the work there was to do.

Chris had been charmed by Sicily from the moment their plane had landed in Palermo on a warm and sultry afternoon some three weeks earlier.

Looking for the perfect locations in which to photograph Irana, he had spent the first few days driving alone across the island. Fragrant citrus groves to barren, sun-bleached hillsides . . . the island's colours and contrasts were soon familiar. On and on he drove, from the elegant seaside resort of Mondello to the lonely and majestic Greek ruins in the Valley of the Temples south of Agrigento. At night, he would turn his little hire car back towards Palermo. A whirlpool of a city, Palermo seemed a strange and noisy mix of ancient splendours and modern misery. Glittering streets of baronial palazzo's overlooked narrow alleys where child beggars roasted wild birds and chestnuts over smoking open fires. Poverty and splendour stood side by side, viewing each other with suspicion.

Yet there was no denying the energy of Sicily, its beauty or its cruelty. As the days had gone by, the island itself had come to remind him more and more of Irana – its complex layers of light and shade, its dark corners giving way to elegance and vibrance.

From the day the photographic shoot had begun, Irana had blossomed. Instantly, she'd turned from sophisticated urban she-devil into a ripe, dark-eyed Sicilian peasant, taking on her role with all the fervour of an actress giving an Oscar-winning performance.

She was loving every moment. When work stopped for the day, she would wander across the parched hillsides like the gangly young goats which formed the backdrop to many of Chris's most atmospheric pictures. Sitting in the shade of a tree, she would listen to the crickets chirruping and watch tiny lizards glide sleepily past. She would lie on her back, gazing up at the hazy blue sky, aware of nothing but the heat of the day and the sounds of nature.

She was dangerous, this woman. Seductive and untamed and dangerous as a woman could be. Yet as he got to know her, Chris began to feel that there was also a generous side to her nature, a side which allowed her to give of her best in every photograph. It was a kinder, softer side, though he felt she struggled to disguise it.

One afternoon, they went for a drive to find the town of Corleone. She'd wanted to go there because she'd seen *The Godfather* years ago when she was a child and remembered it as the town where the 'Don of Dons' was born. Chris was fascinated by her effervescent and childlike enthusiasm. Her excitement as she set out in pursuit of the dangerous and forbidden.

Following a winding road through scorched hills, they came upon Corleone, a small town clamped between two rocks. It was a crumbling and neglected spot with a desolate, wary atmosphere, its quiet, bleached buildings yielding no secrets.

Home to generations of Mafiosi, the once dignified town was deserted in the heat of the afternoon. Stray dogs and a long skinny cat searched for shade in the dusty streets.

Disappointed by its depressing atmosphere and the fact that there was nothing much to see, they turned to go back to the hotel. Irana was map reading. After half an hour, they were hopelessly lost.

To Irana, it was all part of the adventure. Like a child, she had put herself in Chris's hands and, though it took them hours to get back and they arrived hot and dishevelled, she hadn't once complained.

By the time Chris and Irana reached the bar of the hotel that evening, the others had been busily making plans. They were to head for a restaurant that had been recommended by a friend of Suzie, Irana's stylist.

Built on a jetty, it overlooked the sea and it was possible to believe that you were completely surrounded by the ocean. They all agreed it sounded like a good idea.

It was a simple, pretty restaurant which served spicy fish dishes, cous cous and grilled mountain lamb as specialities.

As expected, it was full though not overcrowded, the tables being set far enough apart to make it possible to speak without being overheard.

At the table next to theirs sat a group of men talking quietly, all middle-aged and wearing suits. At last, Irana felt she had stumbled upon the Mafia she had been hoping to inspect and her fascination was palpable.

Chris smiled as she toyed with her *cassata*, the superbitch reduced to a wide-eyed girl, naughtily spying on things that were none of her business.

After dinner, the party declared their intention of going to a club. Irana and Chris declined, choosing instead to stroll along the seafront among the local couples, the young and fashionable out to see and be seen, breathing in the balm of the evening air.

Irana and Chris were oblivious to them all. Locked in quiet conversation, they strolled side by side, entirely relaxed, like a couple of old friends.

He hadn't meant to tell her about Nikki. He hadn't meant to tell anyone. The shoot had been going so well he hadn't wanted to introduce even the slightest hint of negativity. But Irana had seemed so different lately. So relaxed. So human. Chris knew he needed to talk. And Irana seemed happy to listen.

Wandering back to the hotel, he didn't refuse when she invited him up to her room for a nightcap. He hadn't wanted to go to his own room where silence was all that awaited him.

Irana's marble-floored bedroom was cool and quiet, the fresh smell of the night air drifting in through the windows. The balcony was wide open and warm breezes ruffled the curtains.

For a moment they stood silently, awkwardly. Then in a quiet, steady voice, Irana told Chris that since the day they'd met she'd wanted him. She told him that although he'd already taken photographs of her, if he wanted to make love to her she knew that this could only add to the magic that already existed between them. A magic that would show itself in his work and make him the most famous fashion photographer on earth.

Nikki didn't want him, Irana did. And yes, he wanted her. He knew that underneath this gentler exterior she was as determined and ruthless as ever and, strangely, that added to her charms.

To possess this complex, beautiful creature, to master her, to feel her shiver in his arms. That was what he wanted now. 'Why not?' he thought ruefully.

Irana sat quietly on the edge of the bed, her hair framing

her face in a soft dark curtain. Chris walked across to her and knelt before her. Loosening her simple cotton top, his hands found their way to her beautiful shoulders as they had done on that fateful afternoon in the studio. Rubbing and kneading her smooth skin he pulled himself up to kneel behind her on the bed, feeling the soft night breezes blow in through the open windows, carrying with them the distant sound of laughter.

When his hands moved down and onto her breasts, Irana let out a sigh and leant back against his chest. Turning her round to face him, Chris lay back on the bed, lifting Irana onto his body, spreading the folds of her simple voluminous skirt as he slid out of his trousers. He lifted her above him to guide her wet opening down onto his erect prick which slid inside her like a knife through butter.

Her skirts billowed out, covering them both as they moved together. Chris's hand slid under her skirt to stroke her little golden buttocks and, breathing deeply as she rode him, Irana squeezed down on his thick erection. She moved her hips to feel him press and strain against the walls of her deep cavern and, as she took him deep inside her, she rubbed her own nipples, hard against the rough fabric of her simple blouse. Irana jerked her body backwards and forwards in sharp, sudden thrusts, manoeuvring his hardness against the soft lips of her labia. She felt his cock pull against the inside of her passage, each thrust of her body driving her on as she circled his prick with her own hungry gyrations. She looked down at him. His stocky, golden body was a powerhouse of quiet masculine strength, harnessed and focused on nothing but fucking her into oblivion.

There had been no great romance. This was a pure, raw fuck of the most basic kind and Irana loved it. She had been determined from the first that his cock was destined to fill her, that the weeks spent in Sicily would find them fucking like animals on barren hillsides and deserted beaches, and the prospect had thrilled her.

She'd needed all the artifice of which she was capable – from her 'little girl lost' technique one minute, to staying aloof and keeping her distance the next. And at last, he was hers. And this was only the beginning. Before they flew home she intended to have her fill of him. She vowed to discover his every secret, to plunder him, body and soul. It had taken her longer than she'd hoped to bring him to her bed. But now he was here.

Chris began to sit up and, as he did so, he tipped Irana onto her back. Climbing on top, he thrust inside her, slowly and deeply. Looking up, she could see his thick cock as it disappeared between her legs, emerging seconds later to plunge back in again. Chris's hair flopped over his eyes and he slid his fingers into the hairy wet cushion of pink flesh above the slippery cavern he was exploring. His hips moved and his breathing grew faster as his thrusts became more intense.

She laughed delightedly as he rode her, holding her knees apart with his hands to push deeper into her. He rubbed her clitoris with his fingers as his other hand came up to knead her tits. Her pleasure was almost uncontainable as he pinned her down, leaning forward to slip his tongue between her lips. She held him tight as he began to ram hard inside her in little short thrusts. She panted as the tip of his penis plundered deeper, all the time growing thicker and longer as the blood pulsed harder into it and he moved further into her tight little pussy which, though wet and slithery, gave a thrilling degree of resistance. Her muscles tightened around him to make each thrust a voyage of discovery, her body as complex and compelling a journey as the one he felt he was beginning to make into her strange unsettled mind. Irana closed her eyes and held him, squeezing him as a snake squeezes its prey. Yes, he'd been worth waiting for, this blond boy. She'd known it from the start. As usual, she thought happily, she hadn't been mistaken.

* * *

Chris was in the bathroom when the phone rang. As the first rays of sun had crept through the shutters he had woken, moving quietly out of bed in search of toothpaste to freshen his mouth and cool water to wash the sleep from his eyes.

Intending to walk straight back into the bedroom, something in the tone of Irana's voice told him that this was an intensely private conversation. It would be polite to wait till it was over before making his presence known. Though he couldn't make out what was being discussed, he heard Irana say, 'Yes, I'm alone. Come straight up,' before replacing the handle of the telephone in its cradle. Supposing it was her hairdresser or one of the assistants? Supposing it was the client who wished to discuss something with her! She must have assumed he'd gone back to his room.

Chris stood in the bathroom clad only in a towel. He looked for a way out. It would be awkward for her to reveal to the world that she'd spent the night with him and, being who she was, the news was bound to get out. And what about Nikki? Looking round, Chris saw a small cupboard in the corner of the bathroom. Praying that it wasn't full of shelves, he moved across to it. It was a broom cupboard of some sort. Thank goodness. Without a second thought, Chris slipped inside.

There was a knock at the door and Irana called, 'Come in.' Peering out from his vantage point through a crack in the bathroom door, Chris saw a man enter the room, rushing to Irana and throwing himself in her arms, sobbing. Chris looked and looked again and still couldn't believe his eyes. Wrapped in Irana's arms, her fingers stroking his hair, was Marco Lazalle, the world's hottest tennis player and fiancé of Kiki Angelis, Hollywood superstar and one of the highest-paid performers in the world.

'Why have you come here?' he heard Irana say gently.

'I had to see you,' he replied. 'I cannot marry her, the filthy, perverted bitch.' Marco was sobbing heavily, his head buried between Irana's breasts.

Irana rocked him to and fro like a mother holding a baby. Her beautiful hair fell over his face, her hands stroking him as soothing noises escaped from her throat. 'Come to bed,' Chris heard her say, 'and I will make you forget.'

Chris slumped down in his tiny cupboard, wanting to watch no longer. She must have simply assumed that he'd gone back to his room. She'd spent the night screwing him and now it was morning and she was onto the next!

A wave of homesickness flooded through Chris's heart as he sat alone in the marble bathroom of Irana Petrovka's suite, unable to escape either from her nearby presence or his own painful thoughts.

Just a few feet away, Marco Lazalle was slipping out of his clothes, leaving them in a heap on the floor as he climbed into Irana's bed, once again placing his head between her breasts, sucking on her nipples like a petulant baby.

Holding him tight, Irana slid her hand down to his prick. Her little fingers manoeuvred the skin covering its tip back and forth, back and forth, as it swelled and rose beneath her touch. As his hips began to move in involuntary thrusts, Irana looked down to kiss the tears from Marco's face.

'It will all be okay,' she said, extricating her body from his and laying him on his back. Sliding down the bed, she leant over his twitching penis, positioning her body above him so she could brush its tip with the soft globes of her breasts. His growing shaft met the hard little buds of her nipples, sending a tremor coursing through them both. His sticky, white liquid had begun to escape and she rubbed it into her tits, her slipperiness making her more excited as the lips between her legs began to swell.

Sitting up, he took hold of her, turning her around so that her legs were astride his body, her arse facing towards him.

Marco slid beneath her till his face was level with her spread buttocks. Pinching her on each bum cheek, he reached up to slide his tongue into the crack of her arse, licking the tight little hole which contracted sharply in response to his touch.

Moving down, his mouth found her wet and slippery womanhood, his tongue probing deep into her cavern as his hands came up to separate the soft, silky lips which guarded its entrance. Dipping his finger into the pool of her, he spread her juices back towards the crack in her arse, sliding his moistened finger inside her back passage, bringing a gasp and grunt of pleasure from her throat.

Taking his tongue away, he bunched three fingers together, plunging them deep inside her softness. He stretched her wider than she was already, preparing her for what was yet to come.

'Have you . . . ?'

'Yes,' replied Irana, 'in the top drawer.'

Moving quickly from the bed, Marco opened a drawer in the small bureau on the far side of the room, returning seconds later holding a huge, black, artificial penis.

With Irana crouching on all fours, Marco stroked her with it, sliding it across her face, guiding it round the back of her neck and down along her backbone to the entrance to her arse and onto the opening of her eager wet cavern. 'This is too big,' murmured Marco. 'It's huge.'

With a dirty laugh Irana replied, 'I can take it.'

Tentatively, Marco began to push its tip into her body which opened to receive its menacing though welcome invasion.

Marco turned her on her back and knelt above her, his heavy penis level with her face. Irana poked out her tongue, touching his balls with its tip, raising her head to take each hairy, pendulous mound between her lips. She massaged them gently as his prick grew longer and harder, murmurs of pleasure escaping from his mouth as he gave himself up to the sensations pulsing through his scrotum and his fingers worked the huge rubber prick up into her eager canal.

As her hunger and pleasure grew, her mouth moved from

squeezing his balls to take his penis between her lips. Each suck prompted him to plunge the dildo deeper inside her. Pinching her own tits as she sucked him, Irana felt herself to be in paradise – her womanhood stretched and throbbing, Marco's fingers deep inside her arse, her fingers pinching her tits and her mouth full of his heaving cock! All her senses were alive at once, her body straining to squeeze each last ounce of pleasure from what was happening to her.

The dildo was so fat it was stretching her body to a degree that was both painful and deeply arousing at the same time. Her clitoris was sore from the friction, but still Marco plunged. His own prick in her mouth grew more fierce in its demands as he slid the thick artificial penis further inside her.

As she felt the muscles of his thighs begin to tighten, she knew that Marco was about to come, his thrusts into her wet darkness with the dildo mirroring his urgent and frantic thrusting in her throat.

Irana pinched her own nipples harder still and surrendered to the feelings which flooded over her. She felt Marco shoot his hot juices into the back of her throat as her body exploded in a rich, orgasmic wave around the hard black artificial cock with which Marco had violated and so deeply pleasured her.

It was ten a.m. when they both fell asleep and Chris was able to make his escape. He had seen nothing of what had happened in the room beyond. Only the sounds had reached him, leaving him in no doubt that Marco Lazalle had forgotten his troubles.

Chapter 10

Cherry smoothed factor six suntan oil into her breasts and down her taut brown belly and thought how fed up she was.

She hadn't had a good screw or even a mediocre one in ages. Young Jacques had been taken *en vacances* by his doting mama. To make matters worse, last week there'd been a tearful visit from Solange. To Cherry's disgust, Solange had said she'd been banned from seeing Mademoiselle ever again. Her papa, it seemed, had discovered a silver miniskirt and a pair of split-crotch panties. A furious interrogation had followed. Solange was forbidden to go out.

'Silly little bitch,' thought Cherry. 'Why couldn't she hide them?'

Even masturbation had got boring, despite Cherry's secret store of sex toys collected from around the world, each more exotic than the last.

To add to her irritation, Cherry couldn't but be aware of her stepmother's obvious fulfilment. The young man she'd brought with her from England was frankly delicious, his huge cock clearly outlined inside swimming trunks which were carefully cut to protect his modesty but failed spectacularly to do so.

Cherry had tried to seduce him from the moment he had arrived on the yacht. He'd politely ignored her overtures. And now she hated him. Hated him as, in her heart, she hated all men. Today, she knew, he was languishing on the upper deck tanning his dark body, the Contessa having gone into Nice for a couple of hours' shopping. The silly little blonde beauty therapist was somewhere below deck, no doubt, busy sticking her brushes up her arse. How did she manage, Cherry wondered. No one could live in this heat, this wonderful caressing heat, without growing randy as hell. How did that silly cow get by?

Turning the pages of her magazine with an air of terminal boredom, Cherry saw Nikki emerge from the lower deck, an acid-green bikini setting off her tan to perfection, her blonde hair loose about her shoulders.

Her figure was perfect. Even Cherry couldn't deny the fact. She watched as the girl walked towards the back of the boat, heading for the ladder which would carry her down to the sea.

Cherry dozed off on her sun lounger, a burning cigarette falling from her hand and leaving a disagreeable dark stain in the perfect varnish of the deck. She awoke some while later, conscious of the figure of Nikki making her way back along the deck, her blonde hair wet and plastered to her head, her eyes dreamy with obvious enjoyment of the swim she'd just taken.

Nikki hadn't noticed Cherry at the other end of the main deck. Glancing about her, she began to head towards the steps which would take her to the sun deck and into the presence of Pierre, tanning his magnificent body which Cherry now hoped would meet with some terrible accident, rendering him impotent and of no use to anyone, least of all the Contessa.

Curious, though not knowing why, Cherry rose from her shaded sunbed and crept into the full glare of the afternoon. Making her way towards the bottom of the steps, she climbed slowly and gingerly till she could just about see the surface of the sundeck without being spotted.

Pierre was sat behind the little beauty therapist, rubbing oil into her back. Though there nothing in the action itself to condemn them, Cherry knew from the way his fingers pressed into her flesh that his knowledge of her body was total. He was fucking her and no mistake. Cherry's hatred rose in her throat like a wave of nausea.

There'd been two phone calls for that little tart in the past couple of weeks and Cherry made sure that neither message had been passed on. She was glad. The girl didn't deserve this basic courtesy.

Unable to rest, Cherry slipped downstairs and, for some reason she couldn't explain, crept into Nikki's cabin, hiding herself under the bed. Her instinct proved reliable. Within minutes she heard the cabin door open softly and voices whispering above her head.

'This is madness,' she heard the little beauty therapist whisper. 'Pierre . . . this can't go on.'

'I'm going to fuck you,' he replied. 'Fuck you senseless . . . take your body and do what I want with it, when I want. You have no say in the matter. Now lie on the bed on your front.'

'No, Pierre, we have to talk,' Cherry heard the girl reply, followed by a squeal as he slapped her. There were more muffled, though rather half-hearted protestations, and then Cherry felt the springs of the bed stretch above her head as Nikki landed on them, face down. There was a slight struggle and then Cherry heard a deep moan as she felt the bed above her head begin to rock violently. Minutes later, she heard the guttural sounds of Pierre as he came, the bed shaking as he thrust his prick hard into Nikki, as if to punish her, as if to wreak some terrible revenge for the feelings she awoke in him.

Cherry heard Nikki begin to sob quietly and, much to her surprise, she heard Pierre mutter, 'I'm sorry. Nikki, forgive me.' After a few more sobs there was silence.

Nikki fell asleep on Pierre's chest while he stroked her hair in a gesture as unfamiliar to him as the feelings which had begun to stir in his heart. He couldn't care for this girl! He didn't love anyone. That was the reason he survived. The only reason he could live the life he did.

Laying Nikki carefully on her back, Pierre parted her legs with the utmost gentleness, kissing the insides of her bruised thighs, his dark head bent intently to his task, his black hair brushing the golden mound between her legs.

His fingers moved along her inner thigh and he reached between her labia. 'I've really hurt you,' he said.

'I'll be all right,' she replied, her voice a strange mix of emotions.

Sliding down towards the thick, red cock that Pierre had used as a battering ram, Nikki began to lick it from the base of the shaft to the very tip. Long, rasping licks as though she were tasting a delicious ice cream about to melt.

Teasing the tip of his prick with her tongue, revelling in every little dip and undulation, she listened as he whispered his desire and need into her ear, spilling a rich tirade of cruel insults and endearments into her consciousness.

He talked filthy to her and, despite herself, Nikki loved it. He treated her like a bitch and a whore and she responded. Sliding off the bed, she disappeared into her bathroom to return moments later clad in black bra, stockings, suspenders and black stilettos. Her excitement was visible, from her measured panting to the wetness that seeped into her black panties, staining them with her excitement.

Pierre came across and knelt before her. His fingers touched the wet patch then pushed her panties to one side as he slid his fingers between the golden hairs of her pussy. Prising her apart, gently this time, he slipped his tongue into the honey-sweetness of her vulva, sucking on her, sniffing her deeply while his other hand stroked her leg, the silky softness of her stockings causing his erection to grow from large to massive.

Pulling his face away and leading her to the bed, he slipped off her damp panties and parted her legs, revealing the wet pink folds of her pussy and the hole beneath which lay open in readiness for him.

Knowing she was sore, he stroked her gently till the juices

flowed, till her deep pink folds were slippery, her clitoris poking out like a little cat's tongue, its pinkness contrasting richly with the silky black of her stockings and suspenders.

This time, he took things more slowly, entering her gently, holding himself in check for fear of hurting her again. When her legs came up around his waist he began to drive deeper into her, their shared appetite overriding everything but the pleasure of rutting like rabbits, their pants and groans more animal than human.

With her tongue inside his mouth and her nails dug deep into his pumping buttocks, Nikki came with a gasp of pleasure, her abandoned and utterly lascivious moans tipping him over the edge of control as her juices flowed to meet his own.

Lying on her stomach beneath the bed, her fingers rammed inside her own vagina, seeking some kind of relief from this torture, Cherry began to know true hatred.

She would finish them both. Finish them. Ruin their lives along with that of her dear stepmother, the Contessa.

Humiliation, frustration and jealousy burned through her body and soul. They had made her ridiculous, all of them. And she would have her revenge.

Chapter 11

The fact that it would soon be over and he could return to England was all that was keeping Chris sane. But what would he be returning to? An empty flat and no Nikki. She was probably having a whale of a time in the South of France, working her way towards her lifetime's ambition, getting closer by the day towards owning the beauty salon she'd always wanted.

No doubt she'd forgotten about him, putting him out of her mind. He must learn to do the same. It was the only way he was going to survive.

And then there was Irana. Her eyes were full of entreaties and her body language shouted a welcome to him every time he crossed a room. But he hadn't lain a finger on her since that terrible morning when she'd assumed him gone and had invited another lover to her bed.

Disgusted and furious though he was with her, he was angry to find that he still fancied her. He'd decided to avoid further complications by keeping out of her way. Except of course when they were working together.

In the late afternoon, Chris would make sure that he was always attached to the party that was heading down to the beach. In the evenings, too, he went along with the crowd.

Though disillusioned with Irana, the beauty of Sicily still held him in its thrall. Each day, a new and more magical vista revealed itself to his delighted gaze.

One night, they'd gone to visit the Greek theatre at

Taormina, its magnificent columns crumbling against a backdrop of smouldering volcano and snow-capped peaks at the point where the sky and sea meet and blend into one.

In this most romantic of settings, Irana had attempted to talk to Chris alone. Pretending that he had forgotten to finalise some minor detail for the next day's shoot, Chris had headed off in the direction of his assistant, leaving Irana standing by herself in the echoing emptiness.

He woke with a start at four o'clock the next morning, instinctively aware of the fact that he was not alone. Sitting up in bed, his eyes blurry with sleep, he saw a figure seated at the end of the bed. He knew immediately that it was Irana. Though sure of the answer, he whispered her name in the darkness, hearing her reply, 'Yes, it's me,' in strange and muffled tones.

'What are you doing here?' he asked wearily, dreading the answer, dreading her stinging rebuke, the contempt with which she would dismiss him, telling him that he was 'finished' as a photographer. He'd rehearsed it all in his mind and he knew that such a confrontation was inevitable.

Instead, much to his surprise, he heard her sobbing in the darkness. Her slim shoulders shook as the tears rolled down her cheeks and little gasps of misery escaped from her lips.

'Irana,' he said, moving down the bed towards her, 'what on earth's the matter?'

'You no want me,' she replied quietly. 'The whole world want me but no you. The only man I want . . . what I do wrong?'

Chris looked closely at Irana and realised that she was playing the 'poor victim' card for all she was worth. She didn't want him. He was simply the 'one who'd got away' and it had damaged her ego. Chris was angry now, angry with her, angry with himself, angry with the whole damned world.

'I saw you,' he said. 'I was in the bathroom when Marco Lazalle came to your bed. You thought I had gone back to my room but I hadn't. I was there all the time.'

'Then why you no come and join in?' replied Irana, her voice full of mockery. Chris could stand it no longer. Quietly, he took her by the shoulders and looked into her eyes. 'Get out of here,' he said. 'You disgust me.'

'I disgusting? Huh!' replied Irana. 'I disgust you? Lousy hypocrite! You leave girlfriend and soon you sleeping with Irana. Then you make fuss because Irana has other friend! I no pretend. I honest! What you think, Christopher? That I yours alone? That we live happy ever after?'

Chris rounded on her, his voice harsh with fury. 'I'd only just fucked you, Irana, and you let another man do the same! What does that make you?'

'Oh, spare me your petit bourgeois morality!' she spat, jumping to her feet, the tears of self-pity on her cheeks turned to tears of anger. 'What you think it take a girl like me to crawl out of gutter and become famous? Sex mean nothing to me! Sex is currency . . . is power . . . is sometimes simple friendship! But it mean nothing. Nothing at all. But with you . . .' she tailed off, her voice choking in her throat. 'It was beautiful. As I knew would be.'

Chris looked at the complex, angry woman now pacing the floor in front of him and thought again how beautiful she was. Maybe she was right. Maybe he was a hypocrite. His mind was a jumble of emotions but his body . . . well, that was a different matter. He had a huge erection. He'd been fighting with her and it had turned him on. But he wasn't going to sleep with her. No way.

'We promise each other nothing,' said Irana, 'But at least I think we both honest. You have hard-on for me since day we meet and if you deny, you lie!'

At a loss to know what to reply, Chris sighed deeply while Irana continued to pace.

Suddenly, she stopped and, climbing onto the bed, she sat opposite Chris, curling her legs into the lotus position beneath her and pulling up her skirt. Chris's heart missed a beat. Underneath she was wearing tight black rubber panties, a zip running the length of her pussy – a zip which she now began, slowly, to undo. The folds of her labia slipped out from their confinement, the sweet odour of her womanhood escaped from its rubber prison.

Unhooking her legs, she spread them wide apart. She brought her knees up so that Chris had a full view of her in the half-light. Unable to stop himself, he moved closer for a better look. Her vaginal lips were engorged, as fat and throbbing as his prick, the whole encased in tight rubber, a prison of delight waiting to be broken into.

Irana slipped off her blouse and Chris saw that she was wearing a black rubber peephole bra, her little pink nipples erect and sticking out of the bra's two moulded cups. He lifted his hand tentatively and reached out to touch the rubber while his other hand moved down to stroke her arse, tightly grasped in its smooth rubber straightjacket.

Smiling at him, Irana slowly rezipped her rubber panties, hiding her pussy from view.

'But I want you,' said Chris, his voice husky, 'you know I do.'

'Then fight me for it,' said Irana, clambering off the bed, her little rubber-clad arse heading towards the door. In a flash, Chris leapt up and grabbed her by the wrists. Mad with desire, he held her as she struggled to wrench her hands free, his superior strength pinning her to the wall. His mouth was crushed against the rubber bra, his lips frantically seeking her nipples, his saliva making the rubber slippery as his tongue and then his teeth found her left nipple, biting and licking the tiny pink bud till it rose, hard and reddened, from its rubber captivity.

Chris tried to get hold of the zip of her panties but Irana squirmed her way out of his grasp. She ran to the other side of the room where Chris caught up with her, cornering her like an animal.

Kicking and biting, he carried her to the bed, his hand on

the zip. Her fingers were wrapped around his, trying to prise them away, fighting him every inch of the way. Her juices flowed inside the hot rubber and his erection grew harder still.

Pinning her down and straddling her thrashing thighs, Chris managed to hold her hands above her head while his other hand fumbled among the slippery rubber for the zip. The harder he held her, the more Irana fought and the sight of her squirming, the black rubber pinching her golden skin, trapping her little red nipples, sent him into a frenzy of lust he had to satisfy.

With a firm yank, Chris managed to rip the zip partly open, his fingers plunging into the wetness that lay beneath the smooth black rubber surface.

Heaving himself on top of a still-struggling Irana, he stuffed his prick into the small opening in the rubber panties and sank into her body. He'd never felt a woman so wet! He was swimming in her tight little pussy, its grasp firm and hot, throbbing in response to his urgent thrusts, Irana's breathing deep and heavy.

'I'll fuck you whenever I want,' he said.

'No,' she replied. 'Whenever Irana want.'

Chris stroked the smooth rubber that covered her arse and again sought her nipples, breathing in the hot, rubbery smell as he sucked on them, his prick exploring the delicious sensations of Irana through the little hole made by the zip.

'It's like keyhole surgery,' he said, smiling down at her, 'except it's keyhole fucking.'

'Good, is not?' she purred.

He felt her hands come up to lift his head away from her tits, guiding his mouth to meet hers, melting her tongue into his as her body strained against his own, taking him deeper.

'So you are not wanting your Irana then?' she laughed in his face. 'Well, you have funny way to show it!'

The photographs were sensational. In the mobile darkroom

Chris had fixed up as soon as they arrived in Sicily, he looked closely at the images of Irana. Rampant, gloriously sexy . . . a free spirit captured on film. An image with which he knew the world would be enraptured.

Sure, she'd had a million pictures taken of her in the past, but nothing like these. He knew that they would make his fortune and his reputation. What's more, he was sleeping with her, one of the world's most beautiful and desirable women.

With a stab of homesickness, a picture of Nikki came into his mind. Nikki as she looked on Sunday mornings, propped up in bed behind the newspapers, nibbling toast and marmalade as she concentrated on catching up with what was happening in the world. Her coffee would grow cold as she relayed to Chris every juicy scandal as she came across it in the paper, laughing, commenting, speculating . . . always disturbing his own concentration so that he frequently had to tell her to shut up.

How he longed to be at home right now, sitting in bed with Nikki, eating toast and simply being happy. He wouldn't tell her to shut up. Not for a moment.

With a sigh, Chris lifted a strip of photographs out of their developing fluid and stared at them closely. Irana the she-devil stared back at him. Bloody wonderful she looked.

Marco Lazalle had assured Irana that he would leave Sicily and fly back to America. One way or another, his relationship with Kiki Angelis must be resolved.

It wasn't that Irana was in love with Marco or he with her. But as one of the few people she cared for and trusted, Irana hadn't liked to see her old friend so upset, so beset by demons.

Poor Marco! His relationship with Kiki had started so innocently and had so quickly got out of hand. Some media hacks had seen them out together a few times and had put two and two together, creating a Hollywood romance that at first neither had objected to – the added attention doing no harm to either's reputation.

Yet once the publicity machine had begun to roll, its progress was relentless. Their relationship had taken on a life of its own and the public's appetite for more and more news of their lives had become insatiable. The public wanted a 'golden couple'. What had started as friendship became something more complicated and, eventually, sinister.

At the start, neither had wanted to marry. Kiki was a lesbian and Marco . . . well he liked her but saw her as little more than someone who shared the same kinds of pressures as he.

When Kiki's girlfriend had been injured by their 'loveplay', Marco's affection had turned to revulsion. But by this time, Kiki knew things about Marco that his adoring public did not. She wanted to marry him. Her increasingly colourful lovelife made the need for some kind of smokescreen of respectability more urgent than ever. If necessary, she'd blackmail him into it.

Marco had promised Irana that he'd return to America and face the music, however discordant that music turned out to be. He'd said he'd leave immediately. But he couldn't. He had to see her again before he left. He needed the strength she gave him. He needed another night in her arms. And then, whatever happened when he arrived home, he'd take it like a man. And in all probability, when he found the courage to tell her he was leaving, so would Kiki. She was more man than woman. If only her devoted public really knew . . .

Chapter 12

Sitting in the sunshine on her hotel balcony, the girl rubbed lemon juice into her wet hair, turning her face up to the sun and closing her eyes. It was warm and pleasant where she sat, though she'd have preferred to have been on the private beach sipping a *coupe de champagne* and looking forward to lunch.

Lunch was her favourite meal of the day. She liked to sit at an umbrella-shaded table and watch the waiters rushing to and fro with their wicker baskets of fresh bread, their huge fragrant salads and dishes of *moules*. She liked to sniff the air, delicately laced with the smell of olive oil and herbs. The sound of popping corks and relaxed conversation mingled with the noise of laughing and splashing at the water's edge.

'Pure Virgin Olive Oil,' she always thought as she smelt the lunch in preparation. About the only thing on this beach that was virgin.

But they couldn't afford the private beach. Rick had said so. He'd left that morning to 'see to some business' in Nice. He wouldn't tell her what he was doing and, in truth, she didn't want to know.

Her name was Charlotte. Though her mother had christened her Kylie, she'd changed it the moment she left home. At the age of fifteen she'd walked out of her mum's council house in Romford and had bought a one-way ticket to London. Whatever happened, she knew she would not return.

Her mum had told her she'd end up on the game, but Charlotte had known better. She had confidence in herself, confidence in her doll-like looks and what's more she had her head screwed on.

In the summer of '94 she'd decided to try her luck at the Cannes Film Festival. She would be an actress. She would fly over there and be 'discovered'. That's what she'd do.

Her trip to Cannes had cost her all her hard-earned savings and by the end of five days she was skint. She never imagined that anywhere on earth could cost so much.

One night, down to her last hundred francs, she had been chatted up by a fat old man called Conrad. He said he was a film director, though by this time Charlotte's initial enthusiasm for acting had turned to deep scepticism.

Still, at least he had bought her dinner. And though she hadn't wanted to go to bed with him, he'd offered her enough to make her change her mind. Enough money to help blot out the memory of his flabby stomach thumping against hers, his garlic-and-cigar-tainted breath flooding her nostrils as his fat, soft hands pawed at her body.

The rest had been easy. Three days more had earned her enough to fly home feeling that her trip hadn't been a complete waste of time.

Two weeks back in the smoke and she'd met Rick. A small-time crook whose occupation he described as 'duckin' and divin'', he was a true Cockney, a plausible, handsome and highly entertaining man of twenty-six whose attitude to life was much like her own. 'There's plenty for everyone,' said Rick. 'But you gotta be quick.'

Trading in stolen goods, dodgy secondhand cars with suspect MOTs and, occasionally, little packets of white powder stashed about his Essex flat, kept Charlotte and Rick in what they regarded as luxury. They had a huge TV with satellite dish, a well-stocked drinks cabinet and a wardrobe full of designer clothes apiece.

Then Rick began to make enemies. Powerful enemies in

low places, men who'd blow your head off as soon as look at you or carve the London tube map on your face as a warning.

It had been time to get out for a while and Charlotte had suggested the South of France. But they'd been here a month and money was running out. Sighing, she hoped that his 'business' meant they could go home soon. Or even pay the hotel bill. That'd be a start.

The Contessa de Silva had been so loaded down with parcels, she hadn't seen the edge of the pavement. She had tripped, landing heavily and twisting her ankle badly. Though her English, Russian and Italian were fluent, she had never mastered more than a rudimentary knowledge of French. So it was a great relief when she heard an English voice and saw the young man pushing his way towards her through the crowd. He told her to sit still.

'I'll call a cab,' he said.

Preferring not to make a fuss, dreading the thought of hospital, Marianna had persuaded the young man that she wished to return to her yacht where, if necessary, she'd summon a doctor. Insisting that he accompany her if she intended to take this course of action, the young man drove back with Marianna in the late afternoon. He lectured her solemnly on the need for immediate medical help. He flattered her throughout the tedious, painful journey. Most of all, he made her laugh.

Rick was very much at ease with middle-aged women. His good looks and instinctive good manners made him very attractive to them. For three days now he had been leaving Charlotte at the hotel and heading off along the Promenade des Anglais in Nice, his sole purpose being to pick up women of a certain age.

Each evening he'd return to tell Charlotte that once again his 'business' had been delayed and money was as tight as before. But he'd been coining it. Love in the afternoon, he'd decided, was no bad thing.

Once he had made enough money, Rick had decided to leave Charlotte with the hotel bill, returning to his house in Essex to change the locks. The trouble he'd been having should have quietened down a bit, though he wouldn't go home before having amassed enough money to buy himself out of any further trouble. And as for Charlotte? He'd had enough of her. Time to move on.

Rick wished he'd met Marianna earlier. He looked at her during the cab ride back to Antibes and thought how much he'd have preferred to take her money than that of the Honourable Mrs Smithson-Barry, the fifty-two year old nymphomaniac he'd just screwed in her suite at the Laguna Hotel.

For a woman of her age and appearance, Mrs Smithson-Barry had been surprisingly adventurous. Pulling off his clothes as soon as the door had closed behind them and running her hands through her neat, bobbed hair, Mrs Smithson-Barry had looked him over from head to foot. Then, in her cut-glass English accent, she'd announced that she had decided to suck him off while he finger-fucked her, after which he'd be required to tie her to the bed and bugger her. Would he mind, she said, if she phoned her husband and he came to watch?

Simple Essex boy that he was, Rick had felt himself moving into uncharted waters, though three hours and five thousand francs later he'd felt adequately compensated for his pains.

Walking out of the hotel he'd met the Contessa, a stroke of luck and, if he played his cards right, maybe his next assignment. But it soon became apparent that the Contessa was otherwise engaged. She mentioned 'Pierre' in her conversation too often for Rick to feel that here was another serious proposition.

When they got back to the yacht, though, she insisted he come aboard for a drink. She insisted on arranging a cab for him back to Nice. She introduced him to Pierre who immediately rushed off to summon a doctor to attend to her ankle. And then she introduced him to Cherry.

Even by Rick's standards, Cherry had proved to be a bit of a handful. Though he'd got the green light from the moment she'd held out her hand in greeting, he hadn't expected her to be quite so wild, quite so reckless. Still, that's what money and freedom did for you. He'd fancied her like mad from the moment he'd set eyes on her and the attraction, he knew, was mutual.

Taking his polite leave of Pierre and the Contessa he'd arranged to meet Cherry later that evening at a well-known nightclub. Before he'd had a chance to recover from the rigours of the day, he'd found himself in a smoky cavern holding her close, her hard, fat nipples pressing through his shirt.

She'd brought some coke with her, disappearing into the loo within seconds of their meeting and returning sparkly-eyed. It was good coke. He was a connoisseur and this lady, he could tell from the first snort, knew how to buy.

But here they were on the dance floor and she was fiddling with the zip on his trousers. He'd never fucked while he danced before, but that was apparently what turned her on.

Smiling and throwing her head back, she took hold of his prick, lifting it out of his underpants and guiding it under the folds of her skirt till he could feel the hair on her pussy. With a rush of pleasure, he encountered the soft wetness, sliding into the tight chasm into which she guided him with consummate ease.

They circled in time to the music, each change of tempo helping to mask his movements inside her as they danced and fucked. His fingers held her at the waist and, as he felt her tremble, he fought the almost overwhelming urge to ram and thrust – an impulse which, if succumbed to, would have given the game away completely. But the floor was crowded and the nightclub dark. If neither of them did anything too stupid, they'd be okay.

'Isn't this wonderful?' Cherry whispered in his ear. 'You're inside me but you can't fuck me properly. Isn't this the most thrilling thing?'

'This,' thought Rick, 'is the ultimate cock tease,' and twirling her in a circle he guided her towards the edge of the dance floor, whirling her through the swing doors and out in the direction of the gents' toilet.

It was empty. Rick pushed her straight into a cubicle, pinning the giggling Cherry up against the wall and releasing his frustration with six sharp thrusts, a deep groan and a long jet of hot juice which poured out of her, down her leg and onto her satin shoes.

She laughed all the way from the nightclub to the smart hotel where she insisted they spend the night. She giggled as she undressed, stripping off at last to give him his first view of her magnificent full breasts and her dark, voluptuous body. A body to make him forget all about Charlotte, all about everything but another line of coke and the warm, fuckable woman who lay on the bed before him. 'Great body,' he said, advancing towards her. 'And great coke. Where d'you get it?'

'Ah,' said Cherry. 'That'd be telling. But if you're a good boy, I might just let you in on my secret.'

Chapter 13

Cherry had asked Pierre to meet her at the Picasso Museum in Antibes at three p.m. The tone of her request earlier that day had been serious and businesslike with no hint of flirtatiousness. There was something, she'd said, he really ought to know.

It was cool and quiet inside the museum as, side by side, they studied the work of Picasso, Modigliani, Max Ernst and the paintings of many other outstanding modern artists, gathered under the museum's imposing roof.

'This must be serious,' thought Pierre. 'She's wearing a skirt that covers her arse.'

Twenty minutes elapsed before Cherry suggested they go and find a café. Strolling out into the bright sunlight, he noticed that she looked pale beneath her tan. 'What the hell's the matter?' he wondered.

Sitting at a pavement café they each ordered a large espresso. Clearing her throat, Cherry then began to speak, her voice hesitant and quieter than usual, her manner subdued.

'I won't pretend that there is any love lost between my stepmother and I,' she began, 'which, if I'm honest, is part of the reason I've asked you here to talk to you.'

Pierre studied her carefully. What on earth was coming next?

'But,' Cherry continued, 'the real reason I've asked to see you is not because of her, but out of respect for the memory of my dear father.' Cherry cleared her throat. 'You see,' she continued, 'when my father died he left the bulk of his estate to his widow Marianna, the Contessa. Though at the same time I must tell you that as his only child he left me very well provided for. Marianna, sadly, is not the most worldly of women. Foolish investments since my father died have eaten away at her fortune. She has very little left, and what she does have she is squandering with reckless extravagance.'

'She's warning me off,' thought Pierre. But still he listened.

'You see,' continued Cherry, 'she is crazy about you . . . utterly besotted . . . and I know she won't let you go.'

'Oh, really?' said Pierre. 'And what does that mean?'

'She is a very emotional woman,' replied Cherry. 'There has been no other man for her since my father. And though she wouldn't confide in me, I know through others how deeply she feels for you. Now you may think this is all to the good. But if you ever want to move on, it might be . . . difficult.'

'If I wanted to go I would leave,' replied Pierre. 'But I am in love with her.'

'He's clever,' thought Cherry. 'Careful and clever.'

Leaning across the table she stared straight into his eyes. 'It's simply that I want to avoid a family scandal, for the sake of my father's memory if nothing else.'

'What are you getting at?' replied Pierre, becoming exasperated.

'Only that her mother was a murderess,' said Cherry quietly. 'A crime of passion. She killed her husband when he tried to leave her. Or hasn't Marianna told you?'

Pierre returned to the yacht in a state of confusion. He'd taken Cherry's tale of murder with a pinch of salt, though what had worried him was the mention of the fact that Marianna had far less money than he'd believed. 'No,' thought Pierre. 'It's just that bitch of a stepdaughter stirring up trouble.'

Pierre made his way to Marianna's cabin. She was having a siesta. She woke at the sight of him and held out her arms. Like the practised gigolo he was, his response was automatic. His face burrowed inside her cream silk dressing robe to find her warm, tanned breasts, his mouth covered her nipples, his hand moved between her legs which opened to welcome him.

She was a beautiful woman, of that there was no doubt. A rather delicious hors d'oeuvre to the main course that the little beauty therapist had become.

Pierre frowned as he thought of Nikki, the memory of her causing his prick to rise as if by reflex action. He heard the Contessa laugh, a deep, sexy laugh as she felt for his penis and found it rock hard.

'You wake me up with such good news,' she said with a smile, rubbing herself against him.

'Marianna, I'm tired,' replied Pierre, trying not to sound curt. He rolled over onto his back and stared at the ceiling.

Unperturbed, Marianna began to fiddle with the buckle of his belt. 'Then I will have to take care of you,' she replied, her eyes shining, her hands undoing his trousers with all the excitement of a small child unwrapping a birthday present.

He looked at her enraptured face. Could that bitch be right? Was Marianna getting through her fortune and, if so, would there be anything left for him? It was worrying, that's for sure. Pierre simply could not afford to waste a whole summer.

The touch of her lips on his prick brought him back to reality. Looking down, he saw her beautiful head bent over him intently as she got to work, her breasts hanging heavy and firm, brushing his thighs as her mouth began gently to lick and knead his cock. He'd taught her to give good head, that was one thing he'd accomplished. She'd learned to open the back of her throat and take the full length of his prick, pumping at full speed, without gagging. And right now he just wanted to relax and let Marianna do all the work.

She sucked, she licked, but after a while she raised her head, her expression that of a reluctant child who doesn't want to be scolded. 'Pierre,' she began hesitantly, 'I adore loving you like this but . . . I . . . I do need you.'

Pierre hated it when women actually asked to be fucked. It got on his nerves. The humility in Marianna's eyes added to his displeasure. 'Then get yourself ready for me,' he said. 'Go on, Marianna. I want to watch you play with yourself.'

'Oh, Pierre,' she said, blushing.

'Go on,' he replied in a tone that wasn't to be disobeyed.

Marianna slipped out of her silk robe and sat naked on the bed. Shyly, reluctantly, she began to finger her breasts, stroking her nipples into wakefulness. He watched her as the strokes became pinches, as her lips parted and her tongue moistened her lips, her eyes closing as the pleasure built up and she became almost oblivious to his presence.

With the agility of the dancer she was, Marianna pulled her legs up under her to sit cross-legged, her labia gaping open to reveal the deep pink of her clitoris, wet and glistening and poking out from her hairy mound like a tiny penis.

With one hand still playing with her breasts, Marianna rubbed the tip of the slithery little button between her thumb and forefinger, alternating her pinches with slow stroking movements. Two fingers together moved the length of her clitoris, delving deep into her chasm and out again, Marianna's body rocking back and forth as she thrust into herself, bearing down on her fingers, straining to extract the maximum amount of pleasure from each thrust.

The hunger in her was extreme, her battle to quieten it with her own touch alone would be hard. Pierre had awakened an appetite in her that only he could satisfy – and he knew it.

Grabbing her by the arm, wrenching her fingers out of her body as he did so, Pierre dragged her towards him, throwing her over his knee and spanking her tight, tanned arse with the fiercest of blows. Marianna squealed as he struck her, his fingers biting into her reddened flesh with all the stinging intensity of a whip.

As he thrashed her with one hand, his other hand felt for her breasts, squeezing her nipples, causing her pain which coursed through her body. It was pain laced with the pleasure of being submissive. She was a slave to the whims of this dark man – a brooding, secret pleasure that Marianna had never known until this summer.

'Please,' she gasped as he continued to slap her, 'please . . . fuck me.'

'Two months ago,' thought Pierre as he pulled her onto the bed and spread her legs, 'two months ago she'd never have used that word.' He could feel the heat from her arse burning from his blows as he grabbed her buttocks and pulled her body up to meet him, his pubic hair mingling with hers as he thrust inside her.

She was very tight and he felt he would come quite soon. 'A good beating really seems to get her going,' he thought as Marianna began to moan, her muscles contracting around his prick as he sucked her tits and her body sucked him in its grasp. But it wasn't him who was going to be sucked, it was her.

Before he left the South of France he would suck her dry of whatever she had left. But suppose there was nothing? The thought filled Pierre with horror and he began to pump inside her, hard and vicious. A groan of pleasure broke from Marianna's lips, her body pinned beneath him like a rag doll.

'The bitch likes to be hurt,' he thought, 'and if she's got no money, she's certainly going to be.'

Chapter 14

Nikki was awakened by the sound of hammering on her cabin door. Jules stood outside in the cool early morning air, his body language betraying a terrible awkwardness. 'Madame wishes to see you,' he said. 'Straight away.'

'But why?' replied Nikki. 'Is she ill? Jules, what on earth is the matter?'

Jules' somewhat formal facade slipped momentarily. 'I don't know, Mademoiselle,' he said, his tone suddenly softer. 'But I have never seen her like this. She is beside herself. She summoned me five minutes ago and told me that you are to attend her immediately.'

With a sense of deep foreboding and an overpowering feeling of guilt, Nikki dressed quickly, dreading the command to the Contessa's cabin, wishing she could be anywhere else on earth right now and most of all, wishing she was safe at home with Chris.

Knocking gently on the Contessa's cabin door, Nikki was ordered to come in. The Contessa sat at her dressing table, her hair loose about her shoulders, her skin pale beneath her tan, looking every bit as fragile as a china doll. Nikki noticed that her eyes were red. Marianna de Silva had been crying.

The Contessa did not get to her feet. 'Pick up that envelope,' she said, gesturing towards a white envelope which lay on a nearby bureau. 'Pick it up, pack your things and be off this yacht before breakfast. I never want to hear from you again.'

Nikki stood dumbstruck, her eyes on the carpet. She knew what it was that the Contessa must have found out, but she couldn't just leave, not like this!

'Madame . . .' she began timidly, at which the Contessa leapt to her feet, her eyes blazing. 'Get off this yacht, you vile and treacherous little tramp!' she yelled. 'Get out of here! Get out!'

Stunned as though she had been slapped in the face, Nikki turned and left the Contessa's cabin, running along the deck of the yacht, her eyes blinded with tears.

Who had told her? For it could only be that the Contessa had found out about Nikki and Pierre. There could be no other reason for this terrible dismissal, this outpouring of hatred in the early dawn.

Nikki ran back to her cabin with her heart racing, the tears streaming down her face. She had never imagined the Contessa could be like this. There had been a gleam of pure loathing in her eyes and it was this, as much as the fact that she had been dismissed, which had shaken Nikki to the very core.

'What now?' she wondered. 'Where do I go from here?'

The tears still running freely, Nikki packed as if in a dream, stuffing her clothes into cases, sweeping her bottles and jars and tubes of suncream into her holdall, anxious only to get away.

She left the yacht in the early dawn, the sound of her own footsteps echoing in her ears.

The Contessa de Silva's hand was shaking as she reached for the bottle of headache pills, swallowing two with a glass of ice-cold mineral water. Never had she felt so bad as she did this morning. Never had her emotions been in such turmoil, her confusion building like pressure in her head, making her feel as though her skull would split in two.

When Nikki had walked in, the Contessa had wanted to hit her, wanted to scream out her pain at this betrayal by someone she had considered to be a friend.

Cherry had come to her the night before, telling her that Nikki had seduced Pierre. The Contessa had dismissed this as a product of Cherry's sick imagination, but Cherry had persisted, giving the Contessa dates and times, all of which added up, all of which were times when she herself had been shopping or otherwise out of the way.

Cherry had told her stepmother intimate details, such as the small strawberry birthmark she had seen on Pierre's left buttock, details of Pierre's body and how he used it that only a lover or a voyeur could have known. For a while, the Contessa tried to believe that it was Cherry herself who had tried to seduce Pierre, spying on him in the shower, maybe, taking notes, but she knew in her heart that this was not the case.

Cherry had then gone on to tell the Contessa that Nikki had hinted to Pierre that the Contessa was unstable. 'Something about your mother,' as Cherry had put it.

Pacing her cabin, her head aching as if gripped in a vice, the Contessa wracked her brains as to when she had confided such intimate details of her past life to Nikki.

She was sure she hadn't said a thing. But maybe . . . in a moment of weakness . . . after all, they had become very close.

Marianna de Silva did not blame Pierre. Since Cherry had spoken to her the night before, she had lain awake thinking. By the early hours of the morning she had convinced herself that whatever had occurred was Nikki's fault. All soft voice and floaty hair, she was nothing less than a witch. Her seduction of Pierre was the cynical and jealous action of a woman whose relationship with her own boyfriend, so she had let slip in recent weeks, had been going downhill, almost to a point of no return. She was an evil and ungrateful girl who had masqueraded as a friend. Hurt as well as angry, the Contessa flopped into a nearby chair, her anger dissolving into bitter tears of pain and loneliness.

* * *

Nikki walked for hours, wrapped in the quiet of the early morning, strolling aimlessly along pavements wet from where they had been thoroughly swept and scrubbed, seeing nothing, aware only of her own misery and confusion.

After three hours she was exhausted. Flopping down at a table outside a small café, she ordered a croissant and a *café au lait*, suddenly aware that she was hungry.

She opened the envelope that the Contessa had given her. Five-thousand francs. This was all she had worked for, it seemed. She had sacrificed her relationship with the only man she had ever really loved, she had lost her head with Pierre and she had betrayed the Contessa, her only true friend and the one person in the world who might have helped her make something of herself.

Nikki stared at the croissant which sat on the plate in front of her. Suddenly she was aware of uncontrollable sobbing, a wrenching, animal sound that seemed to be coming from nearby. Everyone in the café was looking at her and suddenly she realised that the sound was escaping from her own lips.

Cherry de Silva had completely forgotten the troubles and frustrations of recent weeks. Though she hated her stepmother as much as ever, she was nonetheless grateful to her for falling over because, without her stupid sprained ankle, Cherry would never have met Rick.

At the thought of him, she slid her hand down to her mound of Venus, pushing a finger into her pussy, not at all surprised to find that the mere idea of him had made her wet.

He was the best she'd ever had. The best lover and the most fun . . . and with a little encouragement, as crazy as she was.

Last night had been particularly good. Glad that Cherry had found a 'young man' as she put it, and pleased to have been instrumental in their meeting, Marianna de Silva had invited Cherry to bring him to the yacht for dinner.

The first course had passed uneventfully, then Cherry had felt Rick's hand on her knee. Smiling at him, she'd licked her lips and wiggled closer. Rick needed no encouragement. As the Contessa had told Rick all about her house in Hampshire and he had feigned interest, Cherry felt his hand moving up her leg, stroking her thigh, his fingers 'walking' the last couple of inches across her pubic hair. He found her budding little clitoris just as the Contessa had begun to describe her gardens and how beautiful everything looked in the early spring when it started to come into bud.

It was all Cherry had been able to do not to laugh. Rick's face had displayed no emotion as he took Cherry's own little bud between two fingers, stretching it away from the soft, wet folds which surrounded it, rolling it in his grasp as he asked thoughtful questions of the Contessa.

Oh, how the man could use his fingers! With two playing deep inside her vagina, he used his thumb to tickle every little crevice and fold of her pussy. He ate his dinner calmly while he finger-fucked her till the pulse in her clitoris was racing. Her panties were so wet she felt sure she would leave a stain on the ornate chair on which she was sitting.

She knew she was about to come and reached down for his hand to pull it away, to get him to stop. But he was not to be interrupted. Winking at her with a wicked grin, he dabbled inside her hot little pussy in just the right way, his strokes and pressures down in her throbbing and slithery crack showing no mercy for her obvious embarrassment, designed to take her crashing over the top into orgasm.

Cries of ecstasy had broken from Cherry's lips. In a panic, she had lifted her hand to her brow, feigning a sudden shooting pain, as though her gasps were contractions of sheer agony.

The mime had come off as dramatically as Cherry herself, the assembled company all expressing their deep concern when the 'pains' and Cherry's moaning had subsided. Poor Cherry. Was it really bad? But Cherry felt good. Better than ever.

It had been after the meal that she had gone to Marianna's cabin and told her about Nikki and Pierre. Then, feeling more contented than she'd believed possible, Cherry had gone to meet Rick in a small bar in Antibes. She brought him back to the yacht. Giggling, they'd hidden beneath the tarpaulin of one of the yacht's two lifeboats where Rick had set about finishing what he had begun.

It seemed that Nikki had fainted. At least, that's what they told her when she woke up, floating into painful consciousness in the heat of the afternoon in a small room above the café where she'd stopped for her breakfast.

Panicking for a moment, disorientated and afraid, she'd crept downstairs to find herself in the café. The proprietor had come across to her, leading her to a table in the shade and bringing her coffee.

The woman had a kind face. It was full of concern as she had asked Nikki what was wrong. Unable to begin to explain, Nikki told her simply that she was far from home and had lost her job.

'I think you are ill,' said the woman. 'I think you should rest for a while. Your bags are safe. It is okay. You can rest here.'

Gratefully and without protest, Nikki returned to the quiet room above the café and climbed into cool sheets. She must have slept for many hours, for when she woke it was dark outside and she felt calmer.

She ventured downstairs once again and into the café. The woman said she looked a little better. It was good, she said, that Nikki had woken in time not to miss her supper.

Ushering her to a table, they brought her a carafe of rich red wine, some bread and a steaming bowl of *soupe de poissons*.

The café was crowded, a simple and pleasant pavement café with candles stuck in bottles on each table and checked tablecloths upon which were placed ordinary, functional items of cutlery, cruets and the kind of everyday glasses which Nikki had almost forgotten in her recent weeks of drinking out of crystal.

The rich Mediterranean soup flooded into her stomach and the wine soothed her senses as she sat alone at a corner table in a café she knew not where, a homely-faced woman hovering over her, making sure she ate, though she had a dozen other customers to attend to.

'I don't deserve this kindness,' thought Nikki, the tears welling up in her eyes, distorting the figure of the young man who had suddenly appeared, perched on a stool at the front of the café, a guitar over his shoulder. He wore tattered old jeans and a plain white shirt and his dark, curly hair needed cutting. He wasn't handsome, just pleasant-looking. And then he began to sing.

He sang the songs the tourists would enjoy. He sang the songs of the moment. And then as the evening wore on and the mood of the café mellowed, he began to sing songs of love and loss; the sad and some would say corny songs that cross continents and time barriers, the haunting and unforgettable songs that millions of people know are written for them alone.

In her deep misery, the words comforted Nikki and at the same time caused her pain. But she wanted him never to stop, never to break the magic, never to leave her to silence.

But of course his singing came to an end. And it was then that she saw the woman speak to him and he came over, leaning his guitar against the table.

He was English. A student of agriculture busking around Europe for the summer, he'd happened to arrive in the South of France and had had the good fortune to stumble upon this little café, the owner of which, he informed Nikki, was 'pure gold'.

The proprietress was called Madame Aronson. In return for his nightly singing in the bar, she gave him a room and all his meals. His name was Jake. He was pleased to meet Nikki, he said, but told her he'd been watching her and wondering why she looked so sad and so very tired. 'You look shattered,' he said. 'That's just not on in such a beautiful place as this.'

Nikki asked him to have a glass of wine, suddenly realising that she needed to talk. She needed to unburden her soul and sort out her confusion. It didn't matter who he was. 'If I don't talk I think I'll go mad,' she thought.

It was only when Nikki heard Madame Aronson locking the door that she looked up to see that everyone else in the café had gone. Madame Aronson came across to them. 'Time for bed,' she said, smiling. Picking up their empty glasses, she blew out the candle.

Nikki dragged herself up the narrow staircase. A great sense of relief mixed with her exhaustion, though as soon as she got inside her room and closed the door, a wave of sadness engulfed her. She sat on the edge of the bed, conscious of her own loneliness and the feeling of failure which swept over her like a great tide, bursting out in sobs which shook her tired body, her heart breaking.

She couldn't stay here tonight. She should leave. Just pick up her bags and go. But where to? Where on earth in the world could she go?

'Jake,' she said. Dragging herself to her feet, she made her way out of the room and along the short corridor to the room she'd seen him enter just minutes before.

Knocking timidly at the door she waited, hearing the sound of bare feet as he crossed the floor and opened the door ajar, standing there in the half-light in a faded tee-shirt which came down to his knees.

Without a word, Jake stood to one side and Nikki entered his room. He led her to his bed where, sliding thankfully beneath the thin cotton sheet, she cuddled up to him.

'I'm sorry,' she said.

'What for?' he replied. 'For being sad and lonely?'

Though he had been in bed only a few minutes, Jake already smelt of sleep. Wrapped in his arms, Nikki realised that for the first time in a long while, she felt safe.

Jake made no attempt to caress her. She could feel his heartbeat, feel his breathing and, though his penis wasn't erect, he was polite enough to pull away just a little, angling his body so the outline of his cock merely brushed against her. But she could feel him. And she wanted him. Right now, more than anything on earth.

Cuddling up closer, Nikki made sure that her legs came in direct contact with his. She could feel his prick beginning to stir. Nikki began to undo her shirt, slipping it over her head.

The touch of his skin against her breasts with only her bra between them was more arousing than if she'd been naked. Right now they were still pretending that they were just 'friends' and he was simply comforting her. She knew though that any second his hand would be sliding down the front of her bra, his big fingers groping for her nipples. His hardening cock told her so. And there was nothing either of them could do about it.

Nikki had climbed into bed with Jake fully dressed and now she slid out of her skirt, snuggling up to him with a shiver, winding her legs around his.

Looking up at him in the semi-darkness, Nikki saw his face in shadow, his eyes glinting softly as he looked down at her.

'You don't have to do this,' said Jake. 'If you like, I'll just hold you.'

'I want you,' said Nikki, rubbing her cheek against his own. 'Please, Jake . . . I want you.'

His hands moved across to touch her, tentatively at first. His fingers unhooked the clasp of her bra and she sighed as she felt his lips brush the soft down of her throat. Jake's mouth felt like the kiss of a butterfly's wings softly caressing her flesh, moving down from her neck towards her breast, free at last of its lacy confinement.

His coarse, strangely sensitive fingers tugged gently at the nipple of her other breast, coaxing it into a hard, tingling point. His hands and mouth sent hot thrills coursing through her body as his tongue explored every little undulation of her nipple.

Jake's mouth moved on down her body, covering every inch of her skin with gentle kisses. He kissed her breasts and her belly, nibbled her hip bones, licked the inside of her navel. His lips continued down till he found her panties, wet with her juices, the crotch sticky and clinging, clearly outlining the bulging lips that lay beneath.

Jake nibbled through her panties, his teeth ever so gently catching her clitoris between them, the tiny hard bud slipping out of his grasp as it slithered in its own wetness on the other side of the fabric.

At last, sliding her panties down over her legs, Jake bathed his face in her pubic hair. Drinking in the smell of her, he pushed his tongue between the lips of her vulva which opened to greet him like a flower.

In the semi-darkness of his small room, Nikki could see the outline of his penis standing proud and erect between his thighs. His nightshirt had ridden up his body and now he lifted his head for a moment to slip it off, revealing a broad chest lightly dusted with fine, dark hair.

Nikki's pelvis lifted off the bed, straining towards his touch. She reached down to stroke his skin, running her hand over the silken smoothness of his buttocks and guiding his body towards her own.

Nikki felt her body melt as he moved on top of her. The anticipation of feeling his cock slide inside her turned her to liquid.

The familiar smell of her own juices wafted towards her as she felt the moistness in her clitoris increase and the muscles of her vagina relax as the head of his penis met the soft outer hair which hid its entrance. Sliding in her juices, Jake moved his body to place the top of his prick between the outer folds of her labia.

'Are you sure?' he whispered, at which Nikki moved her body towards him in confirmation. His penis entered her in one sure thrust which slid straight into the depths of her, a thrust so gentle yet so firm that Nikki was overcome with an overpowering lust.

He touched her like he'd known her forever and as he began to pump between her legs, Nikki opened them wider still; holding his buttocks, pressing him into her as her pleasure grew. His moans added to her own excitement as he drove in and out of her, the sweet smell of his skin filling her nostrils.

As she pressed her pubic bone hard against his cock, she felt the first warm flood of orgasm building within. His measured thrusts stretched her as she gyrated beneath him, angling her hot and demanding clitoris against his shaft as the intensity of her orgasm grew.

She felt Jake press and pump against the soft walls of her passage, the pulse in his prick beating in time with her own inner pulse.

They came together, Jake spurting inside her as her own pleasure reached its climax with one deep throb, breaking into a thousand rich pulsations which travelled the length of her womanhood. At last, her exhausted body came to rest in Jake's arms. As she fell into a deep and peaceful sleep, his lips were still kissing her face.

Cherry de Silva heard about Nikki's abrupt departure at breakfast the next day. Jules' subdued manner when he came to bring her her morning coffee set her antennae twitching and, once she had showered and slipped into her shorts, she decided to go and find out more.

Jules was not forthcoming. Though she summoned him four times in one hour on one pretext or another, he skilfully avoided answering her questions, his replies evasive until finally she ordered him to sit down opposite her.

'Jules, I will not be messed about,' she said. 'Something

unpleasant has happened and though I know you won't give me any of the lurid details unless I extract your fingernails first, I want to know *what* has happened, if not why.'

'Mademoiselle Nikki has left,' replied Jules, his tone icy. 'Now if you will excuse me, I must attend to Madame's breakfast.'

Ah! At last! One down, Pierre to go. Cherry ate her breakfast with the utmost enjoyment, savouring every mouthful. So, the Contessa had been convinced by her story and the little beauty therapist was out on her ear. Pity it hadn't been Pierre at the same time, but that would come.

Cherry marvelled at her stepmother's stupidity. No doubt she'd find a million and one reasons to convince herself that her darling Pierre had been blameless, but still, the fact that he'd gone astray must be causing her grief.

Cherry luxuriated in the image of her stepmother which now came to mind. Dishevelled without the nauseating pampering of the little beauty therapist, swollen-eyed and haggard, the Contessa would paint a less then pretty picture to the lover she was so desperate to keep. Marvellous! And soon he'd be off, convinced of her growing desperation and lack of real money. The black-haired gigolo would scarper away to pastures new. Cherry was convinced of it.

And he'd be furious that his little paramour had been dismissed. What fun! The tension was mounting and Marianna was beginning to lose out on all counts. 'Hee hee!' laughed Cherry. 'The Contessa loses on all counts!' The poor joke amused her as she split her second croissant and thought ahead to the rendezvous she'd arranged with Rick for later that day. Yes. Things were really looking up. Life was beginning to be interesting again.

Chapter 15

Marianna had explained everything to Pierre. Her most intimate secrets, the sad story of her mother and father . . . the anxiety in her voice betraying her desperate need to be understood, to convince him that her poor mother had been provoked.

'There was never any other kind of violence in my family,' she'd said pitifully.

'I would think that one murder is enough to be going on with,' Pierre had thought, but held his peace.

Nikki's sudden departure was even harder for Marianna to speak about. She was 'unsatisfactory' said the Contessa. Her work had been getting lazy. Pierre knew she was lying and she was aware that he saw straight through her. 'She's desperate,' he thought. Her stepdaughter was right. It looked like she'd say anything to keep him.

It was late July. By the end of August, Pierre had intended to be on his way, his bank balance fatter, his future, in the medium term at least, assured. Pierre had gambling debts that had to be settled by September or life could become unpleasant. Marianna had been lined up to pay them. Now he wasn't so sure.

They were sitting on deck, watching the sun go down. Jules had brought them a bottle of Veuve Cliquot and some macadamia nuts. Pierre was sipping listlessly and staring aimlessly out to sea. 'I am going to lose him,' thought

Marianna in quiet desperation. 'I must do something.'

With a brightness in her manner that she did not feel, she began to speak. 'Pierre,' she said. 'I want us to go away for a few days. I want us to go to Paris and attend to your autumn wardrobe. Do you think it's too early, my dear? If we go soon, at least the tailors can make a start.'

Much to her relief and delight, Pierre leant across, took her hand and kissed it. 'That would be wonderful,' he said, his mind racing ahead.

They remained on deck until it began to get dark. Jules opened another bottle of champagne, quietly informing Madame that dinner was ready when they were. But Marianna did not want to move. Suddenly, with the mention of Paris, Pierre had looked happy again. 'Let's just sit here a while,' she thought. 'Let's get a little drunk and then go straight to bed.'

Pierre was feeling better. Though he'd been bitter about Nikki's dismissal and had begun to feel irritated by the Contessa, the mention of Paris had shown him a way out. Yes, he'd go with her and let her buy him a whole new wardrobe. Then he'd stage some sudden financial crisis, an urgent call from his London brokers, perhaps, and ask her to raise a temporary loan. A huge loan but one he'd assure her would be repaid in days. If she had no money, he'd find out. But if she had only borrowing power left, he'd use it all. And, if the worst came to the worst, there were other women in Paris of Pierre's acquaintance whom he could move on to. The thought cheered him. One way or another, he'd know if this summer had been a waste of time. And he'd know soon.

But why didn't Marianna understand the rules of the game? He looked at her, starry-eyed and animated as she flattered him, flirting with him like a fifteen year old. Why did she think he'd stay for the autumn? He'd spent the summer with her. If she'd had any sense, she'd have just written him out a huge cheque and seen him on his way. Other women understood this, why not Marianna? Or was she really as poor as Cherry had said? Well, either way he'd discover the truth soon enough.

Marianna was floating on air as they descended to her cabin. He seemed to have forgiven her. His mood had changed when she had mentioned Paris and, for the first time in days, she felt he was back with her again, staring deep into her eyes, touching her hand, making her feel that the world was exciting and new and she, Marianna de Silva, the most beautiful woman on the planet.

Oh, she'd spoil him so much when they got to Paris! He could have anything he wanted. How could she have been foolish enough to think that he'd happily spend all summer on board her yacht? He was a cosmopolitan man, a sophisticated man, he needed contrast, culture, the excitement of the city. He must have been growing bored for weeks. Maybe that's why he'd fallen for Nikki's scheming. How could she have been so stupid?

She'd make it up to him. He could have everything. She'd already bought him presents but nothing to what she would buy him now.

Pierre knew he wouldn't get an erection if he thought he was making love to a pauper. Money turned him on like nothing else, so he must look on the good side, think positive and imagine that Marianna was loaded. Like the true professional he was, he conjured up a picture of her writing out a cheque for five hundred thousand francs. Mmm. That felt better. He could feel his erection beginning to swell.

Marianna was standing before him in stockings and suspenders. They were flesh-coloured; a delicate ensemble above which she wore a matching flesh-coloured bra, her nipples visible through the beautiful lace of which the two cups were constructed. Above the suspenders she wore a pair of silk French knickers, gossamer thin and covering her from belly to upper thigh. The lace trim stopped two inches short of the suspender buckles, leaving a spread of smooth naked flesh beneath the silk.

Pierre sank to his knees before her and simply stared. She stood in front of him, breathing deeply, longing for his approval.

'Five hundred thousand francs,' thought Pierre. Lifting his index finger, he touched her just above her stocking top, moving his finger to trace the ornate lace border of her stocking into which the suspender buckle was fastened.

Marianna shuddered at his touch. He could smell her, scent her arousal, and he knew that his touch had set her body pounding. The silk panties would soon be sodden. She'd be begging for it. Another good reason to take his time.

Standing up and leading her over to the bed, he made her crouch on all fours, instructing her to keep still. Obediently and quietly, Marianna placed the palms of her hands flat down on the bed and dropped to her knees, her breasts pointing downwards, her arse in the air, the silk of her knickers worked into the crack of her buttocks as she knelt quite still. Pierre surveyed her, coming level with her face as he bent to study her tits, hanging down before her in their lacy cage.

Again he simply touched her, the lightest brush from his fingertips across the front of one breast and then the other.

Marianna let out a moan, her nipples hardening at once, her breath coming faster as her body shuddered.

'Where do you keep your stockings?' said Pierre, to which Marianna replied, 'In the drawer over there.' Returning seconds later with a black silk stocking in his hand, Pierre tied it tightly around Marianna's eyes telling her as he did so, not to move a muscle.

He circled her once more. Her French knickers, clinging to the curves of her arse, were now wet with her juices. Stroking his flat palm over her buttocks, he brought his hand down to the wetness, spreading his fingers as they travelled over her smooth bum cheeks and pushing one finger into her gaping pussy.

As his finger moved inside her, Marianna pushed her body backwards, greedily seeking the sensation of being entered, her pussy covering and engulfing his finger which he withdrew in an instant, slapping her hard on the arse as he pulled out of her and leaning across to bite her sharply on the buttock. Marianna cried out but Pierre had no sympathy. 'Do as you're told,' he said. 'Move only when I tell you.'

Leaning across, her he unhooked her bra. He positioned himself beneath her and studied her breasts from below. She knew he was there. She could smell him and feel him breathing. But she didn't know what he was going to do. Her breasts were crying out to be touched, sucked, bitten . . . but all she could do was wait.

Pierre enjoyed torturing Marianna. He lay beneath her breasts for a full minute before poking his tongue out to spread a film of saliva across one nipple, her shudder of pleasure heightened by the tortured anticipation as she crouched on all fours, unable to see what was to happen next.

He took his time, his licks turning to pinches and sucks as Marianna's breathing grew deeper. Eventually, Pierre slid his prick out of his trousers, stroking himself as he played with her breasts, making them wobble and move as his tongue spread across them. The smell of Marianna's hot pussy assailed his nostrils as he worked his prick between his hand, turning occasionally to watch it as it grew huge – the hardest erection he'd had for months.

'Five hundred thousand francs,' thought Pierre, 'that's what I'm going to have.' Sliding out from underneath Marianna's tits, he swung round behind her, ripping her sodden knickers to one side and ramming his cock hard up inside her dripping pussy. A cry of sheer animal lust escaped from her lips as he fucked her hard and fast, her delicate lingerie somehow incongruous as he shagged her like a cheap whore. He pinched her tits hard now and whispered in her ear as he pumped mercilessly. 'You're a dirty little slag, aren't you, Marianna?' he whispered.

'Oh yes, oh yes . . . just fuck me. I'm a dirty slag . . . please . . . shag me, fuck me . . .' moaned Marianna, the language of the gutter coming easily to her lips as her lover pumped her full.

'You're going to come, aren't you Marianna?' he continued. 'You can't get enough of being fucked by me and I can't get enough of shagging you in your tight, dirty little pussy, you filthy little whore.'

That did the trick. With one deep thrust against his prick, Marianna's body exploded in a pulsating orgasm, the contractions from which moved in spasms along his prick like a snake swallowing its prey.

The throbbing in her channel pulled Pierre towards the edge and he plunged deeper, the smell of their mingled bodies exciting him to the point of no return.

'Five hundred thousand francs,' thought Pierre, looking down at the neat little arse poking up at him as he drove in and out of the pussy beneath. 'Five hundred thousand francs,' as he came in one huge spurt, a flood of sperm shooting out of him as Marianna's body responded with one huge contraction.

In her cabin just three doors along from that of her dear stepmother, Cherry de Silva was feeling sorry for herself. Her arm ached and the small scratch on her right cheek stung as she applied disinfectant to it. Still. The other girl had come off worse.

It had all started so innocently but it was strange how quickly things could get out of hand.

As he had told her where he was staying, Cherry had gone to Rick's hotel that afternoon looking for him, only to be confronted by the blonde girl he'd mentioned in passing, the girl who'd come with him from England but was about to return.

For some reason the girl had become very upset when the receptionist had phoned Rick's room. She'd come steaming down to the desk, shouting that he wasn't here and who the hell was looking for him anyway?

Cherry had introduced herself but the girl had just stared at her, eyes blazing. It wasn't Cherry's fault. She was simply making conversation when she enquired exactly when the girl intended to go home.

The girl had started pulling hair first. It was self-protection when Cherry whacked her one, anybody would see that. Though thank goodness she'd had some cash on her to calm the hotel manager. Without it, he'd have called the police.

Rick had been sweet. He'd phoned half an hour ago to ask if she was okay and to say that the girl was no longer with him. The evening ahead was going to be very special. And a silly little scratch wasn't going to upset anything.

Cherry had decided to introduce Rick to her pusher. Rick had been impressed by the coke they'd snorted together and she felt she might be able to put a little business his way. She knew he was a bit short of cash and that he would be grateful. And what could be more delicious than the prospect of Rick 'owing her one'?

Cherry applied a layer of concealing cream to the scratch on her face. A light dusting of powder completed the camouflage and she was ready. She looked good, she felt happy. Life was beginning to get interesting. Even Pierre had begun to notice her more in recent days. She'd caught him glancing at her, a questioning look in his eyes. 'It'll all work out to my satisfaction,' she'd thought. 'I'll just bide my time.'

Charlotte had one hell of a bruise on her face and she'd told Rick it was painful for her to breathe. Cherry had apparently kicked her in the ribs.

Rick had felt a bit sorry walking out on Charlotte, especially as she hadn't known what was happening. Refusing to be drawn either into an argument or into giving an explanation, he'd simply told her that he'd be away for the night on business. While she was in the bath, trying to relieve the aching in her body, he'd packed his case. He'd closed the door quietly behind him and walked out, leaving her with a three-week hotel bill and little else.

But when the going gets tough the tough get going, he'd reminded himself, booking into a cheaper and rather more anonymous hotel six kilometres away.

She wouldn't go back to his house in England, not on her own. She'd be too scared. He reckoned she'd run back to her mum in Romford. That is, if the hotel would let her go. Whatever happened, it wouldn't be safe for Rick to hang around down here for much longer. One way or another someone was going to catch up with him. He needed to make some money and get out fast. He too was looking forward to the evening ahead. Cherry was useful, he thought, and who knows what might happen?

Marianna and Pierre were sleeping peacefully when Cherry and Rick returned to the yacht. Though it was three a.m., Jules was summoned to bring them brandies and Havana cigars, hovering politely over Rick and then Cherry as both rolled their cigars in the matches he struck for them, puffing slowly, giggling and unsteady as they exhaled their smoke into the warm night breeze.

Cherry told Jules to go to bed and leave the bottle. They'd call him when they wanted breakfast.

Cherry looked across at Rick and knew that she had him for as long as she wanted. They were going to buy drugs from a supplier in Marseilles and she was going to put up the money. It was all arranged. Her dealer said all he needed was some money to set the wheels in motion. Rick had whistled under his breath as he calculated how much profit could be made on the quantity they'd agreed to buy.

Cherry was excited by the whole idea but then they'd hit

on the best bit. They'd decided to take the yacht and run the drugs back to England. Rick would then sell them on. He had the contacts. They were both going to be unbelievably rich.

Cherry couldn't believe how everything was beginning to fit into place. After the years of misery following her father's marriage to Marianna, and then his death, she'd begun to feel that life would never go her way again. But now it had all changed. Marianna was taking Pierre to Paris, they'd be out of the way, and all that Rick and Cherry had to work out was how to get the yacht over to the South Coast of England, returning before Marianna and Pierre came back from their trip.

They couldn't take the usual crew. Certainly not Jules! Cherry would have to give them all a few days off once the Contessa and Pierre were safely on their way to Paris. She and Rick could sail the yacht between them but they'd need one extra pair of hands. All this was detail, though, thought Cherry as she sipped her brandy in the moonlight. It could all be worked out. The thrill of danger ran through her, sending shivers of pleasure down her spine.

Excitement and danger were strong aphrodisiacs. Rick poured her a second large brandy and began to unbutton the front of her dress. Moving across to her, he slid his hand into her bra. With a smile on his face, he brought his brandy glass towards her breast, cupping it over one nipple and upending it, then leaning his head forward to lick the brandy from where it trickled, sucking up the last drops of liquor as Cherry's hand groped for the front of his trousers.

'You shouldn't waste good brandy there,' said Cherry, 'it will only spill.' Pulling up her skirt, she spread her legs wide and commanded him to pour. Rick got very drunk that night. Cherry's pussy, he said, took at least a triple. But not a drop was spilt. Not a drop was wasted.

Jacques was lying in his small bed dreaming of the day to come. Tomorrow he would return to the yacht to work with his papa. Tomorrow he would see Mademoiselle Cherry once again. When his mama had told him they were going on holiday to visit grandmama at her home near Bayeux, for the first time in his life Jacques had known true despair. He'd begged his father to tell mama that he was indispensable, to convince mama that he was needed on board the yacht and that without his assistance, his father's life would be impossible. But Jules had said they'd manage. And Jacques and his mama had gone.

Weeks of living at grandmama's! Weeks of frustration without even the hope of a glimpse of Mademoiselle Cherry, let alone anything else. Jacques' senses had been on fire since that afternoon in Mademoiselle Cherry's cabin and he had been unable to think of anything else. Nothing else mattered. Jacques was in love.

By eleven o'clock the following morning, Jacques had been hovering around outside Cherry's cabin for hours but she had not appeared. What was he to do? He felt sure she must have longed for him, too. After all, the afternoon they had shared together had been so very special. Would she marry him, he wondered? He had to know. His life had been sheer torture since he left her.

Jacques' misery was stronger than his fear of consequence. Plucking up courage at last, he knocked gently on Cherry's cabin door. There was no reply. Opening the door slowly and entering, he saw Cherry's sleeping form, her knees brought up towards her chest, her long dark hair spread out on the pillow.

She looked so beautiful. Creeping across to her bed, Jacques sat down and, unable to resist the impulse, touched her hair. Cherry stirred and opened her eyes. For a moment, Jacques thought she'd be angry with him.

'Oh, it's you,' she said, blinking up at the boy who looked down at her adoringly.

'Are you well?' he said. 'I was worried. In case you were sick. It is late.'

'Mmmm,' murmured Cherry, 'I was late last night, that's all. And now I am tired.'

Sensing that he was about to lose her again to sleep, Jacques felt the frustration of recent weeks grip his throat. In a strangled voice, he blurted out, 'Mademoiselle Cherry, if I work hard and learn fast and become a good architect, will you marry me?'

A smile on her lips, Cherry propped herself up in bed on her elbows and looked at him through bleary, half-closed eyes. 'Jacques,' she replied, 'if you go and get me a pot of strong coffee and two aspirin, I will do anything in the world you want.'

Jacques returned minutes later and watched his adored one as the caffeine flooded her body and the pills began to take effect. His heart leapt with delight when she held back the covers and invited him into bed beside her. His hands were all over her in seconds, his erection so hard it hurt. Diving under the covers, his mouth moved towards her warm, wet pussy which opened obligingly to let his tongue inside. Jacques' eyes closed in ecstasy. He'd dreamt of the taste and smell of her throughout the long, frustrating weeks of his visit to grandmama's. But strangely, he hadn't remembered that a woman tasted quite like this. 'My love tastes of brandy,' thought Jacques, and carried on licking.

Chapter 16

Nikki cleared the table and removed the checked tablecloth, adding it to the pile in the corner of the café which was due to be washed that afternoon. It was three-thirty. If she hurried she'd be tidied up by four, giving her two and a half precious hours of relaxation. Then it would all begin again. By seven, the first of the evening's drinkers and diners would start to arrive at the Café Pelican, ready to sample Madame Aronson's plat de jour, Nikki's own friendly and patient waitressing and Jake's music, all of which combined to keep the café busy and Nikki too occupied for much soul-searching thought.

The Café Pelican and Madame Aronson had saved her life and Jake had saved her sanity. When she collapsed in a state of nervous exhaustion they had taken her in, fed and cared for her and kept her occupied.

Her French had improved, as had her self-confidence. Falling into bed each night, she had felt Jake's strong arms around her, soothing her tired body and troubled mind, and each morning when she crept back to her own bed for fear of offending the good Madame Aronson's sensibilities, it was with a sense of having been reborn, renewed.

'Nearly done,' she called to Jake who was sweeping up behind her and was as anxious as she was to complete their chores. For the quicker they finished, the quicker they could 'rest', undisturbed, in each other's arms.

Making love to Jake reminded Nikki of the early days of

her love affair with Chris. Though she knew she could never really love Jake, he was tender and considerate and the feel of him inside her had driven away memories of Pierre and the frantic madness of the last few weeks on the yacht.

Picking up a final ashtray from a table in the far corner, Nikki plonked it down on the bar and headed for the door at the back of the café which led upstairs to their sleeping quarters. Entering her room, she slipped her cotton dress over her head and lay down on the bed, the overhead fan in the ceiling whirring gently, stirring the warm, still air in the silence of the hot afternoon.

Jake would be up in a minute when he'd finished sweeping. It was part of her job really but he tried to help her as much as he could, figuring that the more he did the more time they'd have together.

With a sigh, Nikki closed her eyes and, stretching and yawning contentedly, brought her fingertips to rest against her throat, moving them slowly down until she had made gentle contact with the nipple of her left breast. 'Jake will be here in a minute,' she thought, massaging herself slowly and lazily, feeling the familiar heat of desire stir in her belly as she pictured her lover climbing the stairs.

Sleeping with Jake had strengthened and nourished her. Even now she could feel his sperm still leaking into her panties from their lovemaking of earlier that morning. Her vagina was bruised, the lips of her labia swollen. A day or two's abstinence would make her more comfortable but her lust was so strong that nothing would stop her from welcoming him in.

Deep in her heart she knew she would be leaving soon. There was no urgency to be on her way and Jake would be devastated by the news. But she knew in the back of her mind that all this was simply a dream. Her life could not be resolved until she returned home, came back to reality and picked her way through the ruins of the past few months.

But not yet. Hearing the sound of the door as it opened,

Nikki smiled as Jake's now familiar figure appeared in front of her.

'I have a present for you,' he said solemnly. Unzipping his fly, he released his cock, heavy and swollen, the veins on its surface standing out, its bulbous tip red and moist.

Jake approached the bed and Nikki sat up, her mouth moving across to taste her 'gift' which twitched in response to the touch of her lips.

Jake lay on the bed beside her, his big hand reaching across to cup her breast as he idly stroked her nipple. Her own hand massaged her other nipple until both stood firm and erect and, as Jake decided on looking across, too pretty not to be sucked.

Jake had told Nikki much about his training at agricultural college. He was to be a farmer, taking over from his father when he retired, inheriting a herd of one hundred cows, two hundred sheep and a five-hundred-acre farm in the depths of Devon.

Now he propped himself up on his elbow and looked down steadily at Nikki's breasts. 'On the farm,' he began, 'We have automatic milking machines which we attach to each cow's udders. It's a great relief to them when they feel the machine attached and sucking . . .' and, doing his best impression of a piece of farm machinery, Jake attached his mouth to Nikki's nipple, sucking hard and making mechanical whirring noises in the back of his throat as he did so.

'Now the other udder,' she laughed as Jake moved his mouth across.

'But the cows aren't always just milked, are they?' said Nikki, playing the now familiar game. 'Sometimes that have to be covered by the bull, don't they?'

'Yes,' replied Jake, sternly, 'and the bull is often fierce and angry . . . and he has the most enormous, dangling cock and the cow just has to take it all inside.'

'A cock like this one here you mean?' replied Nikki as he

climbed across her. He straddled her so that she could begin to stroke his twitching penis, his fingers all the while rolling her nipples gently as she lay beneath him, holding his bull-like prick against the palm of her hand.

'How does the cow take the bull?' said Nikki, her excitement mounting.

'Well,' replied Jake thoughtfully, 'she just spreads herself and lets him in . . . lets him bellow and buck inside her till he's done his business . . .'

'Spreads herself like this?' said Nikki, parting her legs, guiding the head of his penis into the hairy crack that lay open to him, bathing its tip in the slippery wetness that he longed to plunge into.

'Yeah,' said Jake, breathlessly, 'that's how she spreads herself . . .' And entering Nikki with one long, slow thrust, he brought his face down to hers and kissed her deeply.

They began to move together, Nikki's clitoris pressing hard against his firm shaft as he began his slow and measured strokes inside her, her excitement growing as she moved her pelvis in circular thrusts, pressing on his cock as it stretched within her, the throbbing in her hungry passage telling him that her orgasm was close.

'Easy, girl,' he said in his softest farmer's voice, his fingertips stroking Nikki's forehead. She closed her eyes and buried her face in the crook of his arm, the smell of fresh, manly sweat enhancing the pleasure she felt as his body bucked and quivered deep inside her own.

It was a busy evening though, strangely, Nikki was not tired when they finally locked the doors and said their goodnights to Madame Aronson. She was unsettled though she didn't know why. Climbing the stairs that night, all of a sudden she told Jake that she wanted to sleep alone. He accepted this as he accepted most things, with a shrug and no questions asked. She just wanted some time to herself, she explained. Jake was not offended.

'See you in the morning,' he said and sloped off to his room, still humming.

Nikki thought again that the time was fast approaching when she'd have to make a move, to leave the Café Pelican and the precarious security she'd found within its warm embrace. Sitting in the semi-darkness of her own small room she decided to see how much money she had. The Contessa's 'parting gift' combined with what she'd earned at the Café Pelican should give her plenty to get home with, plus enough to keep her for a few weeks at least when she got back to England.

Rooting through her handbag she came upon the Contessa's bundle of cash which she tipped out onto the bed along with her wages. Unfolding the notes, she counted them in neat piles which she then replaced in her bag.

The sense of foreboding that had been playing at the edges of her mind during the course of the evening had subsided. She had enough money for her immediate needs. But still she didn't feel sleepy. 'In the morning,' she thought, 'I will go and buy a plane ticket.'

Reaching into her bag once again, she groped around for her passport. It was not there. With a sigh, she got to her feet, reaching inside the wardrobe for the holdall which she'd packed so hastily the morning she'd left the yacht. Ah, here it was. Nikki pulled out a dark booklet. No, this was the little folder which contained her plane ticket from England. It was not her passport.

The uneasiness which had been building up in her mind now flooded to the surface. Tipping all her belongings out onto the bed, Nikki began a frantic search. But it was not there. With a feeling of nausea and despair, Nikki realised that she must have left her passport on the yacht. She even remembered where she'd kept it. She could see it lying in its drawer. 'Oh no,' she gasped in the darkness. 'Oh please . . . oh no.'

Nikki crept down into the bar of the Café Pelican and

poured herself a large brandy. Swallowing it in one, she headed towards the front of the café, undoing the latch, unbolting the door and creeping out into the street. She shut the door behind her with a feeling of regret and fear, not knowing what might happen, what she might have to face before she was safely back inside again.

The cab to Antibes was frighteningly expensive, swallowing up all her hard-earned tips and part of her wages. To make matters worse she felt that each kilometre they covered devoured not only her money but also her new-found happiness.

She asked the taxi driver to drop her at the entrance to the harbour and, her heart thumping in her chest, she walked the familiar path towards the yacht. Every step was agony, every inch of ground she covered filled her with dread.

Nikki had decided to creep aboard the yacht and go to her old cabin hoping against hope that her passport lay where she had left it, undisturbed. Quietly she prayed under her breath that the yacht would be in darkness and her task a fast if not pleasurable one. But as she approached she saw that her worst fears were about to be realised, her most frightful nightmare was coming true. Cherry was on deck with a young man, laughing and drinking and blowing smoke rings into the air as she puffed on a huge cigar. Her obscene laugh ripped through the night sky. Her face was flushed with alcohol and her fat tits spilled over the front of a dress which screamed its obscene price tag as loudly as Cherry's body language yelled her intentions.

Nikki felt sure that Cherry would know of her humiliation and, unlike the Contessa or even Pierre, should she ever catch sight of Nikki she would jeer at her publicly.

But Cherry wasn't thinking about anyone else right now. She stood up and unzipped her dress, letting it fall to the floor in front of her as Nikki heard her speak to the young man who had also risen to his feet and begun to disrobe. 'C'mon,' she said. 'Let's swim.' Grabbing him by the hand, she ran with him along the length of the deck, pulling him in the direction of the ladder at the back of the boat which led down into the sea. Jules had forgotten it as usual, or maybe Cherry had insisted it be left there. Either way Nikki was grateful as she saw her chance to come aboard, hiding and darting in the shadows as she inched her way towards her old cabin.

She dreaded being seen, dreaded being caught, yet at the same time she felt bitter and miserable. Her little beauty cabin stood in darkness and she edged past its door. The faint and familiar smell of oils and lotions assailed her senses, setting up within her a kind of homesickness.

At last she arrived at her old cabin and opened the door, walking quietly across to the bureau which she'd cleared out so quickly such a short time ago. And it was there! Her passport was sitting at the back of the drawer precisely where she'd left it since the day she'd first arrived in France. Thank goodness. Nikki put the passport carefully in her bag and crept out of the empty cabin.

Making her way back in the direction she'd come, she was suddenly aware that her path was blocked, Cherry and her swimming companion having changed their minds about taking a night-time dip. The need for more immediate pleasures had proved too strong for there they stood, wrapped in each other's arms just yards from Nikki's only escape route.

Nikki had seen them at the last minute. Another few seconds and she would have stumbled out of the shadows, bumping into them as they embraced. Sinking back into the darkness, she tried to control her fear, afraid they would hear her thumping heart.

Pulling apart at last, Nikki heard Cherry sigh a deep and contented sigh. She gazed up at the man as her fingers brushed the hair from his forehead.

'It's all going to be fine,' she murmured. 'Just you wait and see . . . I mean, dear papa was *so* respectable! Pillar of the community and all that. No one would ever suspect that his yacht could be used for drug smuggling! My dear stepmama and Pierre are leaving on Wednesday. By this time next week we'll be home and dry. And, my darling . . . we'll be RICH!'

The man grabbed Cherry's head in his hands and kissed her long and deep. Standing in the shadows, her heart racing uncontrollably, Nikki felt her blood run cold.

As if in a dream, Nikki crept back to her old cabin once again and sank into a chair. She didn't care who walked in and discovered her. There were terrible things about to happen and Nikki needed time to think.

She tried to make sense of what she'd just heard. Drug smuggling? Pierre and the Contessa going away? What had happened since she'd left? What was going on?

Admittedly, the Contessa had thrown her off the yacht but even Nikki had to admit she'd had good reason. At heart, she was still a kind and generous woman. She didn't deserve to be implicated in crime. Nikki must go to her and tell her what she'd overheard, whatever the consequences. Miserably, she got to her feet and crept back out onto the main deck. It was still dark and, despite her new found resolve, Nikki was grateful for the camouflage the shadows afforded her. Cherry and the man had disappeared and Nikki was able to make her way to the Contessa's cabin undetected.

Nikki summoned all her courage, opened the door and walked in, fearing a tirade of abuse, steeling herself to stand her ground and implore the Contessa to hear her out. But the bed was made. The cabin was tidy. The Contessa was not there.

Nikki never knew what made her think of it, but seeing the Contessa's cabin as it was she had a sudden premonition that at any moment, the Contessa would return. It was nearly morning. If she were with Pierre, she would come back to her cabin for breakfast.

Nikki was right. Strange though it might seem, the Contessa was deeply conscious of keeping up appearances. Jules and most of the other crew had all worked for her husband, which to the Contessa was reason enough never to be seen in bed with Pierre.

Nikki felt she would return to her cabin by first light. She decided to wait.

Two o'clock . . . three o'clock . . . as the hours ticked past Nikki's courage began to fail her. The initial sense of outrage that had brought her to the Contessa's cabin in the first place had begun to subside. All she could think of was the fact that she couldn't bear it if the Contessa turned on her. To be ordered off the yacht a second time would be too much to take.

But she *must* bear it! The Contessa was in danger, something bad was about to happen and only Nikki could stop it. But no matter how much she reasoned with herself, Nikki knew that her courage was failing. As the sun broke over the horizon, she decided that if she were to remain here then at least she would hide, observing the Contessa and the kind of mood she was in before making her presence known.

Nikki slid herself into one of the Contessa's two capacious wardrobes behind a row of evening dresses. She'd be safe here for a while and as the wardrobe had slatted doors, she could also see out.

By seven-thirty, the excitement and tension of the night had proved too much for Nikki and she began to doze, her cheek resting against the sequined gown the Contessa had worn on the last night they'd all gone out to dinner together. 'What a mess,' thought Nikki as her eyes began to close. 'What a mess this has all become.'

Within ten minutes of drifting off to sleep, Nikki was awoken by the sound of the cabin door opening. She could see the Contessa clearly and was shocked by how thin she looked.

Flopping onto the bed, the Contessa put her hand to her

forehead and heaved a deep sigh. 'Oh, Pierre,' Nikki heard her murmur, her voice laced with despair. 'Oh, Pierre.'

As if in response, the cabin door opened again and a figure appeared in the doorway; the tall, handsome figure of Pierre framed by a clear sky in which the last traces of night were being burnt away by the strengthening sun.

'Marianna,' he said, 'I simply haven't had enough.' Nikki was amazed at the change which took place in the woman who had once been her employer and friend. From the limp rag doll who had entered the cabin just moments before, Marianna was transformed. Sitting up and smiling broadly, she welcomed her lover with open arms.

'We have made love five times tonight and you still come back for more?' she teased him, unable to disguise the delight in her voice, her body poised in anticipation.

Without a word, Pierre stood before her and unzipped his trousers. Marianna fell to her knees, reaching up to release his magnificent cock which sprang forward to greet her, fully engorged. 'But first,' said Marianna, kissing his prick tenderly, 'I must cancel breakfast.'

While Marianna picked up the phone, Nikki stared at Pierre. What was it about this man that attracted her so? For despite the current circumstances, despite the fact that she was worried and Marianna was in danger, all Nikki could think of was how much she wanted to emerge from her hiding place and take Pierre's prick in her own mouth. To suck on the silky hardness of him till he shot his sperm deep into the back of her throat! She longed to feel his fingers squeezing her nipples, his tongue buried deep in her pussy, licking the inner walls of her vagina till she felt her body jolt and shudder beneath his touch.

Nikki knew that she shouldn't look but she couldn't help herself. She watched as Marianna began to kiss the length of his prick, as her kisses turned to long, slow licks and then, with a purr of pleasure, she slid the fat knob of him between her lips. Pierre stood before the kneeling figure of Marianna, moving his hips in slow thrusting movements, holding the back of her head and pulling her closer as his pleasure mounted.

With a sudden, swift movement, he pulled her away from him, lifting her up and placing her on the bed on all fours. Raising her skirts, he pulled her buttocks apart and guided his prick along the valley of her arse and into the hairy forest below, pushing it straight inside her upturned pussy with one determined thrust.

Marianna cried out, her hands reaching behind her to grab his thighs and pull him closer into her, moving her body upright until she was sitting on his cock. She pressed down, moving her body from side to side, her eyes half closed as she luxuriated in the sensation of being filled like no man had filled her before.

Try though she might, Nikki could not tear her eyes away. She knew what it felt like to be fucked by Pierre. How big he was and how the size of his cock heightened every sensation, reaching in more deeply, pleasuring more thoroughly than any other man on earth. Being with Pierre was a kind of madness. An addictive, all-embracing madness in which nothing mattered but the next orgasm. There were no feelings but the sensation of this man pumping deep between your ever-open legs, no tastes but the taste of his cock on your tongue, leaving room for no other kind of appetite.

Nikki's fingers were in her pants as she watched them, the tip of one finger flicking furiously against her clitoris as she probed her body with the other fingers bunched together. But though she came, thrusting quietly against her hand, there was no pleasure in it. Pleasure was beyond this door. Pleasure was out there on the bed. Memories of Jake and Chris dissolved as she watched Pierre's hips thrust and he plunged between Marianna's parted thighs. *There* was pleasure.

Ashamed and yet stimulated at the same time, Nikki watched as the Contessa began the delicious climb up the hill of sensation towards orgasm. Pierre had loosened the front of her dress and her breasts were poking out. His long fingers squeezed each nipple and his tongue licked her neck as she spread her legs wider and worked her body against the shaft of his prick.

Nikki could hardly bear it. She knew so well how good he felt, how exciting, how unpredictable his actions. What an amazing fuck he was. The best any woman could ever have.

Suddenly, as if reading her mind, Pierre pulled the Contessa from on top of him and, dragging her across the bed, placed her face down across his knee and began to spank her buttocks, turning each pink and quivering mound bright red beneath his blows.

Marianna cried out, a mixture of pleasure and pain in her voice as he struck her, her body which had been so close to orgasm seeking its release as Marianna pressed her pubic bone against his leg and the waves of pleasure his cock had created continued to throb through her.

Pierre smacked her harder, one strong arm wrapped around both of her slim legs, holding her still as the palm of his hand made sharp contact with her burning flesh.

Suddenly, he stopped as quickly as he'd started. Throwing her roughly on her front, Pierre spread her arms out on either side of her, holding her pinned beneath him, his hands clasped around her wrists. He rammed his prick back inside her and began to pump, the redness of her smacked arse in bright contrast to the golden brown of his tanned skin.

The sound of Marianna's deep satisfaction broke from her lips just seconds later; the rich eloquence of her moans filling Nikki with a lust and longing that could barely be contained.

Strangely, Pierre withdrew just seconds before he came, squirting his sperm in a slippery jet all over Marianna's buttocks from where he proceeded to massage it into her skin.

'That'll calm the burning,' he said, stroking her gently as she murmured in response.

* * *

They fell asleep again, all three of them; Marianna and Pierre on the bed and Nikki hidden behind her rail of dresses. She couldn't emerge with Pierre in the cabin. In fact she couldn't emerge at all. If the Contessa knew that Nikki had watched them making love, even her faint hope of being heard would dissolve completely.

She would wait till the cabin was empty. There was nothing else for it. Then she would make her escape and think about what to do next.

It must have been late morning when Nikki was woken by voices. Suddenly remembering where she was, she peeped out from between the slats of the wardrobe to see the Contessa and Pierre still lying on the bed wrapped in each other's arms.

'You can have anything you want,' she heard the Contessa say. 'When we get to Paris I will buy you whatever you want. Anything. Anything.'

'Well, that's very nice to know,' replied Pierre, a note of amusement in his voice, 'but I don't ask for anything. You are enough of a gift for me.'

'I know, my dear,' Nikki heard the Contessa reply. 'That is why I have come to trust you, and why I wish to give you so much. Our love is enough . . . and it is that which makes me so happy! But don't deprive me of my pleasure if I want to give you more.'

For the first time ever, Nikki was sorry for the Contessa. The woman she'd thought was so glamorous, so special, was just a woman after all. And from what she'd seen today, a desperate woman, anxious to cling on to this young man by promising him presents, promising him anything.

So. They were going to Paris as Cherry had mentioned. They were going to be out of the way for whatever it was that Cherry had planned. It had to be stopped, but how Nikki would do it, she simply did not know. She had no proof of anything.

Staring out from within her slatted prison, Nikki saw that the Contessa and Pierre had fallen asleep again lying on their backs. His fingers lay between her open legs, his cock resting peacefully against his left thigh. Fascinated, Nikki stared at his cock which even at rest was larger than most men's when fully erect.

Watching him today and seeing the effect he'd had on the Contessa, Nikki realised that Pierre was the kind of man who inspired madness in women. Like a dangerous addiction he was impossible to resist, yet he brought nothing but unhappiness in his wake.

But he was so beautiful. She looked at his cock and felt her own desire stir once more. Despite the fact that her panties were already sodden with her own juices, she slipped her fingers once again between her legs, stroking her body into wakefulness as she imagined Pierre's sleeping cock growing hard, rising from between his thighs, ready to fill her as she came out from inside the wardrobe and climbed astride him. If only . . .

But why was she thinking like this? Where did poor Jake fit into her fevered imaginings? Or Chris for that matter? The answer was, nowhere. She was right. Pierre created havoc and madness. Nikki stared at his cock as her fingers explored the folds of her womanhood and her fingernails teased her clitoris, feeling the pulse of her body beneath her touch as her hunger mounted. Licking her lips and with her eyes firmly fixed on the sleeping Pierre, she came. But when, she wondered, would she be able to go? To escape? To think clearly . . .

It was nearly lunchtime and Cherry de Silva was stretched out on deck. She sighed happily as she turned on her back and felt the warmth of the sun, strong on her face.

All was going according to plan. She and Rick were due to collect a small sample of their drugs consignment that night and, once they had confirmed that they were happy with the quality, the rest would be ready for collection in two days' time. It would have to be stored on the yacht until the Contessa and Pierre had departed. Then, dismiss the crew... and they'd be off.

The only remaining problem was that it took three people to sail the yacht and, so far, a third person hadn't been recruited. Cherry began to think what a coup it would be if the third person could be Pierre. An outrageous idea but one which, the more she thought about it, began to make sense.

Pierre wanted money, that much she knew. He was ruthless and amoral and, most important of all, the sexiest-looking man she'd ever clapped eyes on. Though common sense told her that this was not a good basis upon which to consider getting him involved in such a sensitive endeavour, Cherry thought that to take him along would be the icing on the cake.

She closed her eyes and imagined fucking him on the high seas, unlimited quantities of top quality coke, the buzz of danger, plus Pierre and Rick to roger her senseless with no one but the seagulls to disturb them. Cherry felt the familiar throbbing between her legs at the very idea. Yes, she must get him. To do so would make this her greatest adventure ever.

But what about dear stepmama? Cherry's face broke into a smile as she imagined Marianna distraught and bereft pacing up and down some Parisian hotel room, whatever excuse Pierre had invented revealing itself to be a lie with every moment that ticked past. Oh, that would be almost as good as screwing Pierre and Rick at the same time! And what's more, she would make sure that the Contessa was made aware of her lover's betrayal. There would be no chance of him coming back. Not when Cherry had finished with him. Marianna would be broken and humiliated. What joy!

Suddenly an image came into her mind of Pierre, Rick and herself all 'at it'. She saw herself splayed out in Marianna's cabin, Pierre pumping away between her legs while Rick licked her tits, his cock in her mouth while his tongue tickled and sucked at her nipples. She'd seen how well endowed Pierre was through his swimming trunks. Now she was determined to know for herself how big that intriguing prick could become.

He may have fobbed her off already but she knew that was only because of dear Marianna. They'd have a great time and her stepmother would get hurt. What more could a girl ask for?

But how to persuade him? Cherry lay back in the sun and her mind got to work. Within an hour she'd formulated a plan. Yes, that would do very nicely.

Nikki stayed trapped in her wardrobe till lunchtime when the Contessa and Pierre finally awoke. Sliding his fingers out of her body, he leant across and kissed Marianna between the legs, muttering that he would see her later. He left the cabin without another word.

Marianna sat up on the bed and ran her fingers through her glossy hair. From her vantage point, Nikki studied her face closely. For the first time ever, she noticed that Marianna had begun to look old. 'She doesn't really trust him,' thought Nikki. 'Though she tries to convince herself, she doesn't trust him at all.' Guiltily, she reflected that she herself was in part to blame for the lines of distress and weariness etched into Marianna's face.

Chapter 17

Chris had been having a nightmare. Tossing and turning in his sleep he had begun muttering to himself, his words falling over each other in an incomprehensible stream which had eventually woken Irana from her own happier night-time reverie.

Irana herself had been dreaming about a tennis match. The Men's Finals at Wimbledon to be precise, in which Marco Lazalle had been losing. He was one set down and fighting for his life. In her dream, Irana had decided to persuade the umpire to 'overlook' some of Marco's mistakes. It was a silly fantasy of course, but there in front of the respectable middle-class crowd and in full view of a worldwide television audience, Irana had got up from her seat and drifted down onto the court itself, walking across to where the umpire perched in his high seat, way above the crowd.

She had climbed up to him and slid her hand between his legs. Then releasing his cock, she had taken it in her mouth.

In her dream Irana had felt the sun beating down on her, the thin cotton of her dress damp with perspiration as she sucked. 'Advantage, Miss Petrovka,' the umpire had moaned. 'Ooohhh . . . what wonderful play . . .'

In Irana's fantasy it had been a gloriously hot day, made even more enjoyable when the two finalists in the match had thrown their tennis racquets into the air and had come across to her. Lifting her down from where she was giving her expert blow job, they laid her on the grass in full view of the crowd. Pulling her skirt up and taking their cocks out from deep within their crisp cotton shorts, they lowered Irana's frilly tennis panties (why was she wearing those? she wondered) and kneeling in front of her, their huge tennis player's thigh muscles sandwiching their eager pricks, they stood ready and erect as the crowd roared its approval.

Marco's dusky opponent had been the first to enter her, his thrusts accompanied by the clapping of the crowd of happy tennis enthusiasts which had now turned into an audience of aroused voyeurs. Looking up from where she lay on her back drinking in the sweet smell of the grass court, Irana had stared back at the spectators. The women had their pretty floral dresses dragged up around their waists and were fingering themselves or being fucked by their companions. Sunglasses were askew, white cotton hats abandoned as the oh-so-English crowd rutted in the stands. They rubbed strawberries and cream into each other's bodies, panting and moaning, a frenzy of lust breaking out as one of the highlights of the English social season degenerated into an orgy.

Irana had felt the dusky tennis player's sperm leaking out of her and onto the grass beneath as, within minutes, Marco had moved across to take his turn. 'It can travel at over one hundred miles an hour,' he'd whispered in her ear.

'What, sperm?' she'd replied.

'No, silly . . . the tennis ball . . .'

Sitting up abruptly, stirred into sudden consciousness by Chris, Irana wondered what would have happened next should she have carried on dreaming. She was cross to have been disturbed. She wanted to see who would have won the title.

She shook Chris gently by the shoulders and managed to wake him. His face was pale in the early morning light and though he'd been asleep for hours, his eyes were troubled.

'What is it?' she said, leaning across him and nuzzling his chest with her lips.

'Just a nightmare,' replied Chris. 'A really bad dream.'

Irana's mouth moved across to Chris's left nipple and she began to tease it with her tongue. Slipping her hand beneath the sheet she felt for his penis and found it small and soft, hiding reluctantly in the shelter of his balls. Oh, he *was* depressed!

Irana knew from recent experience that a sudden assault on Chris's body would yield no results whatsoever. Despite the fact that she'd woken up hot and randy, almost expecting to find grass stains on her bum, she knew that if Chris were to bring her to orgasm this morning she'd have to encourage him very slowly, changing into 'sympathetic' mode and coaxing his troubles from him as she fingered and sucked him. Yes, that would be best.

Moving her hand away from his flaccid prick, Irana began to stroke his chest once again. His body was really beautiful. Stocky and thick-set but with all the grace of a Greek statue.

Her voice soft and concerned, Irana looked down into Chris's face and, with the best expression of sympathy she could muster, asked him what was wrong.

It was Nikki, of course. The soppy little girl who'd taken off for the South of France and with whom he'd been living before they left England. Chris had told Irana that he'd tried to contact her and she'd ignored him. Now he was banging on about feeling 'guilty' saying that if he'd taken better care of her, thought about her more, things might have worked out.

Irana disguised her exasperation behind a kindly smile. The girl sounded like a total bore, though for some reason even the mere mention of her irritated Irana to screaming point. Why was Chris so concerned about her? She was a nobody, but even though Chris was now on his way to becoming the world's most celebrated photographer, even though she, Irana, had done all she could to hasten his progress, he was still prattling on about some silly girl who by now he should have grown out of and forgotten.

But Irana knew that it would not do to tell him this.

Plastering her sweetest expression on her face, Irana looked down at Chris once more and stared earnestly into his eyes. 'Poor Christopher!' she said. 'I see how bad you are feeling about the girl and I see how much you care. If only Irana could work magic, I bring her here for you right now! Oh, Christopher . . . I do anything to make you happy.'

Irana's apparent generosity of spirit had exactly the desired effect. Chris's cock began to stir under the sheet and he turned to look at her, seeing her suddenly in a different light, as a woman capable of generous as well as her usual selfish impulses.

He leant across and kissed her deeply, his hand reaching out for her breast. His mouth moved from her lips to take one hard, pink nipple between his teeth, nibbling it oh so carefully as Irana's body moved in gentle upward thrusts in response to his touch. With luck, thought Irana, he'd soon get bored and stop thinking about the silly bitch. If so, then Irana would keep him around to screw her for the rest of the summer. If he carried on whingeing then she would soon stop wasting her time. For, she reasoned, if pining and moping for some cheap beautician was to stop him getting an erection, then it wasn't worth the effort.

But whatever Irana had said to soothe him this morning, it had worked like a dream. He was kissing and sucking her like he meant it, his fingers probing the slippery canal between her legs, his penis huge and hard.

She closed her eyes as his mouth left her breast, his fingertips taking over as his lips moved down her belly, brushing through the downy hair which gave her skin its peachlike quality. Every tiny little hair stood on end in response to his touch as his mouth glided down her body and on into her pubic hair. His fingers slid out of her pussy as his mouth took over, his tongue inside her labia, its slightest pressure sending a pulse of pleasure shooting into the softness of her dark chasm.

Chris used his tongue like a snake, darting in and out of her pussy, dipping into the folds of her labia and pulling back again, each gentle probe leaving her body crying out for more. Unable to stand the tension a second longer, Irana grabbed his hair and held his face firmly between her legs. Chris's little teasing probes turned to long, deep licks which sent the pleasure tingling through her in waves. The moisture at the entrance to her pussy was now running so free that Chris's tongue slipped and slid within her like a puppy on ice.

'Please, Chris,' murmured Irana. Knowing exactly what she wanted, he swung his body full circle into the *soixante-neuf* position, his smooth, thick cock in its cradle of golden hair directly above her face. Reaching up to move her hand behind his buttocks, Irana guided him into her mouth, her eyes still closed so she could concentrate on every sensation. The musky, masculine smell of him filled her nostrils and fired her lust as she slid his thick penis straight into her throat, burying her face in his soft pubic hair which smelt of a mixture of fresh sweat, body shampoo and sperm.

Imagining herself back on the tennis court, Irana sucked him slowly and rhythmically. Occasionally she paused to slide her lips the length of his warm prick and towards its tip, running her tongue around the soft and sensitive head which was leaking a slimy trail of fluid which she spread with her mouth. His prick felt even silkier then as it pushed instinctively between her lips, and she ached to take it back into the depths of her throat.

He was wonderful, this man, she thought as she felt her orgasm begin to gather momentum; his tongue and lips responded to every quiver of her body, coaxing and licking her where she throbbed till she throbbed some more. Though he had no idea how good a lover he was, his tongue alone could control her orgasm.

Instinct told him to delay his licks and sucks until exactly the right moment, at which point he lifted her body from the bed, angling her pussy so that he could penetrate it deeply with his tongue. Flicking inside her in circular, lapping movements, he gave Irana an orgasm of such intensity that she felt her juices would flood his mouth, drowning him in her pleasure.

As her pleasure began to subside, he slid his prick out of her mouth and, turning deftly in a semicircle, brought his face level with her own, slipping his prick deeply into her welcoming pussy as his moment of climax approached. As he kissed her cheeks and her eyelids, she felt his thrusts deep inside her body. Much to her surprise, her receding orgasm found a new life.

The feel of Chris's thick penis caused a hot wave of lust to build again in her body. Her thighs came together to squeeze the most sensation out of this beautiful body of his as, with a groan and a final thrilling thrust, Chris came deep within her, their sticky juices trickling onto the rumpled sheets upon which they fell once again, their bodies exhausted. As Irana lay stroking Chris's hair, her eyes closing, she thought about their earlier conversation. Yes he must forget this stupid girl and concentrate on what was important. She hadn't finished with him yet. And he wasn't going anywhere until she had.

Marco Lazelle watched as Chris emerged from Irana's room two hours later. He'd been meaning to phone her but his courage had failed and he'd ended up booking into her hotel and taking a room across the hall, intending to knock on her door and surprise her.

He didn't know who the fair-haired young man who sloped off along the passage was, but he knew he did not like him. Something told him that this man was more important to Irana than the others. No, he did not like him a bit.

Moving along the passage towards her door, Marco held up his hand ready to knock. But then he felt that maybe now wasn't the time. He turned on his heels and slunk away, back to his room. Lying on his bed he took his penis in his hand, rubbing it gently. 'I will see her tonight,' he thought, 'yes, tonight.'

Chris glanced at the piece of paper upon which Nikki had scribbled the address and phone number where she could be contacted. Though she'd informed him that the yacht would be sailing the Mediterranean, she'd also intimated that the Contessa was reluctant to stray far from this particular stretch of coastline and that though they might be making short trips, the yacht would always return, sooner rather than later, to its regular mooring.

Gazing at the scrap of paper in front of him, Chris stared closely at Nikki's handwriting. She had been so upset when she'd scribbled these details down. Maybe he should just get on a plane and go to her. But what would he say? 'I'm sorry,' seemed like a good place to start. But then Nikki had made it clear she didn't want to speak to him. He'd phoned four times now and she hadn't called back.

He'd go home. That's what he'd do. Now that the shoot was over he'd return to the flat. Then at least if she had a change of heart, she'd be able to ring him there. He didn't hold out much hope, but he'd be around. Just in case.

He would book his flight to London and then take his leave of Irana. They would meet again in England, though he knew that whatever the final outcome of his relationship with Nikki, he could never return to the dark-eyed beauty whose body had almost succeeded in making him forget his past. Almost, but not quite.

His affair with Irana was just 'one of those things'. Did he feel guilty about sleeping with her? Maybe a little. Since he'd first met Nikki nearly four years ago, Irana was the only other woman he'd touched. But in her way she'd helped him through the last few weeks. Without her body blocking out the torments in his mind, he might never have survived. Nikki need never know. Deceitful though it was, it was best she never knew about Irana.

On reflection though, what did it really matter? he thought sadly. It was all over with Nikki if only he'd face it. She didn't want him after all.

Chris booked a ticket to London for the following Thursday afternoon. Though Irana had dropped less than subtle hints about his spending the rest of the summer in Sicily, he just wanted to go home and get his feet back on the ground. And if he had no real home to go to then at least he had the satisfaction of returning with a triumphant photographic campaign under his belt. Surely that would provide some compensation? But he wasn't convinced. Oh, how difficult everything had become! He'd tried to forget his unhappiness in the arms of Irana, he'd tried to disguise his own feelings even to himself but nothing, nothing had really worked.

There were three days left. He would spend them with Irana and make sure she had a good time. He would try and do the same before he flew back to London and finally back to reality. They'd take a trip around the island, they'd eat and drink and make love. No, he didn't feel guilty about his affair. After all, it wasn't Irana who had left him, it wasn't Irana who had ignored his phone calls when he tried to make peace, it wasn't Irana who had abandoned him, leaving him all alone.

Irana was in the bath when Marco Lazelle finally plucked up the courage to knock on her door. It was crazy! He had no fear in most situations, yet this business with Kiki had turned him into a nervous wreck and the thought of Irana being angry with him had made it even worse.

Thinking that it was Chris, Irana called out, 'Come in,' not bothering to stir from the huge white marble bath in which she was having a soak.

Marco advanced nervously towards the bathroom, pushing open the door and walking in to find Irana lying on her back, her nipples poking out of a sea of pale blue scented water, her pubic hair like a little sea anemone floating in a sunken golden island of tanned skin.

Much to his relief, Irana didn't yell at him or throw a bar of soap in his direction. Turning the tap on with her toe, she simply looked at him wearily and shook her head.

'I couldn't go back without seeing you again,' said Marco.

'I'm sorry.' Irana stroked the bubbles from her long, tanned arms and sat up in the bath.

'What I going to do with you?' she said. 'You promise one thing and do another.'

Marco shivered involuntarily though the bathroom was hot. Taking pity on her old friend in his obvious distress, Irana handed him a loofah and ordered, 'Come . . . scrub my back and we talking about it.' His relief at being forgiven was evident from the enthusiasm with which he set about his task. 'Ow, you hurting me!' yelled Irana as he scrubbed too hard, fighting him off by splashing water at him and soaking his trousers.

Leaning forward into the bath, he scooped up two handfuls of foaming suds and threw them in her face. Within seconds, the scene in the bathroom degenerated into a childish water battle with the marble floor awash, Marco soaked and Irana giggling wildly.

There was nothing for it but for Marco to get into the bath with Irana. Climbing out of his clothes, he stepped in behind her, snuggling up and wrapping his arms around her waist. With his face pressed against her back, he told her how glad he was that she hadn't sent him away and how much he needed her advice.

'Is that loofah I sitting on?' said Irana, wriggling as Marco moved closer.

'No,' he replied, 'I'm just glad to see you.' Picking up a bar of soap, Marco began to lather it into Irana's breasts, carefully spreading the thick foam over each nipple and massaging it into her skin. As he splashed the water up and over each hardened nipple, Irana sighed gently, turning around to face him and thrusting her breasts towards him.

'Still no washed . . . again,' she commanded at which he picked up his bar of soap once more and lathered each breast, this time rinsing them rather more quickly in warm water and then giving each a final licking with his tongue.

'Clean, do you think?' he said solemnly to Irana.

'Oh no,' she replied, mock-seriously. 'No anything like real clean . . .'

Marco leant forward and took each of Irana's wet breasts in his mouth, one after the other. He could smell the soap on her body and feel the tip of his prick brushing against her soft wet mound of pubic hair as his legs circled her own. They sat facing each other in her steaming bath, the water caressing their limbs as they began to play with each other. Irana plunged her hands beneath the water to squeeze Marco's swelling prick as his hands continued to soap her breasts which Irana still declared to be 'filthy', however much he washed them.

It was strange how silky his pubic hair felt under the water and how his balls seemed to float as she held them in her hands. Irana touched him tentatively, fascinated by the sensations as his fingertips continued to stroke her hard shiny nipples which were covered in tiny bubbles. They were both getting too aroused to stay playing like a couple of kids for much longer. Wiping the wet hair from her face, Marco got up and lifted Irana from the water, standing her on the floor and wrapping her in a thick, white towel.

He carried her through to the bedroom and began to dry her, rubbing the towel carefully against her soap-scented skin, the slightest touch making her nipples spring to attention.

He stroked her belly with the towel, wiped her long legs dry and then moved slowly towards her bush of dark hair, parting the lips of her labia with the utmost care. Though he knew that strictly speaking he didn't need to dry her there, he began to rub her gently with the towel. Irana's body responded immediately to the pressure between her legs, moving her clitoris against the slight roughness of the cotton as Marco dabbed painstakingly between each fold of her, like a fussy old woman dusting a precious table.

'I think I already dry down there,' she said, laughing.

'Mmm,' replied Marco, moving the towel to one side and bringing his face close to her pussy. 'I don't agree. I think you're wet and getting wetter all the time.' With studied concentration and a pretend-serious expression on his face, Marco began his inspection of her body. 'Breasts dry, tummy dry, legs and arms dry . . . but pussy? I can't understand it,' he said jokingly. 'I bring you out of the bath and dry you off, but you're still wet!'

Her body completely aroused by all the rubbing and stroking, Irana reached up towards Marco and pulled his face towards hers, opening her mouth to meet his in a long, satisfying kiss. They'd known each other so long and so well. There were no secrets between them. And as he moved his body on top of the familiar and beautiful one that lay beneath, and guided his firm prick into the wetness that opened up to take him, Marco felt he was coming home. He was safe. 'I'll talk to her about Kiki later,' he thought, closing his eyes and burying his face in her breasts.

Chris walked along the corridor to Irana's room. He wanted to talk to her. To tell her that he'd be flying out on Thursday and to suggest that they spend the days in between together.

She'd worked really hard in the last few weeks. They both had. And without her, he thought, he might still be one of many good but unexceptional photographers doing the circuit, making a living but precious little else.

He owed Irana a lot and he knew it. He also suspected that she'd be upset when he told her the he was definitely leaving. Pausing outside her door he heard the sounds of laughter from within. 'Oh, Irana . . .' he muttered to himself and, with a shrug of resignation, turned and walked away.

Chapter 18

Since her papa had found what he'd termed 'whore's clothes' at the back of her wardrobe, Solange had led a less than comfortable existence. She went to work each day and returned home each evening and if she happened to be five minutes late her papa would interrogate her mercilessly until Solange began to cry.

She knew she'd behaved badly with Mademoiselle Cherry and, thankfully, her papa would never know the half of it. But as she'd come to realise during the long boring evenings at home with her brothers and sisters, life simply wasn't worth living without a little excitement. She missed Mademoiselle Cherry, oh, how much! She was in love with her – something that papa would never understand and, if she told him, he'd be offended and outraged.

Solange knew that she had see her lover once again. The need grew with each week that passed, each suffocating dawn and predictable dusk making her more determined to escape, to go to Cherry and see if she could stay with her. Even if it meant taking a job on her yacht as some sort of servant, Solange would be happy.

Papa was an old-fashioned man who thought that a woman should want no more than a family and children. But Solange knew she was different, which was why, one Wednesday afternoon, she stared her papa straight in the face and lied. She told him that she had been asked to work late, to help with a stocktaking exercise, and would he mind if she stayed over afterwards at the apartment of a friend?

Of course, papa had to phone this friend who had obligingly agreed to give Solange an alibi. And Solange had asked his permission so very humbly. Papa was reassured.

And so it was that on a hot summer's evening in late July, Solange set out to see Mademoiselle Cherry, to throw herself at her feet and on her mercy, to beg her to take her back again, to be like they used to be.

Cherry was curious when Jules knocked at her cabin door and told her that a young lady was waiting to see her. Walking out to greet the unexpected visitor she was surprised and delighted to see that it was Solange. She looked a little thinner and definitely more subdued, sensibly dressed in a simple cotton skirt and blouse.

Cherry led Solange to the nearest deck lounger, insisting she sit down and tell her all her news. Jules was sent to fetch them a bottle of champagne and within minutes, Solange had agreed that it was beginning to feel just like old times.

Cherry was highly embarrassed when Solange began to cry, telling her that life had ceased to have any meaning since last they'd met.

'Oh, hell,' thought Cherry to herself. 'She used to be fun but I can't take much of this.'

With the utmost humility, her huge eyes shining with tears, Solange asked Cherry if she could find her a job. Just to get away from papa, just to be near to Mademoiselle . . . that was all that Solange asked, all that she'd ever want.

'And the rest,' thought Cherry, remembering that Solange's appetites were every bit as voracious as her own. Yes, she'd been a true soulmate. But Cherry simply didn't need her any more. Watching her though, sitting in the sunshine, Cherry decided to have some fun. She would be meeting Rick later that night but in the meantime she had a little time to spare.

Cherry knew that Jacques was back on board the yacht, helping his father and dreaming of her. At every opportunity

Jacques would appear at her cabin on some pretext or other, though thankfully his father kept him sufficiently busy to stop his visits becoming a nuisance. Sometimes when he called, Cherry would give him a lesson in love. At other times she'd simply send the boy away.

He was pining for her and so, apparently, was Solange. They'd both do anything to please her.

Cherry left Solange sitting on the deck while she went to look for Jacques. Luckily he wasn't with his father but was fixing a seat on one of the lifeboats on the lower deck which, thought Cherry, a smile on her face, had possibly been damaged in a moment of passion by her and Rick.

Telling him that she had a job for him in her cabin in fifteen minutes time, Cherry left Jacques in a state of high excitement and returned to Solange. Taking her straight down to her cabin, Cherry told the girl that she was obviously in need of a new wardrobe and, throwing open the doors of her own, told her to choose whatever she liked.

Solange went almost pathetic in her avarice, thought Cherry. Her eyes bulging out of her head, she fingered Cherry's clothes, pressing her face against the fine fabrics and breathing in the soft smell of expensive perfume which hung about them all. 'Try something on,' said Cherry.

Without further encouragement, the girl stepped out of her clothes, standing in the middle of the cabin in lacy bra and pants as she pulled one after another of Cherry's dresses over her head.

Solange was admiring herself in an ivory silk evening dress when there was a knock at the door and Jacques appeared. He was surprised to find that his mistress was not alone.

'Jacques, meet Solange,' said Cherry as the boy stepped forward to take her hand.

'She's pretty,' thought Jacques, 'but not as pretty as my love.'

Cherry flopped down on her bed and told them she had a task for them to perform. It would be a test of their love for her. Anxious and willing to do anything to please, they listened attentively as Cherry told them that she wished them to make love to each other, using all the techniques that she'd taught them both, so she could be sure that they'd learned their lessons well.

With dismay, Jacques and Solange glanced at each other. They'd both wanted to be alone with Mademoiselle Cherry. But if this was what she wanted . . .

Cherry lay back on her bed and declared that the show should begin. Reluctantly, Jacques moved towards Solange, his boyish hand touching her shoulder, his mouth moving awkwardly to cover her own. Oh, this was crazy. Jacques felt like a fool standing in front of the woman he loved and kissing another. Solange felt no such awkwardness. This was an audition and she thought that if she pleased Mademoiselle Cherry, she would get to stay. Her whole future depended on it.

Her lips moved expertly against the boy's reluctant ones, her hand reaching for the front of his trousers.

Jacques felt his prick start to harden as her fingers began to stroke and rub him. Her pert little nipples squeezed against his chest as Solange pressed her body close to his. He felt his cock being lifted from the front of his trousers and, as it made contact with the girl's skin, he realised that she had stepped out of her clothes. The explosion of sensations that she created within him was enhanced a hundredfold by the smell of her, the touch of her and the knowledge that just inches away from his grasp was a wet pussy.

Suddenly, Jacques had forgotten his embarrassment. He could smell this girl whose body was held against his own. His hard cock was touching her soft flesh. Her hot little pussy was wide open and just waiting for him. She smelt different from Cherry. The same, but different. Oh, what a mystery women were. What a delicious surprise!

Solange took the boy's hand and led him to the bed. His prick had grown huge and stood out from his young body, hard and horizontal, looking somehow too big and grown up for the slim-shouldered youth who carried its weight. 'Oh, yes,' thought Jacques. 'I want this woman now.' He closed his eyes and sniffed her as her lips began to explore his chest. He wanted to pin her down and stuff his hard prick into the depths of her softness. Oh, yes.

Would she be as tight as Mademoiselle? Or even tighter? 'No,' thought Jacques. 'I mustn't think about that. I mustn't come till we're both ready.'

Laying the young boy down, Solange climbed on top of him, bringing his hands up to touch her tits. They were so different from Mademoiselle Cherry's! Jacques' fingers strayed across Solange's delicate nipples and small, firm breasts, his cock jerking in spasms of arousal as she held him between her thighs, her pussy resting against his legs like a little furry animal with its tongue out.

Solange leant forward and began to lick the boy's chest in long, firm movements. Watching them, Cherry had become aroused and, sitting just inches away on the bed, had begun to masturbate, her hands inside her shorts, her fingers buried in a pussy that was longing to join in with the action.

'Solange,' she whispered into the girl's ear, 'let's tie him up.' With a giggle, both women slipped off the bed, returning seconds later clutching the silk scarves which Cherry kept in readiness.

'What are you doing?' said Jacques, sitting up on his elbows as they approached.

'Just a little game,' replied Cherry. 'Now lay back and relax.'

Tying his wrists to the bedpost, both women stood back and surveyed their prize. He was gorgeous and so eager, his prick looking like it would burst out of its skin, his neck a deep flush of red as he squirmed beneath his bonds.

'Are you going to leave me tied up like this?' complained Jacques as Mademoiselle Cherry leant over him and carefully licked one of his nipples. 'Mademoiselle, please! Untie me and I will give you such a good time . . . both of you!'

'Oh, you'll do that,' replied Cherry, sucking the tip of his cock very briefly as one would suck a finger that had just been dipped into a favourite sauce to taste for seasoning . . .

Jacques thought his mind and his cock would explode with frustration. By now, both the women were naked and they stood before him, licking and kissing each other, Cherry's fingers buried in Solange's vulva while her mouth nibbled at the girl's breasts. Solange began to moan. They looked so wonderful together, thought Jacques, and had he not been firmly tied to the bed he would have been unable to stop himself touching them both.

Breaking apart at last, the women walked towards Jacques. They stood on either side of him as he lay pinioned, unable to move. 'Which of us shall go first?' said Cherry.

'Oh you, Mademoiselle,' replied Solange.

'No, I insist,' said Cherry, standing out of the way for her old friend.

Climbing onto the bed, Solange positioned herself above the excited boy, lowering her open body onto his erection. She swallowed his prick inside her as a hoarse moan escaped from Jacques' lips. Coming up behind Solange, Cherry wrapped her arms around the girl's chest and, as Solange rocked backwards and forwards against the boy's throbbing shaft, she pinched Solange's pretty tits. All the while she rubbed her clitoris against her friend's buttocks, her pleasure mounting as she felt Solange shudder, her body taut with expectation.

'Oh, he's good,' murmured Solange. 'I can feel him . . . so deep.' Reaching down between her own legs, she opened the lips of her vulva wide, greedy for this man-child whose fresh young cock was filling her with a pleasure she'd missed so much in the lonely weeks she'd pined for Cherry, pined for their shared adventures, their naughty escapades.

'Now me,' said Cherry, urging Solange to move over, to climb off the boy. Solange moved away reluctantly and

Cherry spread herself on top of him, his cock – already wet with Solange's juices – sliding easily into her eager cavern.

How good he felt! His juvenile prick responded to every contraction of her body as she urged him on, sucking and squeezing him inside her.

Cherry had taught him well. Jacques was able to delay orgasm until both women had ridden him to their own satisfaction, slipping him in and out of their bodies as they straddled him in turn, each extracting maximum pleasure from the fact that he wasn't simply well endowed, but he was also so very young.

Cherry had corrupted them both and she was proud of her handiwork. They were her slaves, sexual playthings to do with as she pleased. But life had moved on from the days when she needed Solange. So when they dressed again and Cherry sent Solange home, promising that she'd send a parcel of the clothes she'd chosen within days and the firm offer of a job within the week, Cherry didn't mean a word of it. She never intended to see Solange again. But it had killed a few hours. And it had been an interesting way to say goodbye.

Yes. Life had taken a turn for the better for Cherry. Now all she needed was to get Rick to organise the forging of a letter, and the plan to persuade Pierre to take part in their imminent drugs deal would be firmly in place.

Nikki never wanted to see the yacht again. Escaping at last without detection, she had wandered the streets, wondering what on earth to do next. Calming herself eventually, she had found a small hotel and had booked in for the night, grateful to have her passport with her at last, able to take a room with no questions asked.

She knew that Jake would be worried and so would Madame Aronson. Phoning the Café Pelican immediately, she told Jake an edited version of the truth – that she'd discovered her passport was missing and had panicked, leaving the Café Pelican to return to the yacht where she'd been trapped on board, unable to escape for hours without being seen.

Jake sounded cool and distant, which he had every right to be. Why hadn't she asked him to go and collect her passport? After all, she was perfectly entitled to it. Nikki couldn't answer his question. 'I'm sorry,' she said.

How could she ever make him understand about her affair with Pierre? The answer was she couldn't. No man would really understand the craziness that could seize a woman, the passion that had destroyed her reason and was even now destroying the Contessa de Silva.

She'd told Jake and Madame Aronson that she'd simply been sacked from the yacht, that her employer had changed her mind about having her own personal beauty therapist and had paid her off. Nikki had been honest with Jake, but only up to a point. He knew of her relationship with Chris. But she'd never mentioned her affair with Pierre. Jake might have behaved very differently to her if she had told him the whole truth and frankly, thought Nikki, who could have blamed him?

Jake was no fool. From his point of view there was no reason why Nikki had needed to hide on the yacht after dark like a thief in the night. He knew that there was more to her sudden departure than she was letting on. But he didn't press her, didn't ask questions. And when Nikki simply said that she'd be back in a couple of days and hung up, he accepted it.

Nikki put the phone down after talking to Jake, knowing full well that he no longer trusted her. Why was it that everything good in her life seemed to get spoiled, she wondered? It was all her fault. But out of this mess must come something positive or it was all a waste of time.

There was a drugs deal about to take place and the Contessa's yacht was going to be involved. Nikki didn't know how but she had to stop it. She didn't know when it was due to happen but she had to try and find out.

Since leaving the yacht, she'd had time to think and had decided not to try and involve the Contessa. It had been foolish from the start to think that Marianna would have any time for Nikki or what she had to say.

Hiding in the wardrobe, Nikki had seen for herself the full extent of the Contessa's obsession with Pierre. If she was to be saved from involvement with the bad things that Cherry was planning then it was Nikki alone who could save her.

She knew her life to be in a desperate state. But suddenly, and without warning, Nikki found a feeling of strength and confidence returning, a sense of purpose and a clear idea of what she must do.

She would return to the yacht that night and every night. She would eavesdrop on Cherry's conversations, chart her movements and, if necessary, follow her. She would find out what was going on and put a stop to it. She owed it to herself and to the Contessa, and in a strange way she also owed it to Chris.

With a renewed sense of purpose, Nikki decided to enjoy the day. Leaving the hotel, she made her way to a nearby boutique and bought a bikini. She may as well enjoy the sun. There was nothing she could do without the cover of darkness. She'd laze in the sun today and go to work tonight.

Cherry never ceased to marvel at Rick. The more she got to know him, the more fabulous he was, the more he revealed himself to be a resourceful as well as a clever criminal, a man with a finger in many pies and contacts everywhere that mattered.

She'd gone to him, telling him that she needed to forge a letter from one of the major banks, informing the Contessa that her overdraft facility was cancelled and that the bank was demanding payment of the massive debts she'd run up. The tone of the letter needed to be both highly professional and cautiously threatening. It was Cherry's intention to leave it in a prominent place in the Contessa's cabin so that Pierre would accidentally discover it, leaving him in no doubt that he was wasting his time with Marianna.

Once she'd softened him up, Cherry would then introduce him to Rick and recruit him to become the third member of their little team. There'd be no advantage to him in reporting them. No advantage either in staying with the Contessa. They'd have him where they wanted him and, as an added bonus, Cherry would have him in her bed at last. It was all coming together so well and very soon life would be even better still. For a split second, Cherry thought about Solange, laughing quietly to herself as she imagined the girl waiting for the post, waiting for the phone to ring, waiting and waiting in vain. Pierre would feel every bit as bad as Solange by the time Cherry had finished with him. He'd be promised a fortune as part of his 'cut' but Cherry would see to it that he ended up without a penny. She had it all worked out in her mind. It was just a matter of time.

Chapter 19

Chris had left Irana a note. He'd placed it on her pillow while she'd been out for a swim and then he'd simply disappeared. His note told her that he was going home and he thought it best to leave without a fuss. He said he'd see her when she was back in England. At the bottom of the note, there were three little kisses.

Much to her amazement when she'd read his note, Irana found that there were tears on her cheeks. He had every right to leave, of course. Their work was over and they were both adults, both aware that their affair was no more than a fling. Her own words came flooding back to her from the night she had yelled at him. 'What you think, Christopher? That I yours alone? That we live happy every after?' She'd sneered at him when he'd objected to her sleeping with Marco. She'd jeered at his sense of propriety. And now he'd gone and she was crying. Even Irana could appreciate the irony . . .

It had been a difficult journey for Chris. Airport delays, a baggage mix-up, but at last he had arrived back at Heathrow, the familiar and comforting sounds and smells making him feel like he'd never been away. As usual, there were long queues for taxis and the traffic moved into central London at a crawl. 'Yes, I'm definitely home,' thought Chris as the cab driver chattered aimlessly.

Marianna de Silva had decided that she and Pierre would

take the train to Paris. It wasn't really a long journey and a train was so much more romantic than flying. She'd phoned the bank earlier that day and arranged for some money to be transferred from one of her many deposit accounts. She'd then taken a phone call from her stockbroker in England. One of the companies in which she had shares had been swallowed by a larger consortium. The price of her shares had rocketed and Marianna had made a quarter of a million pounds overnight.

This afternoon, while Pierre was sunbathing, she'd go into Nice and buy him a present. The shops would close during the early part of the afternoon but if she arrived as soon as they re-opened she'd have plenty of time to choose something rather special before returning for dinner.

Nikki was lying on the beach, reading a book and trying to concentrate. Though the umbrella under which she sheltered gave sufficient shade from the glaring mid-day sun, she still found she couldn't keep her mind still. She wanted to leave, to fly back to the rich green fields and cool fresh air of England. But there was still so much to do and, for now, all she could do was wait.

Everything seemed to be on hold. Everyone seemed to be waiting. The day was still. It was a glorious summer. But everywhere from Palermo to the palm-shaded boulevards of the Côte d'Azur, unrest was in the air.

The forgery was quite perfect. Rick had appeared at the yacht soon after lunch to find Cherry lazing on deck as usual, a full ashtray and an empty wine bottle beside her. Her hair was scraped back from a face partially obscured by a pair of the season's most fashionable 'shades'.

Cherry told him that the Contessa had just left for Nice and Pierre was stretched out on the upper deck. There was no one to disturb them, no one to prevent their masterplan from being put into action.

Rick had arrived at the yacht with a holdall slung over his shoulder. Sitting down beside Cherry, he calmly informed her that it contained eight packets of cocaine, one of which they were to select at random in order to do a quality check. If all was well they could pick up the rest of the consignment in two days' time. The day after the Contessa and Pierre were due to leave for Paris.

Rick hadn't objected to the recruitment of Pierre as the third member of their group. 'But what if the Contessa won't go without him?' Rick had said.

'Don't worry,' Cherry assured him. 'She will.'

Sitting in the sun, Rick had removed a carefully forged letter from his holdall, handing it to Nikki who first wiped her hands for fear of covering it in suntan oil. The paper was heavy and embossed, the golden logo of the Banque Centrale glittering in the sunshine as Cherry read the letter carefully. It informed the Contessa de Silva that her overdraft had been cancelled and the massive debts she had accrued in recent months could no longer be permitted to remain unpaid. The language was formal and stern, the message of the letter unequivocal. It told Marianna that she was skint. Anyone who read it would be in no doubt.

Cherry looked at Rick and a wave of lust shot through her. He was clever. He could get anything done and she adored him for it. They'd lay the trap for Pierre, snort some of the coke he'd brought with him and then . . . Cherry felt herself grow hot at the thought of the afternoon ahead.

When Jules came up to Pierre an hour later telling him that there was a phone call for him, he was surprised. No one knew he was on the yacht apart from the Contessa and she was shopping in Nice. It must be her, asking him what colour shoes he'd like, what kind of shirt . . . she'd really begun to get on his nerves lately, her desperation almost palpable.

Pierre was beginning to miss the little beauty therapist more than he'd imagined he could miss anyone. There had been something about her that was different from the rest. Not only was her body beautiful but she'd had a certain quality, an elegance of spirit which most women lacked. Whenever he'd been fucking Marianna lately, he'd had to imagine it was the little beauty therapist. He'd think about the money he would squeeze out of the Contessa and then he'd think about Nikki. The combination gave him a hard-on that even he was impressed by. And he knew that it was these performances in bed that kept Marianna scuttling off to buy him more presents, anxious to hold him, desperate to keep his interest.

With an air of total boredom, Pierre made his way to Marianna's cabin. He'd told Jules that he'd take the call in there as there was no phone in his own cabin, a deficiency that Marianna had promised to rectify.

Her cabin was cool and uncluttered, save for a few papers lying around. He picked up the phone. He listened. There was no one there. How strange! With a sigh, Pierre turned on his heels and prepared to leave the cabin, to return to the sun deck and kill a few more hours before he had to exclaim in pleasure over Marianna's latest gift.

As he went to leave though, a flash of gold caught his eye. There was a letter sticking out of one of Marianna's handbags. Recognising the bank crest, something told him to look at it.

Five minutes later, putting the letter carefully back where he'd found it, Pierre left Marianna's cabin. His mind was racing yet, from his demeanour, no one would have been able to tell a thing. Returning to the upper deck he lay down and began to think. The bitch. The stupid, senseless bitch. The deadline by which he had to pay his debts was just weeks away and the consequences of not paying them were too serious even to contemplate. He must think, and think fast. But he must not panic.

Cherry watched Pierre leave Marianna's cabin and sneaked

inside, taking the fictitious letter and disappearing as quickly as she'd come. Her first instinct was to destroy it but she thought better of the impulse and decided to keep it, to relish it as a trophy.

Rick had returned from the phone box and was waiting in her cabin. Good coke, a lazy afternoon and Rick. Cherry decided that she was closer to perfect happiness than she'd ever been.

As she opened the door and entered her cabin, Rick was selecting one of the many little packets from his open holdall. Coming up behind him she wrapped her arm around his waist, feeling for the front of his trousers, happy to find that his prick was already half-hard, his mind moving in the same direction as her own.

She handed him a mirror from the top of her bureau and watched as he cut a line of coke – a straight, perfect line of pure white power which he handed to her. Rolling up a banknote, Cherry snorted the coke greedily, holding her head back as it flooded through her body, sending her senses reeling. Oh, this was good. This was pure genius.

As Rick snorted his own line, Cherry began to giggle. She was looking again at the forged letter she'd just removed from the Contessa's cabin. 'You're brilliant, you know,' she said to Rick, moving across to him and pulling his hand inside her shirt, guiding his fingers till they latched on to her fat brown nipple. 'You're plain fucking brilliant.'

'I'm hungry,' he said as she nibbled his earlobe. 'Didn't get a chance to stop this morning. Shall we call that Jules guy for some lunch?'

Dismayed at the idea of being interrupted yet aware that Rick wouldn't be able to perform at his best if he needed food, Cherry moved away from him reluctantly and walked across to her little fridge. 'Taramasalata, houmous, bread, chocolate . . . will that do till later?'

'Sure thing, babe,' he replied as Cherry began to remove the food, placing it on the table beside her bed.

They sat on the bed together, the little banquet spread out between them, and Rick began to eat. Idly, Cherry removed her shirt and, with a smile on her face, began to spread a dollop of the taramasalata across her breast. Rick dipped his bread in it, wiping it from her skin and then licking the rest away, his matter-of-fact attitude betrayed by the huge swelling which had now appeared at the front of his trousers.

Cherry dipped into the pot again, spreading tarama on one breast and then houmous on the other. Lying on her back, she licked her lips as Rick bent over her and began sucking his lunch from her tits, his hand moving down her body and between her legs. 'Got any butter?' he said quite suddenly at which she replied yes, she thought she might have.

Rick got to his feet and went to the fridge, returning seconds later with a pot of unsalted creamery butter.

Pulling her shorts and panties down over her legs, he spread her wide, smearing a little of the butter on one forefinger and pushing it into her pussy.

'Ow, that's cold,' said Cherry as Rick then spread some more taramasalata and houmous over her body.

'You look like a fucking feast,' he said, his mouth beginning to work its way across her breasts, licking the soft gooey mess, his tongue wiping it along her body as he went. He filled her navel with houmous which he then licked out, moving down to her pussy, sliding a small piece of pitta bread between her legs to find the butter hidden there. The butter slipped, it moved, it crept deeper inside her. The bread wouldn't work. He must use his tongue. Brushing the crumbs from his mouth, Rick moved down to the foot of the bed, spreading Cherry's legs even wider till her clitoris poked out at him.

'The butter,' he reminded himself, poking his tongue straight into Cherry's vagina in pursuit of the knob of butter which he knew would melt at any moment. He felt it . . . it slipped away. He probed deeper, Cherry growing more excited as his tongue pursued it, contracting her muscles to keep it hidden from him so he'd have to keep up the search. In the end he had to remove it with his fingers before it melted.

'Don't want to leave anything stuck up there,' he said.

'No,' she replied. 'Nothing except you.'

Popping a chocolate into her mouth, Rick kissed her deeply, curling his tongue around her own to dissolve the chocolate between them, rubbing it till it exploded in a shower of strawberry flavour, coating both their mouths as their tongues intertwined.

'Now *I'm* hungry,' moaned Cherry, dragging her lips away from Rick's and moving down the bed towards his cock, pulling impatiently at the front of his trousers to release it as it sprang forth like a jack-in-the-box from the confinement of his boxer shorts. Leaning forward, she began to lick his cock in long strokes from base to tip. The pressure of her tongue caused a little spurt of white to appear at its knob, over which she placed her lips, moving down to absorb the length of his penis in her mouth.

'Mmmm,' he moaned, 'you could give head for England.' Thrusting against her tonsils, he came in the back of her throat, too deep for her even to need to swallow, his juices slipping straight down into her stomach.

She lay with her head against his chest, listening to his heart. 'It's all going to be wonderful,' she said.

'Yes, I know,' he replied. 'A few more days . . . that's all.'

Stroking his chest with her fingertips she watched his cock begin to swell, fascinated as in a matter of seconds it grew again, rising from his belly to stand proud and ready for action.

'What makes it swell?' she asked, her childlike question sounding more than a little silly.

'Blood,' he replied.

'Yes, I know that,' said Cherry, 'but what do you think about to get the blood going?'

'I think about the taste of your pussy. I think about how soft your nipples are until I touch them and how they turn into little fleshy bullets. I think about the smell of you and what it feels like to open you and take my cock in my hand and stick it in you. That sort of thing.'

'Oh, you love me then?' said Cherry and as they both began to laugh she sat up, moving her leg across him and spreading her body wide, tensing her thighs to lift her opening level with his prick, hovering just above it.

She began to stroke the tip of his cock against her clitoris, the soft, rounded head of him brushing the lips of her labia. Leaving a trial of wetness across him, she guided him through the soft bush of her hair and into the most sensitive creases of her pink and puckered flesh. She lowered her body to skim his prick one minute, coming down harder the next to feel its firmness against her as she dragged its head through the crack between her legs, squashing him roughly against her labia, putting pressure on the pubic bone beneath which responded by sending a shiver through her which pulsed the length of her vagina, causing a fresh wave of moisture to flood through her swollen chasm.

Holding his prick and kissing its tip, she moved it down through her bush, guiding it at last into the entrance to her womanhood. She experienced that familiar sensation as he eased himself into her body – a feeling that she knew so well yet which never ceased to thrill her like it did the very first time, like it always did.

Beginning the familiar rocking movements which she knew would bring her to orgasm, Cherry looked down at the man whose dark pubic hair was tangled with her own. He had a curious expression on his face. One which she didn't recognise.

'What are you thinking?' she said. 'You look strange.'

'How what you said a moment ago was true,' he replied. Cherry couldn't remember what he was talking about.

'When I described what I felt like, when I got an erection,' said Rick. 'And you turned round and said that I must love you. And you were joking. Well, I do. I do love you. I've never met a woman like you. I love you and I want to stay with you for ever.'

Cherry leant across and kissed Rick deeply, thinking this was the best way to avoid having to make a similar declaration. She did not love him. She did not love anyone and felt only embarrassment on his behalf. Thinking that her action was her way of confirming that she felt the same, Rick's arousal reached the point of no return and, with a series of short, rapid thrusts, he came inside her, his cry of pleasure telling Cherry that as orgasms go, this had been a good one.

She buried her face in his shoulder and cursed quietly to herself as she held him tight. 'Damn,' she thought. 'Damn his stupid sentimentality.' She'd have to get rid of him and bring herself off with the dildo.

Up on deck, stretched out in the sunshine, Pierre had been masturbating. The shock of the letter he'd read in the Contessa's cabin had made him feel that he'd never get an erection again which, in his particular line of work, would be like an artist losing his paintbrush.

All was in working order, though. If anything, his prick was growing bigger, and now he'd left the tool of his trade out in the sunshine to dry off, the slippery fluid which had shot out of him still leaking gently from beneath his foreskin.

Closing his eyes he considered his options, none of which looked too appealing. There was a rich American widow of his acquaintance who lived in Paris, though she had a penchant for being buggered which Pierre did not find to his taste. There were others . . . but no one from whom Pierre could guarantee to obtain all the money he needed in the time he had available.

Pierre lay back as the full weight of his problems continued their relentless march through his mind. Thump,

thump, thump they went, much as his creditors would do if he were unable to pay his debts. Of this he had no doubt. They were gambling debts, owed to the type of men who wouldn't be fobbed off by excuses.

Pierre sat up with a start, a sudden attack of panic causing him to catch his breath, the sunlight sparkling on the sea shooting darts of pain into his skull. What the hell was he going to do? With time, with a few months in hand, he could have wined and dined and seduced another woman. But he knew now that it was too late and that though he'd soothed himself with the prospect of other conquests in Paris, he hadn't seriously believed that such drastic measures might be necessary.

Staggering to his feet, Pierre made his way to his cabin to lie down. He would stay here tonight and try to be calm. He wouldn't panic. Something would always turn up. It must.

Cherry had invited Rick to stay for dinner, knowing that the Contessa approved of this 'nice young man'. Despite Rick's poor performance of the afternoon, Cherry had thought it might give them both the opportunity to talk to Pierre – if, that was, it proved possible to get him on his own. They had to speak to him soon as time was running out.

Marianna was completely confused and more than a little unsettled. She had returned to the yacht loaded down with parcels to find Pierre up on deck where she'd left him hours before, staring out to sea and sipping a gin and tonic. To her knowledge, Pierre didn't drink spirits and, what's more, he appeared to be a little drunk. Usually by this time he was showered and dressed for dinner, a smile of welcome on his face, telling Marianna how much he'd missed her.

She'd brought him a light cashmere jacket and a pair of gold cufflinks. He appeared to be pleased though, much to Marianna's distress, he didn't thank her in the usual way. 'The usual way' brought a flush to her cheeks and a glow to her backside. Tonight, though, they did nothing to work up an appetite and when they gathered for dinner, for the first time ever Marianna was glad that Cherry and her new boyfriend were there to help lighten the atmosphere.

By midnight, they were still sitting on the deck drinking brandy. Pierre showed no inclination to go to bed and had been drinking heavily throughout the evening. 'What's wrong, my dear?' Marianna had enquired during one of the brief moments when Cherry and Rick had both been away from the table.

'Nothing,' he had replied. 'I have a few things on my mind, that's all.'

It was a quarter to one when Marianna finally accepted the fact that Pierre was in for a hard night's drinking. Saying goodnight she made her way to her cabin and, for the first time in months, allowed herself to cry. Things hadn't been right between them for a while now. But what was she to do? In quiet despair, she undressed and decided to try and get some sleep.

Despite her apparently relaxed and carefree demeanour, Cherry had been watching Pierre closely all evening. The letter had affected him more than she'd dared to hope for. His ready wit and easy charm had evaporated and, during dinner, it had been as much as he could do to join in the conversation or give polite answers to the Contessa's many anxiety-laden questions. He was drinking heavily, too. Perfect. It couldn't be better.

Pierre made it easy for her. 'You were right,' he said, with no preamble or introduction. 'Marianna is skint. I saw a letter.'

Cherry looked at him and saw a man with nothing to lose. Had he nurtured even the faintest hope of extracting money from his mistress, such a comment would never had been forthcoming. But his cards were on the table. He freely admitted he needed money. And within minutes, a whole new world had opened up to him, along with a way of getting his hands on enough cash to solve all his problems.

Hiding on deck as she had been since eight that evening, her heart thumping, Nikki heard Cherry and her smooth, East London boyfriend outline their plans to Pierre, taking him totally into their confidence, knowing there was no risk at all. When they told him how much they stood to make out of the drugs deal, Pierre's mood had altered immediately. Even his voice had changed, the customary elegance of phrase and sexy laugh returning as he saw, for the first time, a bright light at the end of the tunnel, a way out of his own private hell. Then, surprisingly, the conversation had turned to Nikki.

'How will stepmama manage without you *and* her beauty therapist?' said Cherry spitefully.

'I was sorry about that,' replied Pierre. 'What happened to her?'

'I have no idea,' replied Cherry. 'Maybe she went looking for her boyfriend.' Seeing the effect her words had on Pierre, she rammed her point home spitefully. 'Oh, she definitely had a boyfriend,' continued Cherry. 'He phoned here a couple of times. Most anxious to speak to her he was. I think it was serious.'

Standing in the shadows, it was all Nikki could do to stifle her cry of despair. Chris had phoned here? No one had ever told her. Suddenly she felt the full force of Cherry's jealousy like a kick in the stomach. Chris had tried to speak to her and she'd never known.

At three a.m. Pierre went straight to Marianna's cabin. He found her staring anxiously into the darkness, her eyes unusually bright.

'Pierre,' she said, sitting up at once. 'What is the matter? Please don't tell me it's nothing because I know you and you've been unhappy for days. What is it, my dear? Tell me what you need and you can have it.' Holding out her arms, she beckoned him to her and, much to her relief, he came.

'It's my mother,' he said. 'She's dangerously ill in a hospital in Marseilles. I've been wondering how to tell you, how to break the news. I can't come to Paris with you, Marianna. I must go to her.'

'Oh, Pierre,' said Marianna, the tears spilling down her cheeks, 'why did you feel you couldn't tell me?'

'Because you'd be so disappointed,' replied Pierre, at which Marianna's tears turned to sobs of compassion mixed with relief.

'Then I will come with you,' she said.

Pierre held her sternly by the shoulders and looked into her eyes. 'You will go to Paris as planned,' he said. 'I want to meet you in Paris. It is the most romantic city on earth and there is a question I wish to ask you, but only in Paris. Will you promise me that you will go, and wait for me there?'

Marianna's unhappincss of thc last fcw days turncd to joy. He wanted to meet her in Paris because he wanted to propose to her. That much was obvious. 'Oh, my darling,' she said, clasping him to her, burying his head in her breasts.

With all the skill of a true professional, Pierre began to kiss Marianna's breasts, holding each in turn in the palm of his hand and addressing it with his mouth with the reverence due to a sacred object. She was more aroused than he'd ever seen her. A little anxiety did her good, he thought.

Ordering her to kneel on the bed, he crouched beneath her, spreading her buttocks, parting the dark furry mound till her little clitoris came poking out of the shadows and he licked it with his tongue.

Pierre reached inside her arse, his fingers groping downwards for her slippery hole. She was wet, so wet. Sliding two fingers into her crevice, he spread her juices from the depths of her pulsating vagina back along the length of her arse till Marianna was a slippery mass.

Her body swayed backwards and forwards, leaning against his fingers which plunged ever deeper into her upturned canal, his thumb toying with the hole in her arse as she began to moan and press against him.

Pierre unzipped his fly, grabbing hold of his swollen cock which he began to rub in rhythm with Marianna's gentle swaying. Stroking it between her buttocks, he heard her sigh as she moved her arse higher in the air, positioning her body so that her pussy was gaping, its juices lubricating the shaft of him as he squashed his penis between the cheeks of her bum like a hot dog inside a bun. 'I'd better keep the silly bitch happy,' he thought to himself. 'Then at least she'll do as she's told and go quietly.'

Chapter 20

By morning, Nikki felt she must surely have cried herself out. But still the tears came until she thought that she would never stop. Chris had phoned her. He'd phoned her more than once and he'd obviously left messages, maybe even a number for her to call him back. She'd waited for his call and she'd thought it hadn't come. And it was then that she'd finally slept with Pierre.

Oh, how cruel it all was! And even now she had no way of finding out where he might be, of contacting him and telling him that she was sorry. How would she find him in the whole of Sicily? What should she do?

It was eight o'clock when she finally phoned Jake. Her voice was trembling though she tried to control it, telling him that everything was fine and she'd see him very soon. She'd simply wanted to hear his voice, to be comforted by the sound of him, to hear the ordinary, everyday gossip of the café and to send her love to Madame Aronson.

Jake didn't pry. He didn't demand to know what was going on or why she hadn't returned. He just relayed all the news, such as it was, and when Nikki felt she'd said enough, he'd returned her goodbye.

Dressing wearily and picking at the breakfast she'd asked to be sent up to her, Nikki wondered what to do next. There were drugs on board the Contessa's yacht and more to come. Pierre was involved and the yacht was about to make a shameful voyage to the South Coast of England, the

Contessa having been safely bundled out of the way. How they were managing that, she did not know. And what about the crew? What about Jules? Surely, she thought, he would not be a part of their evil plan.

Nikki paced her room, wondering what to do for the best. There was no alternative. She had to go to the police. It was the only course of action open to her and the only thing she could do to help the Contessa. Yet she knew that she would not be thanked for it when Pierre was exposed as a criminal. The Contessa hated her already. If she went to the police, Marianna's heart would finally be broken.

By lunchtime, Nikki was wondering how much worse things could get. She'd pulled herself together, applied make-up carefully around her swollen eyes and made herself look presentable. Then she'd gone to the police station and, after a lengthy delay due to a recent 'major incident', she had finally been seen. Her story was listened to with the utmost politeness. But she knew they hadn't believed her.

What real evidence did she have for saying that there were drugs on board the Contessa de Silva's yacht? Had she seen them? Did she realise who the Contessa actually was and who her husband had been? And what was her relationship with the family? 'Ah,' said the policeman and smiled. 'You worked for the Contessa and you were sacked, *non*? That is what you are telling me, Mademoiselle. Why were you sacked?'

Nikki realised it was hopeless and that no one would believe her. She should go back to England. There was nothing else for it. But the drugs deal was due to take place tomorrow night! They would sail to England with their packets of white poison, shattering the lives of thousands of people in pursuit of their own wicked aims and ruining the Contessa's life into the bargain. And all Nikki could offer the police was her own 'evidence', the testimony of a girl who had been sacked for misconduct and, for all they knew, was poisoned by jealousy and a desire for revenge.

She walked out of the police station crying, not caring who saw her. Stumbling back to her hotel she pushed her way through the double doors at the front entrance and straight into the waiting arms of Jake.

The Contessa de Silva was very worried about Pierre's mother. She was also deeply relieved that his recent moods had been the result of concern about their planned trip to Paris and his regret at the prospect of having to let her down.

She packed carefully and, when she was ready, asked Jules to summon Monsieur Valbon, who had said he would accompany her to the station and put her on the train. Pierre would then be setting out for Marseilles to see his mama. He was devoted to the frail old lady he'd described so lovingly to Marianna the previous evening, that much was obvious. 'But does he really love *me*?' Marianna asked herself. The answer was yes. It must be so. Anything else was unthinkable. Because without his love, there was nothing.

Cherry was waiting for Pierre when he returned from the train station. She'd waited for him for over an hour, expecting him back sooner. But in the scheme of things, this was nothing compared with how long she'd really waited. She'd wanted Pierre since the moment she saw him and now she was going to have him. And Rick would be here soon. All would be complete.

Pierre stepped on board the yacht like a man who had just been saved from the gallows. There was a new spring in his stride, the same lightness of manner that Cherry had noticed the first time they'd met. He had seemed so confident then, so full of life and natural charm. Now he was back to his usual self and they were going to have some fun.

'I've given the crew double wages and told them to come back next week,' she said. 'Jules made a bit of a fuss but as none of them know where Marianna is staying, they can't go bleating to her. Did she go quietly, by the way?' said Cherry, a smile on her lips.

'She hung out of the train window with tears in her eyes,' replied Pierre. They looked at each other and burst out laughing.

'Ugh! How sickening,' said Cherry, pouring them both a drink.

Cherry smiled at Pierre and the message in her eyes was clear. Pierre wasn't here for his sailing skills alone. That much was understood. 'This man is going to fuck me till I can hardly stand,' she thought, smiling sweetly. She swallowed her drink in one, hoping it would go straight to her head.

'C'mon,' she said, unable to wait any longer and leading him down to her cabin she opened the door. 'I want to film you,' she said, 'and then I want to film *us*.'

On the bed lay a camcorder of the very latest and most sophisticated kind. 'I'm going to make you a star,' said Cherry, laughing her careless laugh. But she felt nervous. Or was it excited? The palms of her hands were damp.

Picking up the camcorder and switching it on, Cherry pointed it straight at Pierre. 'This is Pierre Valbon,' she said. 'He is mine and will do anything I ask.' Smiling at him, Cherry then ordered him to get undressed, going up to him with the camcorder and filming a close-up of his penis as he removed his boxer shorts. Cherry felt herself grow hot. It wasn't even erect yet and still it was enormous. Maybe she should stop the filming and just get down to business . . . but no, she checked herself. The recording must be made.

'Pierre,' she said, 'I want you to walk out on deck and go towards the cabin of my dear stepmother, the Contessa Marianna de Silva.'

Without a murmur, Pierre did as he was told, walking along the deck with Cherry following behind, filming his bum as he walked, occasionally swinging round to get another view of his penis which swung from side to side as he padded across the deck.

Arriving at the door of Marianna's cabin, Cherry ordered him to enter and sit on the bed. 'Now, Pierre,' said Cherry, 'I want you to take that wonderful prick in your hand and pleasure yourself, just for me.'

Once again Pierre made no objection, wrapping his long fingers around his penis and rubbing it vigorously till it stood hard and firm. 'I can't believe it,' whispered Cherry from behind the lens, 'he's hung like a bull,' and with a hand that grew increasingly unsteady, she continued to film.

Pierre brought himself to climax in less than two minutes. As instructed, he shot his arc of slippery juice over Marianna's bed and wiped his prick on her pillow. Cherry took her time to capture the scene, filming the rumpled, damp pillow with the utmost care.

Leaving the camcorder running, Cherry came round to stand in front of it. 'Now I will take my clothes off,' she announced, the pleasure of being filmed as she did so adding spice to her enjoyment. Peeling her shirt and skirt off in seconds, she stood pinching her nipples and announced to the whirring machine that she was now going to have some fun with Pierre.

'Pierre and I have been lovers since he came on board,' said Cherry as the tape recorded her every move. Winking lasciviously into the lens, she strolled across to the Frenchman. 'He is my slave,' she said. 'And will do anything I ask.'

Spreading her legs as she stood before him, Cherry guided his nose and mouth towards her vulva, feeling the firm probing of his tongue as his mouth explored between her pussy lips. She saw his prick begin to stir again and felt a strange mixture of desire and fear. He was so huge! She licked her lips in anticipation. It was time to find out what she'd been missing. 'Fuck me,' she breathed into his ear. 'Treat me rough . . .'

The camera whirred softly as Cherry felt the juices of her arousal, sticky between her thighs.

She felt herself being grabbed roughly by the wrists as Pierre pulled her down. His weight pinning her beneath him, the full force of his hand met her bare brown arse, sending shock waves of pain coursing through her body, each blow sweetened by the rich flood of arousal that was buried in its bite.

Writhing and struggling, Cherry was dragged to her feet and across to a nearby bureau. Of course. They were in dear stepmama's cabin. Pierre would know where things were kept. Cherry watched as he opened a drawer and drew out a length of rope.

Pulling her back to the bed, Pierre threw Cherry down. Her pulses racing, she struggled as he climbed on top of her, tying her hands to the bedstead, moving down to secure her ankles tightly so that the ropes cut into her if she moved even a little. Cherry panted as she stared up at Pierre, knowing that he wanted her as much as she wanted him.

She could see the lust in his eyes and knew she looked good tied up like this. Her bush was slightly parted, a tiny glimpse of her clitoris poking out of the curls. Her tits looked good too, she knew they did – great heavy globes lying spread against her chest, her hard brown nipples big and juicy and pointing straight up in the air.

She could see he was excited by the enjoyment he'd got from beating her and tying her up. She knew she was sweating. Her expensive deodorant could not cover up the smell of fear as Cherry watched him circle the bed, looking down at her.

She watched him disappear into the bathroom. She knew he was taking his time, leaving her to grow more excited and apprehensive.

When he sauntered back into the room, Cherry saw that he was carrying a bottle. Remembering that they were still being filmed, he smiled straight at the camera.

'This is one of the dear Contessa's many creams and potions,' he said, holding up a long, thin bottle and moving across to the bed. Cherry watched as he removed the cap of the bottle and ran a stream of the cool, viscous liquid the length of her body.

When he began to rub it in, Cherry closed her eyes and lust took the place of fear and reservation. His hands were pure magic. His long, probing fingers slid and slipped in the cool scented liquid, gliding over her nipples and between her thighs. His fingers delved into her crack to spread the slipperiness he found there across her thighs along with the lotion, and as her body leant upwards towards him she strained against her ropes, her tongue moistening her lips as she writhed in ecstasy.

He could do whatever he liked with her and she was no longer afraid. Not even when he went back to the bureau, returning with a riding whip which he brought down hard across her slippery skin. She closed her eyes and felt the tears prick her eyelids as he whipped the insides of her thighs and on across her belly, each blow sending a quiver of pleasure shooting into the depths of her womanhood.

Straining at her bonds, she turned her body over so that the blows would fall on her full and rounded arse. Cherry cried out at each blow, her bum cheeks wobbling as the red streaks criss-crossed each other in a pattern of pain and pleasure which, the more he beat her, the more she knew she wanted. She fought and yelled but they both knew she liked it rough. The rougher the better.

She wanted him inside her now, more than she'd wanted anything, ever. She turned on her back and spread her legs wide. She knew she was dripping, that he'd slide inside her like an eel in a current. She'd suck him right into her, giving herself up to the fuck of her life.

Cherry cried out as he entered her. She'd had some big men in her time but Pierre was something else! At first she thought that he was just too big and might injure her but, as her body opened up to take him, she realised that never before had she felt such a sensation, such a deep and satisfying fuck.

Cherry began to understand why her stepmother had gone crazy for this man. The beautician too for that matter. She didn't have to move a muscle to feed him into the right position within her. He filled her completely, the knob of him pressing into her womb while at the other end of his huge and delicious member, its very firmness and size meant that the lips of her labia and her clitoris were squashed and rubbed by every jolt and thrust he made. The whole length of her womanhood was stimulated at once, leading her towards the orgasm which she knew would explode within her at any second.

Suddenly there was a sound behind them and, opening her eyes, Cherry saw Rick standing by the bed, looking down. Expecting to see disgust or even pain in his eyes, she was relieved to see only curiosity mingled with lust.

'Move over, mate,' he said to Pierre. 'Let's have a go.'

Cherry felt Pierre's huge prick withdraw from her to be replaced by Rick's smaller one. Now she did have to move her body to feel him, but the change of size and pace had come as something of a relief, helping Cherry to delay the orgasm she'd been so close to and had wanted to savour that much longer.

She looked up and saw Pierre moving towards her. She felt his hand on her face and the pressure of his fingers opening her mouth. She saw his prick moving in the direction of her lips. As he slid between her teeth and into her throat, the smell of her own pussy filled her nostrils, his penis still wet with her juices.

Pierre moved gently inside her mouth for fear he might choke her. Though her jaw was aching, she sucked greedily on him, closing her eyes and surrendering herself to the sensations that threatened to overwhelm her.

Rick was fucking her, her mouth was full of Pierre and he

even had his fingers on her tits, squeezing her to greater excitement as she writhed beneath Rick's body, his rock-hard cock rammed up her pussy, pumping away as his fingers grasped her buttocks and he gyrated deep inside.

She was coming . . . oh, yes . . . she was coming like never before and both men seemed to sense the fact, alert to her responses and excited by her gathering climax. She thought the orgasm would go on forever. As the throbbing intensified, she felt first Rick and then Pierre squirt inside her, their yells and moans driving her on as the pleasure rocked her like a giant earthquake. This was what it was all about. And they hadn't even started on the coke!

Exhausted, they fell apart at last and lay panting wordlessly. The camcorder continued to whirr, the only sound in the room apart from that of the sea, lapping lazily against the yacht.

Chapter 21

Nikki had told Jake the truth at last. The whole truth and nothing but. He had left the Café Pelican that morning informing Madame Aronson that he would be straight back, arriving at Nikki's hotel intending to persuade her to return with him, whatever the problem.

He'd known there was something very wrong, he said, from the sound of her voice on the phone. With uncharacteristic forcefulness he had demanded to know what was going on. She'd had no choice but to tell him.

He frowned deeply when she told him about Cherry de Silva and her accomplices and their plan to smuggle cocaine over to England. He sighed and put his head in his hands when she told him of her lack of success with the police, but agreed that she'd had precious little evidence with which to convince them. He told her sternly to do nothing more and then he told her that she looked exhausted. She need to eat and then sleep. He would see to it.

Dear Jake! Nikki had never been so happy to see anyone as she was to see him. Like an obedient child, she allowed herself to be led upstairs, undressed and tucked into bed. A tray arrived with a bowl of soup and a fresh brown roll. Jake watched while she ate and then told her to rest.

She couldn't sleep without him, she replied, looking into his anxious face as he sat on the side of the bed supervising her lunch. Jake told her it was no time for sex. Nikki leaned forward and nibbled his earlobe, sliding her hand down to stroke the thick lump that bulged through his jeans. Oh, he smelt so good this man and she wanted him so much! Putting her tray on the floor, and with a wicked expression on her face, Nikki moved out from under her covers. Hitching up the simple cotton nightdress Jake had brought her along with some of her other clothes, she waggled her butt in his direction.

'You deserve some lunch, too,' she said in a lisping, babyish voice, lifting his hand to place it firmly on her left buttock, guiding it down to trace the contours of her shape, feeling Jake's fingers respond to the touch of her skin.

'Your arse is like a fat peach,' said Jake, a note of amusement in his voice as he stroked the soft downy hair of her bum cheeks.

'Eat me, then,' she replied, turning to face him with her best 'little girl lost' expression of innocence.

It was strange how a crisis could make you think of sex, thought Nikki. Apparently, in wartime when life is in danger a normal reaction to fear is frantic copulation. She'd never felt so stressed out as she did at this moment. And she'd never felt so randy, either.

Jake still hesitated. She knew he was worried about her wellbeing and thought that her tired and puffy eyes needed some rest. But Nikki knew her mind would not rest until her body had been satisfied. 'Please, Jake,' she implored him. 'Comfort me in your arms.'

Jake closed the blinds and shut out the day, standing silhouetted against the light and pulling off his shirt. When he stepped out of his trousers and moved towards the bed Nikki saw that he was already fully erect, his long, incongruously elegant penis standing firm in a straight horizontal line away from his body. Spreading her arms as he climbed between the sheets, she welcomed him into her embrace, holding him tight and drinking in the reassuring smell of his skin. For a moment they lay together in silence, Jake's heart thumping gently. Then, very slowly, he moved his curly head down on to her chest, his mouth gliding across the softness of her breast to fix itself on a yearning nipple, hard and pointy and longing for his touch.

Jake was as hot as she was. His fingers caressed the softness of her inside thigh and then slid themselves within her, moving in and out in slow, regular thrusts that rubbed against her clitoris on the way in and on the way out. She felt the heat and the throbbing begin as he stoked her deeply inside, then without warning she felt his hands on her hip bones as he lay her flat on her back. He rolled his body on top of hers, lifting his heavy prick from where it lay squashed against her belly and pushing its thick and rounded end ever so gently into the entrance to her chasm.

A great throb of longing shot through her as he hesitated, just for a second. Spreading her legs wider she wrapped them around his back and with onc dclicious thrust he was deep inside her, moving his hips in a steady motion which ignited her deepest longings.

She closed her eyes and let go completely, her body like that of a rag doll as he drove into her in the slow, measured and deeply sexy way that he went about everything. As her mounting pleasure caught the breath in the back of her throat, making her groan, he began to pump more forcefully, driving her over the edge of orgasm as she bit into his shoulder, their sweat mingling as her nipples rubbed against the hair of his chest, its very coarseness adding to her stimulation.

When she had finally fallen into a deep and untroubled sleep, Jake got dressed and crept out of the room. There was something he had to see to. And it wouldn't wait.

Cherry de Silva sent the parcel by courier, ensuring that it would be treated with the utmost care and would be delivered personally to the name shown on the label.

Then she returned to the yacht and waited for Rick and Pierre who were due back at five o'clock. They would sail at seven. Everything was in readiness. And life would never, ever be the same again.

After all these years, Cherry was to have her revenge on the woman who had stolen her father's heart. After the death of her mother, Cherry had been daddy's favourite little girl, scheming and plotting to make sure that none of daddy's lady friends stayed the course. Until this one had turned up and daddy had fallen hopelessly in love.

Cherry had spied on them through keyholes, watching as her father fucked this woman, grunting like a pig as his sperm shot into her and she moaned, her dark hair plastered to her forehead with perspiration. Even though she was only a child at the time, Cherry had known that this woman had a hold on her father that none of his other amours had ever managed to secure.

Her sticky little pussy kept him enslaved. And it was through this particular orifice that Cherry had decided, one day, to take her revenge.

She'd dreamt of creeping up on Marianna and raping her with a red hot poker. She'd fantasised about hiring a gang to carry her off and plunder and humiliate her before finally slitting her throat. But instead, she'd decided that the ability to fuck well was the key to success and if that was what Marianna possessed, if that was her secret, then Cherry would make it her own. When she was still at school, Cherry had decided to learn to fuck like the best. Then maybe she'd ensnare a man like daddy. Or even get her daddy back. She wanted her daddy back. To be the centre of his world like before.

Cherry remembered the evening when, aged fourteen, she'd gone into her daddy's bedroom. Marianna had been away somewhere and Cherry had thought that maybe here was her chance to turn the tables, to win back her daddy's love. She'd gone over to his bed and climbed in beside him, rubbing her body against his own. But daddy had woken and, seeing what she was up to, had recoiled in horror.

The expression on his face that night had lived with her forever, burned into her consciousness like a brand of hurt and shame. In her mixed-up mind, it was Marianna who had turned her daddy against her. Marianna who'd made sure he never touched her again like he used to when she was small, hugging her and bouncing her on his knee and telling her she was the best girl in the world.

She hadn't held her daddy's hand ever again. Not until he was dead. And then she'd gone into the room where his coffin lay and squeezed his hand just one last time. But it was cold. Daddy was cold. And it was all because of Marianna.

Cherry snapped out of her reverie and realised that it was getting late. She should go and dress. But still she sat, the memories of her early life coming back to haunt her.

She'd fucked everyone! She'd seen her ability to get a man, any man, as a mark of honour. And the more respectable and 'unlikely' her conquests, the greater the thrill they gave her.

Her headmaster at school, two of daddy's closest friends and business associates – one straight after daddy's funeral – even her Uncle Claude who was a magistrate and pillar of the community. Not so much a pillar as a little worm as it turned out, but he'd still managed to get it up. Cherry smiled at the memory.

Cherry stood up with a sigh and wandered slowly in the direction of her cabin. Five minutes later she was in the shower, soaping her smooth flesh and playing with her nipples. Her breasts were large, though try as she might she'd never been able to lift them quite far enough to reach her own nipple with her mouth. That would have been sensational! If she could have sucked herself and combined this sensation with the dildo she now held between her legs as she stood under the shower jet, oh that would have kept her happy on many miserable nights.

But she still needed men and, more to the point, they needed her. Even if her daddy hadn't.

Bearing down upon the dildo, she imagined that it was

Pierre and that he had her up against a wall. But he was even bigger than this rubber monstrosity, she thought, casting her mind back, feeling him once again inside her. And she *really* had him! He was bound to her by the crime they were about to commit and, even though she'd make sure he got no money out of the deal, he'd be bound to her forever. She'd make certain of that . . .

In all the bad years of her life, Marianna de Silva had never seriously considered suicide. Even when her mother had murdered her father and the terror of facing the world alone had made her stumble, her dancer's body crumpled in a heap of grief, she had always known that there was hope.

Frightened, insecure and unsophisticated, she had striven in the darkness of her days, holding on to she knew not what until, one day, Dimitri had arrived and rescued her.

When he died, the warmth of him still wrapped her close. The fact that he had devoted his life to ensuring that, materially at least, she would be safe had given her some comfort. But as the years had gone on and the cold howling wind of loneliness had crept under her door, she had found herself increasingly unable to shut it out. Then she had met Pierre.

She played the video film straight through, three times.

'This is Pierre Valbon and he is my slave,' she heard Cherry say as she grinned at the camera. 'We have been lovers since he came aboard this yacht.'

Sitting in her elegant hotel suite just off the Faubourg St Honore, Marianna looked around her at the flowers she'd ordered to fill the room, the clothes she'd bought for Pierre hanging in the wardrobe, the pretty new lingerie that lay spread out on the bed. No. She had never considered suicide until now.

But as she walked to the window and looked out onto the sunshine of another beautiful summer's day, she wondered if it would be for the best.

* * *

Pierre and Rick had arrived back at six-thirty. Cherry had begun to get anxious, fearing that something untoward may have happened. But here they were, the first and most dangerous part of the mission accomplished.

Though they were longing to try the 'merchandise' again, Pierre had decided that they should all keep clear heads until the delivery of the drugs had been made. They could snort on the return journey to France. They could relax then, but not before.

Cherry and Rick agreed with him, though secretly she would have liked to be stoned throughout the whole trip. And thinking about it, they didn't really need her to navigate or anything . . .

Cherry suggested she go below decks for most of the journey to England. She could snort quietly and if either of the men felt like a 'rest' she would be there. They nodded at her suggestion but weren't really listening. For now, Rick and Pierre had other things on their minds.

Nikki awoke in her darkened room to find that Jake was not there. She felt pleasantly sticky between her legs and, for the first time in days, peaceful and relaxed. There was nothing she could do about Cherry and her plans. If the police didn't believe her, then what more could she do?

Nikki got out of bed and pulled on some clothes. Should she catch a train and go to Paris, to the British Embassy? To the British Consulate, maybe? Where would that be? There must be a Consulate somewhere in the South of France. Her mood of tranquility had lasted only a moment, broken by her return to reality and the banishment of sleep. She was unable to convince herself that there was nothing more she could do to stop the drugs deal and help Marianna. But where was Jake when she needed him? Where the hell was Jake?

The young waiter had only been on duty for five minutes

when the call came from Suite Nineteen. A bottle of champagne to be sent up. Nothing more. No food.

He knocked lightly on the door and heard a woman's voice call 'enter'. Balancing his tray complete with two glasses and ice bucket, he used his security card to open the heavy oak door to the spacious suite that lay beyond. The woman's voice called 'in here' and carrying his tray carefully, he walked into the bedroom of Marianna de Silva who lay propped up on two cushions, her face pale, her eyes staring vacantly into the distance.

On seeing the young waiter, she sat up and asked him to put the tray by her bed.

'I didn't need two glasses,' she smiled at him. 'It is only me now.' Glancing at her more closely, the young man saw a face he thought he recognised. When he was a child his mama had taken him to the ballet and if he wasn't very much mistaken . . .

'You are right,' said Marianna in answer to his hesitant enquiry. 'I used to be a dancer.'

'Oh, Madame! You were a prima ballerina!'

'Yes,' said Marianna wearily, 'I suppose I was.'

Bowing politely the young man turned to take his leave.

'Stay with me for a moment,' she said. 'You have brought one glass too many and . . .' Her voice trailed off and the young man turned to look at her again. He'd be sacked if he was discovered, but this was only a temporary job. He weighed the risks against the advantages and, as Marianna gestured for him to sit on the side of the bed, he decided to take the gamble.

What on earth was a woman like this doing alone in one of their best suites, drinking champagne with a waiter? He didn't know and frankly he didn't care. The wine was superb, one of the best vintages in the hotel cellar, and after two glasses he began to feel quite incredible. They'd be missing him by now, wondering where he'd got to. He'd have to make up some story about 'Madame' being ill, or something.

She didn't want to talk, this one, only to listen. She asked him all about his home and his background, all about his future and what he had planned. And then, quite without warning, the beautiful woman leant across and kissed him.

Sure, he'd had many fumbled kisses with girls in the past and had even slept with one or two – if frantic shagging in a borrowed apartment when the owner is out can be classed as sleeping with someone – but he'd never felt lips like these or skin so soft. She smelt so expensive, too, her hair tumbling around her shoulders as waves of delicious perfume enveloped him and he felt his hand being lifted and placed against her breast.

Terrified in case she changed her mind, he climbed quickly out of his uniform, conscious of his slightly off-colour underpants which he'd washed once too often in the same tub as his dark sweatshirts. She didn't seem to notice.

Silently, she moved off the bed and knelt before him, her pretty head reaching down between his legs to take his penis in her mouth, that mouth from which such a mellow accent emerged. Her red nails held his thighs as her tongue explored the tip of him, feeling him tremble and grow between her lips as each pressure was met with another surge of his manhood, the softness of her mouth coaxing from him an ever-hardening response.

He couldn't believe what was happening. And when she stood up and led him back to the bed he thought he was in a dream as, sinking down onto her back, she invited him to make love to her. Her skin was so fine, her body so supple and golden brown and as he pulled her lingerie up over her legs, leaving her belly clear, he revealed a triangle of dark hair which for a moment he felt he lacked the courage to touch. But she took his hand and guided his fingers into her delicate bush, the contact sending his cock shooting upward in jerks and spasms till it stood horizontal to his body, thick and pink.

It was as though she was made of pure silk. His arousal overcoming his feelings of awe, the young man carefully lifted

Marianna's slip up and over her head to reveal her nakedness. His hands and mouth touched every inch of her, his tongue moving through the dark bush to taste the sweetness of her vulva as he gobbled between her legs, lapping her up, savouring every sensation, dreading the thought that he'd suddenly look up and find her no longer there.

He saw that she was smiling softly, a faraway look in her eyes. When he moved up her body and pushed his penis against her furry mound she did not object.

Groping clumsily inside the curls, he found the little opening he was searching for and, with all the haste and gaucheness of a relatively inexperienced twenty year old, he entered her with one clumsy thrust, the tightness of her pussy exciting him so much that he thought he would lose control, that it would all be over too soon.

Dismayed, he tried to slow his thrusts but the roller coaster ride towards orgasm had already begun. The contractions of this beautiful woman's body were drawing him on to the point of no return.

He felt her fingers at the base of his prick and realised that she was squeezing him gently. Immediately he felt the climax begin to subside as the heat inside him turned to warmth and her fingers reached out to slow the pace, her clear eyes gazing into his own.

He made love to this woman for what felt like an eternity, until the final shudder could no longer be held back and he burst like a dam inside her, flooding her body with his juices as a great cry broke from his lips.

The boy who had walked into her suite emerged a man, closing the door carefully and puzzling on her final words to him as he left. 'Pierre wasn't the last,' she had said. 'I am glad of that.'

Chapter 22

Nikki was exhausted. Her head ached, her feet ached, everything ached but she didn't care a bit. She'd never danced with Jake until this evening and had been unaware of his 'hidden depths', as she put it.

All around them people were dancing, the waiters weaving in and out of the crowd in time to the music, balancing their trays of fluorescent-coloured cocktails above their heads and swaying their hips in time to the Jamaican band. Couple after couple took to the small dance floor and those who could find no room spilled out into the street of the pavement café in Juan les Pins, where at midnight the night was still very young and the world shone bright like the sparklers that fizzed in a hundred cocktail glasses.

Jake had come back to the hotel earlier that evening to find Nikki pacing her room in a state of high anxiety. He'd told her to get dressed and that they were going out. It was only when they got to the café that he broke the news. And they'd been dancing ever since, Nikki holding him close, their legs entwined, pressing her hips against his body and feeling his manhood rear and strain against his jeans.

Madame Aronson had been very kind, said Jake. She'd been like a second mother to him for ages now, but this time she'd really excelled herself. 'You don't run a café like mine for twenty years without getting to know some of the right people,' she'd said when he'd gone to visit her earlier that day. 'And besides,' she'd added with a smile, 'there is my son.'

Then she'd bustled off to make a few phone calls. And that was that.

Nikki didn't believe him at first. How could he be so sure that the yacht would be intercepted? 'Because,' he'd told her, 'Madame Aronson has friends in the police.' Nikki still wasn't convinced. 'And her son is a senior customs official,' added Jake nonchalantly, at which Nikki began to cry with relief.

The yacht would be stopped that evening and, if drugs were found, its crew would be arrested. It was quite reasonable for the customs to wish to board a yacht and check it over. And though Nikki still kept her fingers crossed, she had allowed herself to believe that it would really happen. She had allowed herself to trust.

It had been an evening of magic laced with sadness. On his return from the Café Pelican, Jake had stopped at the airport and bought Nikki a plane ticket to London. 'You're trying to get rid of me then?' she'd said lightheartedly, her eyes full of tears. But they both knew that she had to go home and Nikki knew at the moment he handed it to her with his love, that Jake really did care about her. Cared enough to let her go.

She was flying home the next morning at eleven o'clock. And it was already two in the morning. Strolling back to the hotel, Nikki felt a great wave of sadness engulf her as she realised that tonight would be the last time she and Jake would make love. The last time she would lay safe in his arms.

Cherry de Silva had heard some yelling and then the door of her cabin had burst open. She had been so stoned that it wasn't until she was led up on deck and handed over the side of the yacht and into a customs launch, that she really got the message that something was very wrong.

The night air had been cool against her face as the boat sped through the water. Pierre and Rick sat alongside her. No one had spoken a word.

* * *

Nikki had woken, her face wet with tears as she reached out for Jake in the half-light of the early morning. She had slept fitfully for only a couple of hours and her dreams had been haunting and sad.

'Oh, Jake,' she murmured. 'Am I doing the right thing?Tell me.'

Wrapping his arms around her he held her tight. 'You've got to go home,' he said. 'I want you to stay but I know you can't.'

'Make love to me then,' said Nikki. 'Make love to me before I go,' and with a sob she had lain her face against his chest and cried and cried.

Kissing her tears, Jake had held her close in his arms, listening to the sounds of the day outside – the noise of shutters being raised, brooms sweeping across pavements and the chatter of local people out on the streets returning home with their warm baguettes, stopping to exchange the gossip of the morning.

Still sobbing, her chest heaving with sadness, she felt his lips press upon her own. His wide, generous mouth engulfed hers in a kiss of both comfort and desire. Hungrily she sought for his tongue, sliding her own in circles around his, teasing him to kiss her deeper, to squash her lips and bruise them as her need for him grew, pushing the sadness she felt to one side as her body cried out to be taken.

She felt a change of mood in Jake as he sensed her own raw hunger. Suddenly, his gentle kisses became firmer, his tongue driving deep into her mouth as his fingers pinched her nipples with an unaccustomed hardness.

'Jake,' murmured Nikki. 'Oh, darling . . .' But her mouth was stopped with kisses as he lifted his heavy body onto hers. Holding her down, his pinches turned to nips and she felt her juices run and then pour into her vulva, swelling her hot pussy lips till the entrance to her womanhood was so swollen she feared his path would be barred.

'Don't leave me, Nikki,' he growled, 'not now.' Forcing his big hand between her legs, his fingers fumbled till he found his way through the swelling of her inner lips and into her chasm, her juices breaking over his fingers like a waterfall.

'But, Jake,' whispered Nikki. 'You just said . . .' His answer was to fill her mouth once again with his tongue, his fingers working inside her, opening the swelling she felt had closed her body till she lay wide and welcoming, the pulsing of her womanhood waiting to beat in time with the sweet throb of Jake's own sturdy prick.

'I must go home,' she murmured, her resolve weakening as the tip of his long, engorged penis probed between her legs, toying at the entrance to her hungry body.

'Fuck Chris,' she heard him say and couldn't believe her ears.

'But, Jake . . .'

'Oh, fuck everyone but us, Nikki. You can't leave,' he replied, as with one forceful thrust he was inside her. His strong body silenced all further protest as he began his slow, rhythmic build-up to orgasm, sweeping Nikki along with him. His huge hands clasped her small body and he held her, his hips thrusting her into submission as his prick moved deep inside her, driving all thoughts of Chris from her mind.

'Fuck me then,' she said. 'Fuck me and fill me forever,' and, closing her eyes, she meant every word.

But when they woke in the morning, they both knew it couldn't be and that the night before had been their final goodbye.

Without a word, Jake leant over to brush Nikki gently on the lips. He drew his mouth away for a moment to look down at her, returning to kiss her lightly, exploring the corners of her mouth with tiny kisses and nips, teasing her with his touch till she felt she would melt with desire.

His fingers brushed her nipples, his hand laid flat as he stroked each hard little pink pellet in an unbroken sweep which set her shuddering, her pelvis lifting off the bed as the juices of desire began to trickle into her bruised and painful vulva.

When his mouth moved down to her breasts, Nikki thought she would come, the tingling as he sucked her nipples and rolled them with his tongue making her reach for his manhood. Suddenly she was desperate to feel him inside her, needing only to sigh that great shuddering sigh as she spread herself wide to welcome him in. There was no feeling on earth like it, thought Nikki. No substitute for the pleasure of giving yourself to a man who loves you.

Finding him firm beneath her touch, Nikki worked the foreskin of Jake's penis backwards and forwards in her hand. She could feel the satisfying slide as she massaged it against the thick swelling that lay beneath.

Her eyes were tightly shut as she felt him lift her, turning her onto her stomach and pulling her to her knees, his hands reaching for her breasts as his prick knocked gently at the entrance to her pussy.

As he pinched her nipples, she worked her body against him, taking his prick between the cheeks of her buttocks, feeling it tease the little hole of her arse before it slipped down and into her pulsing opening with a sudden thrust that made her catch her breath. Jake gave four or five quick, sharp thrusts to get himself fully inside her and then, buried deep within her womanhood, he began his slow and delicious lovemaking.

As Jake stroked her breasts, Nikki twisted her body in delicious slow circling movements which put pressure on the walls of her vagina. Her inner lips squashed against the base of his penis, the throbbing in her clitoris increased, pounding like the pulse rushing through her veins, only to slow again into deep, rich contractions of pleasure as her orgasm finally reached its crescendo and she closed her eyes tight and sighed a deep sigh.

Cherry never saw the newspapers which told of her arrest.

She never saw the lurid headlines which described her as a 'well-known party girl', their unspoken implication supported by less than flattering photographs of Cherry emerging from any one of a thousand nightclubs, casinos and bars.

Her father had been a well-known and respectable man. His daughter's arrest on a drug offence was hot news.

The yacht had been stopped, heaving with drugs, and they'd been caught red-handed. Cherry had been incoherent, out of her brains on drugs, and hadn't even known what was going on when they'd taken her to the police station and put her in a cell. She'd been full of coke and 'other substances' as the papers had put it. Not even the best lawyer that money could buy could rescue her from this mess. It was too late even for regrets. And now she was stuck in a cell with two other women, one weighing at least eighteen stone and the other with a shaven head and a tattoo just above her ear. No, this hadn't been meant to happen. It was all a nightmare.

They laughed at her, too. Laughed and spat their contempt for her good clothes and the suntan which marked her out as a 'lazy cow'.

'Fucking bitch,' they'd exclaimed, delighting in her discomfort and her fear.

She would be in here forever, she knew. And as she lay on her bunk, with no one in the world caring whether she lived or died, she knew that the next few months would be the worst of her life.

Jake drove Nikki to the airport in silence. They had finally managed to tear themselves away from each other and get showered and dressed, emerging into the sunshine of the day in optimistic mood. A phone call had been made to Madame Aronson and Nikki had said her tearful goodbyes. Madame Aronson had sounded excited and said that her son the customs official was 'very proud' of his mama. The tip-off had been a good one. The drugs haul was considerable. All three occupants on board the yacht were now in custody.

'Had they seen the papers?' enquired Madame Aronson. '*Très* shocking!'

As they got out of the car at Nice airport, Nikki thought back to the day she'd first walked into its bright and bustling arrivals hall. It seemed like a lifetime ago and during that time everything in her life had changed.

They arrived early and had half an hour to spare. She took Jake to the same café where she'd sat alone, sipping her cappuccino all those weeks ago, waiting to meet the Contessa and the new love in her life.

With a sudden sense of panic, Nikki realised she might never see Jake again. Grabbing his hand, she pulled him to his feet and rushed towards . . . she knew not where. There were people everywhere! Yet, within minutes she had found a hidden corner, out of sight of the main thoroughfares, away from the glittering brightness and the thousand holidaymakers who would land at the airport that day, stepping out of their planes to be embraced by the heat and sparkle of a coastline which in all the world had no equal in beauty.

'Kiss me,' she pleaded.

As Jake's mouth met her own, she felt him lift her skirt, running his hand up her bare brown thigh to grope for the crack between her legs. He pushed his fingers into the lips of her labia and held her apart as he pulled his cock from the front of his shorts. For the last time in his life, he would know the sweet wetness, the softness and smell of this woman. He knew he would miss her like no other woman he had ever known. His lips rubbed against her nipples, the dry roughness of her simple cotton shirt denying him the feel of her flesh in his mouth. He moved his face up to nuzzle against the scented softness of her neck as he pumped her full of him, standing against a wall in a hidden corner of the airport at Nice.

She asked him to go before the flight checked in. To leave

her where she stood, her panties soaked as his sperm leaked out of her, pouring down the inside of her thighs. She would clean herself up on the plane. She wanted her last memory of him to be the feel of him inside her, not a sad little waving as she disappeared out of sight. 'Go,' she said and closed her eyes. And when she opened them, he was gone.

The young waiter had been unable to concentrate, despite the fact that the hotel restaurant had been busy that night.

As he'd waltzed between tables in his usual manner, his facade of professional concern had deserted him and he'd failed to respond with the necessary degree of obsequiousness to the relentless demands of the chic clientele. Steaks had been sent back, sautéed potatoes had arrived instead of *frites* and had been rejected. He'd even served a bottle of fizzy mineral water when still had been called for.

'*Garçon!*' they had yelled and he'd seemed not to hear. The head waiter had muttered darkly about 'last chances'.

The young waiter hadn't been able to put the Contessa out of his mind. Though he'd left her hours before, smiling and relaxed, he was troubled and he knew that something was wrong.

'Pierre wasn't the last,' she had said. 'I am glad of that.' All day these strange words had haunted him.

He didn't even bother to knock on the door when he arrived at Marianna's suite. Letting himself in with a pass key, the young waiter went straight to her bedroom.

He despised himself for not coming before. But still, he might not be too late. There was still a pulse. If the ambulance came soon, there might be a chance.

Jake hung around the airport long after Nikki had gone through into the departure lounge. Despite the fact that she was flying home to an uncertain future, he knew that whatever happened she would not be coming back to him.

He tried to imagine Nikki living on his father's farm.

Nikki, exquisitely groomed among the cowsheds and the mud? No, it just wouldn't work. And besides, she didn't love him. Not enough to give up her life and her ambition.

Jake dreaded the thought of returning to the Café Pelican. He dreaded the lonely nights ahead when the closing of a door or the creak of a floorboard would wake him with false hope, making him believe, if only for a split second, that she was coming to him, finding her way to his bed and into his arms, wrapping her lovely body around him till morning.

Jake, who hardly drank, decided to find a bar. A little emotional anaesthetic and then he could face the now exuberant Madame Aronson who, he felt sure, would still be full of the excitement of playing her part in bringing three 'big-time' drug smugglers to justice.

Solange hadn't been working as a prostitute for very long and she knew that she had a lot to learn. But she knew, the first time that she stood up against a wall down a dirty back alley and took money for being pawed by a middle-aged businessman from Rheims, that nothing could hurt or humiliate her more than Mademoiselle Cherry had done. Not even this. Not even the hateful touch of strangers.

Solange had seen the papers. Far from being glad that Mademoiselle had found the punishment she so richly deserved, Solange had grown more bitter then ever. Even though she'd sunk as far as it was possible for her to go, she'd still nursed a faint hope that Mademoiselle Cherry really loved her. That there'd been some terrible mistake and that one day she would come for her, taking her away from a life lived in a haze of alcohol and on the back seats of cars.

She noticed the young Englishman when he came into the bar. By the time he'd ordered his third cognac she was smiling at him and, as he called for his fourth, she got up from her seat and went over. Would she be good enough to join him?

'Yes,' said Solange. He looked sad. But that was none of

her business. They all had a tale to tell.

Yes, this young Englishman would do for the night. He was a punter, that's all. Yet, try though she might to harden her heart, as she began to talk to him something prevented Solange from treating this man as just another paying customer. Something told her he was hurting inside like she was. And though she knew it was unwise, she longed to talk to him.

Half guiding, half carrying a highly intoxicated Jake to a nearby hotel, Solange managed to get him up to her room. She brought him water and headache pills and watched while he slept. When he eventually woke up his head was clear and it was dark. 'I am the prostitute you met in the bar,' she said. 'My name is Solange.'

They talked for hours with the honesty of strangers who will never meet again. She told him of her life and he told her of his own. When she mentioned Mademoiselle Cherry and the scandal in the papers, Jake said he knew about it and explained his connection.

'She was a bad woman, your Mademoiselle Cherry,' said Jake. 'You mustn't let her hurt you any more.'

'He is right,' thought Solange. 'I must forget her or I will go under.'

When the dawn began to break, Solange moved closer to Jake and touched him.

'You don't have to do anything,' said Jake. 'I will give you money. Please. I'd like to help you go home to your family and start again.'

Solange had never really loved a man but, looking down at this handsome, tousle-haired Englishman, she felt cared for and no longer so lonely. 'I want you,' she murmured. 'Please . . .' And leaning forward to where Jake lay on the bed she began to unzip his trousers.

'I don't . . .' began Jake, to which Solange put her hand to his lips and shushed him like a baby.

'No,' she said, 'what you want is Nikki. You need not make

love to me. I am just a prostitute. But please . . . let me love you.'

With the utmost gentleness, Solange reached inside Jake's trousers and slid her hands around his prick. Warm and thick, it responded to her touch, swelling quickly as she began to stroke it. Solange sighed with contentment as she felt it grow in the palm of her hand, her fingers applying gentle pressure like a potter at a wheel pulling clay into shape, turning a lump of raw material into a proud and erect creation of great beauty.

Jake's penis grew beneath her fingers and as Solange guided his trousers down over his hips, leaving him naked but for his white shirt. Jake did not object. Propped up on a pillow, he watched fascinated as Solange's pretty head leant across him and her lips made contact with his throbbing member.

A deep sigh of pleasure purred in her throat as Solange placed his prick between her lips, her hand cupping his heavy balls in their dark forest of hair.

Her fingers kneaded and squeezed softly as Jake's hips began to reach off the bed and his body began to thrust, the blood coursing through his cock, stretching it to fill Solange's eager mouth, probing the softness at the back of her throat.

Solange guided his hands towards her breasts, opening her shirt to place his thick, coarse fingers either side of each nipple, not needing to tell him how to squeeze or stroke her. She closed her eyes and surrendered herself to the pleasure of being touched by this kind and gentle man to whom the mysteries of love were second nature.

No one had touched her womanhood, not even herself, yet such was her arousal that as Jake began to moan as she sucked him, Solange found that she too was about to have an orgasm. The seams of her panties pressed against her clitoris and the deep desire she felt for this man excited her in a way she would never have thought possible.

They came together, slept peacefully in each other's arms

and in the morning they left together. Jake kissed Solange gently and pressed sufficient money into her hand to keep her for a while without needing to 'work'.

For the first time in a long while the day looked good to Solange. This stranger had given her the help she needed to save her own life. Mademoiselle Cherry had been wrong. All men weren't bastards.

As Jake headed off back to the Café Pelican and a morning of telling white lies to Madame Aronson, Solange turned and walked towards the nearest phone box. With her hand trembling, she reached into her purse to find some change. She would need all her courage to make the call and she knew it may not be welcomed. But if he wouldn't speak today then she'd phone again tomorrow. One way or another, she had to talk to papa.

Chapter 23

Irana Petrovka and Marco Lazalle had issued a joint press release before leaving Sicily. It told the world that they had known each other for many years and had finally decided that they wished to spend the rest of their lives together. They were getting married and would fly to London to do so. 'As soon as possible,' the press release had said. And they'd packed their bags.

It had seemed the best way out for Marco. The world would be just as happy with 'famous tennis star marries supermodel' as it would have been had he married 'famous actress' Kiki Angelis. They arrived at Heathrow to be greeted by the popping flashbulbs of a hundred paparazzi and a barrage of questions, both of which they'd been anticipating.

'What about Kiki?' the reporters had yelled, to which Marco had replied sweetly that there had been certain 'insurmountable problems' but that they remained 'good friends'. Both he and Irana had decided that this would be the safest way to prevent Kiki's threats of blackmail from becoming reality. Anything she said about him now would simply not be believed. 'Hell hath no fury' and all that. It had been a brilliant plan.

Irana had surprised herself when the idea of their marriage had come to her. It was a few days after Chris had left and, much to her amazement, she was still thinking about him. She missed him. She was lonely. And Marco was in trouble.

Neither of them would alter their lifestyles, that was agreed. They'd just need to become more discreet about their various liaisons. And strangely enough, the more she thought about it the more the idea of being Mrs Lazelle appealed to her. A married woman! 'How wonderfully respectable,' thought Irana, with an ironic grin.

They were marrying in four days time at Chelsea Registry Office, after which the happy couple, plus an entourage of press and reporters, would set off for Mauritius for three weeks. But first, Irana intended to see Chris. She needed to see him. 'To discuss the advertising campaign,' she had said to Marco.

Since his return from Sicily, Chris hadn't even bothered to unpack or shop. His suitcase was still where he'd left it in the hall, the kitchen was piled up with pizza cartons and greasy tin-foil containers from the local takeaways which promised speedy delivery and, in the sitting room, empty wine glasses made sticky circles on the glass-topped table which itself was littered with a dozen videos which Chris had watched but barely seen.

He'd phoned the advertising agency and told them he'd returned from the shoot with flu, but that the pictures were all fine. He'd be in to see them next week, he'd said. But he'd have to get dressed first. And right now that was the biggest effort in the world.

Irana knocked on his door at nine o'clock the morning after she and Marco had arrived in England. Too depressed even to be ashamed of the state of his flat, he'd let her in, standing opposite her in the hall, floppy blond hair falling over a face that was a picture of sadness.

'My Christopher,' she had said, with not a trace of the expected bitterness and resentment in her voice. 'Why you run out on Irana? Why you leave only note?'

Chris wrapped his arms around her and held her tight. 'You're just too much for me, Irana,' he said. And without a trace of malice, he added, 'And besides, I don't love you.'

'That important, I think,' she had replied. 'Yes . . . to my Christopher, I think very much . . .'

Running him a bath, Irana ordered him to get in it and then to get dressed. She then set about clearing up the flat. When Chris emerged an hour later still wrapped in a bathrobe, the smell of fresh bread filled his nostrils and he was surprised to find the flat looking neat and clean with not a trace of an empty bottle to be seen.

'I find frozen bread at back of freezer,' said Irana. 'I cook you breakfast.' Looking at her standing there, this impossibly beautiful and exotic looking woman playing housewife in his little kitchen, Chris felt a sudden wave of affection for her.

'Come here,' he said, opening his arms. He held her then, clasped against his newly bathed body. He regretted leaving her in Sicily without a word, knowing he must have hurt her. But he was so confused himself, so mixed up.

As if reading his mind, Irana looked up at Chris. 'She be home soon,' she said. 'Then you try work it out.'

'Too late, my love,' he had replied sadly. 'I think it is too late.'

'Then,' whispered Irana, 'you must be happy just for now.' Taking his head in her hands she kissed him deeply and tenderly.

For the first time in a long while, Chris felt the familiar prickly heat of desire as the blood stirred in his cock. It strained against his towelling bathrobe as Irana laughed her deep, throaty laugh, her hand coming down to touch and stroke the swelling tribute to her beauty.

Chris slid her dress over her shoulders and touched the warm, fragrant skin that still carried the smell of the sea. The memory of Sicily filled his mind as his lips skimmed her throat, kissing her along the length of her breastbone and down, down to her yearning breasts. The rosebud nipples hardened beneath his touch as his mouth sought her hungrily, sucking on her breasts and breaking away to cover her mouth with his own.

'I think we fuck now, no?' said Irana.

'You're such an elegant girl,' laughed Chris, lifting her and carrying her through to his unmade, rumpled bed. Placing her on the crushed sheets, he grabbed the panties she wore, ripping them apart at the hip and climbing on top of her, straddling her body.

'You hot for me, my beautiful blond boy,' purred Irana as Chris pushed his penis against her crotch, seeking frantically for the opening and finding it at last.

With a deep sigh, he sank into the warmth of her open chasm which closed about him, drawing him in as he clasped her beneath her buttocks, pulling her towards him till his prick had burrowed into the depths of her and his mind had been numbed by the sheer relief of fucking and forgetting.

Irana closed her eyes and gave herself up to the pleasure of feeling Chris drive himself deep inside her. She felt his prick at the edge of her womb, each thrust sending tingling messages flooding through her, thumping the length of her slippery canal to resonate at the very tip of her clitoris with a steady throb which only the next thrust could satisfy. She knew she would never fuck him again in the whole of her life. She would leave here today and see him only professionally. However many more assignments they did together, she knew that this would be the end of their affair.

Irana also knew that she loved him. It was a strange and unfamiliar feeling, a mixture of elation and hopelessness that she had never experienced before. 'The quicker it go, the better,' she thought, viewing it as some kind of unwelcome affliction, liable to play havoc with her flippant and superficial approach to life. No. She could do without all that.

This was goodbye. They both knew it. And it added a melancholy piquancy to their final coupling. Chris held her and sucked her and fucked her till she moaned, his juices filling her mouth and her pussy till she thought she would overflow.

She left at lunchtime and Chris showered and dressed for the first time in days. He would go out. He would take a walk and clear his head. He would think about the rest of his life tomorrow.

As the plane taxied in to Heathrow airport, Nikki had made up her mind to disembark, buy another ticket for somewhere else – anywhere else – and leave again immediately. She couldn't face the thought of returning to the flat. Would Chris be there? And if so, what on earth would she say?

Once she'd landed, she knew that she couldn't run away. The air smelt like home and as she heard the English voices around her she felt she would cry with an unexpected relief.

The taxi to Earl's Court cost far more than she'd expected and as she climbed the stairs to the flat, her heart was beating so fast she could feel it reverberate in her skull. Her hand shook as she reached for her key and undid the front door.

'Chris,' she called but there was no answer. Walking into the flat she saw that it was neat and clean, the remnants of breakfast cleared away and piled carefully in the washing-up bowl, the bed carefully made, the bathroom smelling faintly of soap. She touched the white bath towel that lay over the heated rail. It was still damp. With a lurch in her stomach she realised that Chris hadn't long left the flat.

In the kitchen on the shelf there was an envelope addressed to her. It was an airmail letter and, with beating heart, she recognised the Contessa de Silva's handwriting. Ripping it open, Nikki saw that it contained three pages, closely written.

'My dear Nikki,' it began, 'I am writing to tell you that I am so sorry . . .' Nikki felt the tears welling up in her eyes as she read the letter in which the Contessa de Silva told of receiving the video tape which Cherry had made, of having been sent to Paris on a fool's errand, of being humiliated in ways that she hinted at but never clearly spelled out.

The Contessa apologised to Nikki for her dismissal and

said how much she cared for her. As she went on to read of the Contessa's suicide attempt, the words swam in front of Nikki's eyes. 'It was so foolish,' said the Contessa. 'I feel so ashamed . . .'

A young waiter had found her, apparently. Just minutes before it was too late. He had gone with her to the hospital and sat by her bedside all night. It was Jean Claude, in fact, who would be posting this letter. Jean Claude who was with her right now, bringing her meals on a tray, taking her out for afternoon drives in the hills above Cannes, Jean Claude who was helping her to get better.

'Please . . . not another gigolo,' thought Nikki, but something in the way Marianna wrote about Jean Claude made her feel that the Contessa de Silva might at last have found someone she could depend on.

'I have tried to pay him for his time and his trouble but he will take no money other than his living expenses,' Marianna had written. 'And if, when we're out driving we stop for a meal, he will not let me contribute, so we must always go somewhere he can afford.'

Nikki smiled as she thought of Marianna taking her meals in ordinary cafés among working people. Yet she knew that this was where Marianna had come from. A simple, peasant background. She would cope.

Marianna went on to say that she hoped 'the enclosed' would compensate for all that had happened. She didn't once mention Pierre. And then she said goodbye.

Nikki reached again into the envelope and pulled out a cheque for thirty thousand pounds. Far, far more than she had been promised. Enough to get her on her feet. Enough to start her business and buy her the time she needed to build it up to become a success.

When Chris walked back into the flat an hour later, he found Nikki sitting at the kitchen table, sobbing as though the world was about to end.

He'd stood there looking at her, not knowing what to do

or say as, tears streaming down her face, Nikki had raised her eyes to his. 'It all went wrong,' she said. 'I didn't know what to do. I was lonely and lost and you weren't there and I didn't hear from you. It was only just before I came home that I knew you had tried to call me. They didn't tell me. Nobody told me.'

Nikki cried so hard that she could barely breathe, but though his instinct was to rush to her and take her in his arms, Chris simply stood where he was, swallowing deeply and trying to control the emotion which rose like a lump in his throat.

'I tried to phone you many times,' he said. 'The woman called Cherry said you always got my messages.'

'I didn't,' she sobbed. 'Never! Not once . . . I thought you never wanted to speak to me again . . . Oh, Chris, if only I could have called you . . .'

'Maybe if I'd listened . . .' he replied, his voicc trailing off. 'It was important to you, going away, making your own way on your own terms. It was more important than I'd ever realised.'

Slowly and quietly, Chris walked into the bedroom and returned with some tissues which he handed to Nikki. He opened a bottle of wine and came back to the table with two glasses.

It was twilight by the time Chris had told Nikki everything that had happened to him during the past few weeks and she had told him of the Contessa and Cherry and Pierre and all that had taken place on the yacht. She spared him the details of her affair with Pierre saying only that she had made a stupid mistake.

Though in the past Chris had always been honest with her, he told her nothing of his affair with Irana and when she came to talk about Jake, she told Chris that he had been 'a friend' she'd met at the Café Pelican.

Both knew that they'd come too far to go back to where

they were and both had learned an instinctive wariness, a realisation of what each was capable of doing to hurt the other.

'I've never had secrets from him before,' thought Nikki, feeling that one day she would tell him everything. Or would she? 'I'll think about that later,' she said to herself as she sipped her wine.

She looked well, thought Chris. Despite her sadness she looked wonderful. Leaning forward, he brushed a strand of hair from her eyes, his fingers touching her skin; her soft, familiar skin, now tanned a golden brown.

'Come to bed with me,' she said, and taking the wine bottle with her she walked into their bedroom, stepping out of her clothes to stand before him, her eyes holding his with a new confidence, almost a challenge, glinting in their depths.

Chris felt his prick begin to move as he met her gaze, finding her both familiar and somehow new and exciting at the same time. Moving over to the bed, she sat down and, still looking straight at him, she brought her legs up under her knees. Her vulva was wide open to his view, the pink cushion of her inner folds inviting him to touch. She moistened her lips with her tongue as she watched him fumble with his clothes. The zip of his trousers got stuck over his huge prick which burst out of the front of his jockey shorts as soon as the zip could be coaxed over it.

She could tell as soon as he touched her that there had been someone else. The thought excited her. He bit and licked her in a new and more assured way. As his mouth moved down to explore between her legs, she knew that some other woman had taught him exactly how to fold his tongue in half and slip it between the folds of her pussy, moving it back and forth as he lapped and tickled and sucked her into quivering arousal.

'Turn around,' she said and he swung his leg across her belly, his neat arse pointing at her as he slid his prick towards her mouth and she took him between her lips. The taste of his sperm on her tongue, the familiar shape of him as he thrust against the back of her throat . . . oh, how she'd missed him. How she loved him.

Chris had taken a shower after Irana had left and he was glad. He hadn't expected this to happen and even now, lost in the softness of Nikki's pussy, rolling her wonderful little clitoris between his lips, he felt unsure of himself, wondering if she'd just come back to say goodbye or if she would stay.

'Who has he been sleeping with?' wondered Nikki. 'She has woken him up whoever she is.'

Breaking apart for a moment they came to look at each other, their eyes full of secrets, their hearts full of jealousy, each wondering what the other had really been doing and feeling since they parted.

Chris began to lick the sweat from Nikki's body. He drank in the sweet smell of her as his tongue moved down to stroke the insides of her thighs, the strong smell of her pussy juice filling his head. Moving up her body, he knelt over her and placed the head of his prick tentatively at the entrance to her wet canal. 'Nikki, do you really want me?' he asked.

She parted her legs and smiled up at him and he slid his prick deep into her. His mouth closed over hers, his tongue pressing hard against hers as she stretched against him, her mouth making long slow circles as she wound her fingertips into his hair. Their lips slid and slipped and bruised against each other as passion made them forget.

Nikki loved him. Not like the girl who had left him but as the woman who had returned. Her body writhed as she squeezed his prick against her clitoris, swivelling her hips as she lay beneath him and he rammed his cock against the inside of her pussy from every angle. She pulled his mouth to her hungry tits as her body demanded to be touched, fucked and satisfied on her terms.

Sweating and panting, she climbed on top of him, riding him like a rodeo horse, bucking and twisting and fixing him between her thighs as the juices ran from her throbbing pussy and she guided his hands to her breasts, telling him to pinch hard then harder still.

As Nikki scratched and clawed at his back and his buttocks, Chris felt his body on fire as he began to bite and scratch her in return.

'Oh, yes . . .' she moaned. 'Fuck me, Chris . . . fuck me and have me and hold me . . . oh . . .'

She was a different woman and he was glad. As she clung to him moaning out her needs, occasionally biting his mouth as her excitement grew, he knew he fancied her like no other woman on earth. He'd always fancied her. But somehow they'd just lost their way.

Things would be different from now on, that much was obvious. There was a new sense of anticipation in the air, an atmosphere of excitement, a new buzz. Yes, things would be different. Whatever happened.

Nikki's tears were dried and her eyes were sparkling and, for the first time in ages, they were making love and having fun.

'I want us to get dressed,' she said when they woke some hours later to find that it had got dark outside. Chris did as he was told and when they were both fully dressed she led him through to the kitchen and out onto the fire escape.

'What are we doing here?' he asked her, a puzzled expression on his face.

'Don't you remember?' she replied, lifting her skirt and ripping a hole in her tights. She reached for his hand, sliding his fingers past her already sticky panties and deep into her pussy, working her body against his hand till a flush spread across her cheeks and a smile played about her lips.

'Oh, yes,' replied Chris as he looked up to see one of their neighbours closing his window two floors up. 'I remember, Nikki. I remember.'

A Message from the Publisher

Headline Liaison is a new concept in erotic fiction: a list of books designed for the reading pleasure of both men and women, to be read alone – or together with your lover. As such, we would be most interested to hear from our readers.

Did you read the book with your partner? Did it fire your imagination? Did it turn you on – or off? Did you like the story, the characters, the setting? What did you think of the cover presentation? In short, what's your opinion? If you care to offer it, please write to:

The Editor
Headline Liaison
338 Euston Road
London NW1 3BH

Or maybe you think you could do better if you wrote an erotic novel yourself. We are always on the look-out for new authors. If you'd like to try your hand at writing a book for possible inclusion in the Liaison list, here are our basic guidelines: We are looking for novels of approximately 80,000 words in which the erotic content should aim to please both men and women and should not describe illegal sexual activity (pedophilia, for example). The novel should contain sympathetic and interesting characters, pace, atmosphere and an intriguing plotline.

If you'd like to have a go, please submit to the Editor a sample of at least 10,000 words, clearly typed on one side of the paper only, together with a short resumé of the storyline. Should you wish your material returned to you please include a stamped addressed envelope. If we like it sufficiently, we will offer you a contract for publication.

More Erotic Fiction from Headline Liaison

VOLUPTUOUS VOYAGE

Lacey Carlyle

The stranger came up behind her and slid a hand round her waist while the other glided over her breasts. Lucy stared out into the darkness as he fondled her. She knew she should be outraged but somehow she wasn't . . .

Fleeing from her American fiancé, the bloodless Boyd, after discovering he's more interested in her bank account than her body, Lucy meets an enigmatic stranger on the train to New York. Their brief sensual encounter leaves her wanting more, so with her passions on fire Lucy embarks for England accompanied by her schoolfriend, Faye.

They sail on a luxurious ocean liner, the *SS Aphrodite*, whose passenger list includes some of the most glamorous socialites of the 1930s. Among them are the exiled White Russians, Count Andrei and Princess Sonya, and the two friends are soon drawn into a dark and decadent world of bizarre eroticism . . .

0 7472 5145 2